Praise for the Jaya Jone

"Charming characters, a hint of romantic conflict, and just the right amount of danger will garner more fans for this cozy series."
— *Publishers Weekly*

"With a world-class puzzle to solve and riveting plot twists to unravel, *Quicksand* had me on the edge of my seat for the entire book...Don't miss one of the best new mystery series around!"
— Kate Carlisle,
New York Times Bestselling Author of the Bibliophile Mysteries

"A delicious tall tale about a treasure map, magicians, musicians, mysterious ancestors, and a few bad men."
— *Mystery Scene Magazine*

"A joy-filled ride of suspenseful action, elaborate scams, and witty dialogue. The villains are as wily as the heroes, and every twist is intelligent and unexpected, ensuring that this is a novel that will delight lovers of history, romance, and elaborate capers."
— *Kings River Life Magazine*

"Forget about Indiana Jones. Jaya Jones is swinging into action, using both her mind and wits to solve a mystery...Readers will be ensnared by this entertaining tale."
— *RT Book Reviews* (four stars)

"*Quicksand* has all the ingredients I love—intrigue, witty banter, and a twisty mystery that hopscotches across France!"
— Sara Rosett,
Author of the Ellie Avery Mystery Series

"Pandian's second entry sets a playful tone yet provides enough twists to keep mystery buffs engaged, too. The author streamlines an intricate plot....[and] brings a dynamic freshness to her cozy."
— *Library Journal*

The Cambodian Curse & Other Stories

**The Jaya Jones Treasure Hunt Mystery Series
by Gigi Pandian**

Novels

ARTIFACT (#1)
PIRATE VISHNU (#2)
QUICKSAND (#3)
MICHELANGELO'S GHOST (#4)
THE NINJA'S ILLUSION (#5)

Short Stories

THE LIBRARY GHOST OF TANGLEWOOD INN
THE CAMBODIAN CURSE & OTHER STORIES

The Cambodian Curse & Other Stories

A JAYA JONES TREASURE HUNT MYSTERY COLLECTION

Gigi Pandian

HENERY PRESS

Copyright

THE CAMBODIAN CURSE & OTHER STORIES
A Jaya Jones Treasure Hunt Mystery Collection
Part of the Henery Press Mystery Collection

First Edition | October 2018

Henery Press
www.henerypress.com

Trade Paperback ISBN-13: 978-1-63511-418-8
Digital epub ISBN-13: 978-1-63511-419-5
Kindle ISBN-13: 978-1-63511-410-1
Hardcover ISBN-13: 978-1-63511-411-8

Printed in the United States of America

To the memory of the authors
from the Golden Age of detective fiction,
who made me fall in love with
the puzzles of locked room mysteries.

ACKNOWLEDGMENTS

Apart from "The Cambodian Curse," the short story that leads this collection, each of the stories first appeared elsewhere. Thank you to Gary Phillips for inviting me to contribute a story to Asian Pulp, and to the editors of the anthologies where the stories originally appeared: Ramona DeFlice Long (editor of "The Hindi Houdini" in Fish Nets: The Second Guppy Anthology and "The Shadow of the River" in Fish Tales: The Guppy Anthology); Dana Cameron (editor of "The Haunted Room" in Murder at the Beach); Tommy Hancock and Morgan McKay (editors of "The Curse of Cloud Castle" in Asian Pulp); Naomi Hirahara, Kate Thornton, and Jeri Westerson (editors of "Tempest in a Teapot" in LAdies Night); Verena Rose, Barb Goffman, and Rita Owen (editors of "A Dark and Stormy Light" in Malice Domestic: Murder Most Conventional).

Before these stories were accepted for publication, my critique readers were essential in helping me figure out if my twists were successfully executed. Thanks to Nancy Adams, Paula Benson, Stephen Buehler, Shelley Dickson Carr, Kim Fay, Emberly Nesbit, Susan Parman, Brian Selfon, and Diane Vallere.

Luci Zahray generously gave me insights into poisons. The Guppies chapter of Sisters in Crime provided me with the tools I needed to become a writer and gave me my first publication credit, "The Shadow of the River"—my only Jaya Jones story with a different narrator!

As always, I'm grateful to the team at Henery Press, especially Maria Edwards and Meagan Smith who helped me with the stories in this collection, and Kendel Lynn, for being part of my journey from the start. To impossible crime literature expert Doug Greene and master of mystery Laurie King for giving their time to introduce this collection. To my husband James, for providing ongoing support even when I would disappear for hours at a time as I worked out these puzzles.

And to my readers, whether you're picking up this collection because you're an existing fan of Jaya Jones, a short story enthusiast, or someone intrigued by locked room mysteries—thank you for making this such a fun undertaking, and I hope you enjoy the mysteries in the coming pages.

Introduction

Why Do We Like Our Rooms Locked?
Laurie R. King

In the mystery world, there is a spectrum. At one end is the cerebral detection story, a delicious puzzler over which we linger; at the other is the fast-paced, heart-pounding thriller, where the pages turn so quickly the reader barely has time to breathe, much less reflect. In that spectrum, at the narrowest tip of the detection end, lies the locked-room mystery: a puzzle demanding attention and thought, a story that pits reader against detective—and (more to the point) against the author behind the scenes.

At its purest, the locked-room tale presents a face of bland impossibility. We have a crime; we have a suspect; we may even know the means and motive and time—but there is simply no way for that suspect to have performed the act. Therein, of course, lies the trickery. We readers see (as that greatest of rational minds, Sherlock Holmes, chided his companion) but we do not observe. For that, we require a detective.

Locked-room mysteries are among the oldest of stories, with "Bel and the Dragon" placing the Prophet Daniel in the role of sleuth. In the early exemplars of the type, divine interventions and last-minute revelations were permitted, but when "mystery" became a genre, ground rules had to be established (such as Ronald Knox's tongue-in-cheek "Ten Commandments of Detective Fiction"). A writer had to play fair. The reader must be able to solve the crime, at least in retrospect. Hiding clues from the audience is cheating.

Of course, this still meant that the solution could be based on a fragment of arcane knowledge that one's detective just happens to possess, or on his (occasionally her) inexplicable determination to follow a tortuous and patently unlikely path, ignoring logical possibilities right and left, until he discovers that diabolically complex piece of machinery, previously unsuspected doppelganger, or drug-unknown-to-science that explains it all.

Sometimes a writer's reach outdistances his grasp, and plausibility snaps. (I'm looking at you, Edgar Allan—no way an orangutan would do that. And as for playing fair with the reader, really: an orangutan?) The key to a locked-room story is to walk the very edge: a solution is indeed there for the observing, but it is tucked away inside the story's details, invisible both to the characters in the story and to the reader looking over their shoulders—until S/He Who Observes points out an overlooked item that sheds new light on the conundrum. The crime is impossible, until one reconsiders some tiny element, and realizes that the solution was indeed there all along.

When the locked-room story turned from razor-wielding orangutans to a more subtle use of befuddlement, it grew into its own, and a game of wits was born. Misdirection came into play, the story's effectiveness resting on the skill of the writer as a trickster, the author's ability to manipulate the reader into grasping the solution mere moments after the story's detective.

All kinds of means to this end come into play. The writer's tool might be a distracting sub-plot, or an eye-glazingly lengthy info-dump that encourages the eye to skip over it (what reader notices a landscape artist's lack of white paint amongst a tedious list of all the other colors?). It could be the use of some multisyllabic descriptive term that only a reader with a background in a specific field—or one who reads with a dictionary in hand—would catch in passing. A writer might also shine a powerful light of evidence on one particular answer to the puzzle, enticing the reader to ignore the other evidence accumulating in the shadows.

Naturally, the more experienced the reader, the harder to trick. A modern audience that turns up its nose at the rejuvenating properties of langur-blood (What is it with monkeys and monomaniacs, anyway?) has also learned to resist the obvious villain—although this introduces yet another set of possibilities in the writer's tool-chest, that of the double-fake: I load a ton of accusation and evidence on the despicable X, so that you the reader know it has to be the sympathetic Y, when in fact it's the colorless Z framing Y by over-framing X...

Yes, the game is truly afoot once the writer begins to play not only with the eyes of the reader, but with the heart. I want the villain to be X, the slimy one, the one who hurt our protagonist— but I'm afraid that's too obvious, that it's going to be Romantic Interest Y instead. But then again, I remember that this writer has a history of trickery. So maybe that means...

A locked trunk, behind a locked door, on an island locked in by storm: can it get any better than this?

As we said, the spectrum of crime runs from intellect to emotion. The highest praise a thriller can receive is a close of the book's covers and a puff of exhaled breath as the pulse slows to normal. The highest praise of a locked-room story? A wry smile followed by a shake of the head, acknowledgment that the reader never saw it coming.

What follows will bring a number of wry smiles and shakes of the head, as Gigi Pandian takes us into a series of rooms, and locks the doors behind us.

—Laurie R. King

Stories mentioned: (Holmes) Arthur Conan Doyle, "A Scandal in Bohemia"; "Bel and the Dragon" is from the first-millennium BCE Septuagintal Book of Daniel; (orangutan) Edgar Allan Poe, "Murder in the Rue Morgue"; (paint) Dorothy L. Sayers, The Evidence in the Case; (langur monkey) Arthur Conan Doyle, "The Adventure of the Creeping Man."

Foreword

In the Tradition of John Dickson Carr
Douglas G. Greene

Many years ago at a mystery convention in London, I chaired a panel on locked room mysteries. Among the participants was the late Bob Adey, the bibliographer of books and stories featuring locked rooms. I asked Bob why they remain so popular, and he responded, "Because a locked room always guarantees that the story features a puzzle." And the detective story in its most fundamental incarnation is centered around the puzzle.

The locked room mystery is one type of "miracle problem," a story in which a murder or some other crime is committed that seems humanly impossible. At its most atmospheric, as in the novels of John Dickson Carr, the reader is led to believe that the only explanation is supernatural, that the crime was committed by a witch, a demon, a vampire or some other denizen of the nether regions, until the detective steps in and shows how the murder was actually done by humans for human motives. He acts almost like an exorcist, banishing the supernatural and restoring order.

In a locked room story, a murder is committed within a room whose doors and windows are locked, sometimes even sealed, on the inside; but only the corpse is there, as the murderer seems to have vanished. And speaking of vanishing, another form of the miracle problem is the disappearance of one of the characters seemingly into thin air. Someone walks into a hallway, with observers at both the entry and the exit, but doesn't come out. In one spectacular variation, a man dives into a swimming pool and disappears. The pool is drained and no one is there. In yet another novel, a corpse vanishes from a sealed vault. An intriguing story is based around a street that vanishes. Other variations include death by no visible cause, and a murder committed in a house surrounded by unmarked snow or sand.

It is fair to say that the miracle problem has attracted the most ingenious of all mystery writers. Indeed, it began when the detective story form itself emerged from the gothic story. The very first detective story, Poe's "The Murders in the Rue Morgue," is a locked-room mystery. Half a century went by and Sir Arthur Conan Doyle gave Sherlock Holmes a disappearing weapon problem. In 1898, L. T. Meade published A Master of Mysteries, the first short story collection dedicated entirely to miracle problems. A bit more than a decade later, in 1910, two writers emerged who specialized in seemingly impossible crimes. One, G. K. Chesterton, was a master of prose style; the other, Thomas W. Hanshew, wasn't. Chesterton set Father Brown to investigate winged daggers, disappearing murderers and corpses, a murderous book, seemingly genuine spiritualist phenomena, family curses, and much more. And all of this in Chesterton's paradoxical, sometimes ornate and often indirect storytelling, enlivened by Father Brown's cryptic remarks. Also in 1910, Thomas W. Hanshew, an American dime novelist living in London created Hamilton Cleek, the Man of the Forty Faces, who has what is described as a "weird birthgift," that is, he can writhe his features so that he can look like anyone he chooses— leading to the "Forty Faces." Scotland Yard becomes touchingly dependent on Cleek's ability to solve seemingly impossible crimes, and an admiring Inspector brings him cases that seem to have no rational solution. And what cases they are—locked room after locked room, impossible disappearance after impossible disappearance—including a man who vanishes while turning a somersault, and a huge statue that disappears from a locked museum, and on and on.

Chesterton and Hanshew were important not only for their own contributions to fictional impossible crimes but also for their influence on John Dickson Carr, the greatest creator of locked rooms and other miracles. Carr so admired Chesterton's stories that he based his great detective, Dr. Gideon Fell, on Chesterton. Carr didn't base any characters on Hanshew—no one has forty faces, and his female characters are not all that pure—but he said that, though he recognized Hanshew's faults as a writer, the creator of Hamilton Cleek had extraordinarily imaginative ideas.

All this is leading to the book you hold in your hands. In The Hollow Man (aka, The Three Coffins), Dr. Fell stops the story to lecture on the locked room. He describes no fewer than eight methods to kill someone in an apparently locked room:

1) The murder is not a murder, but an accident that looks like one;
2) The murder is committed by a poison gas, which causes the victim to go into a frenzy throwing things about, thus creating the appearance of the murderer having been in the room;
3) The murder is achieved by a mechanical trap;
4) It is a suicide which is set up to look like murder;
5) After committing the killing and leaving the room, the killer impersonates the victim, thus confusing who is in the room when the crime is done;
6) The murderer has left his victim unconscious (stunned or drugged), and left the room. He is the first one back into the room and commits the murder at that time;
7) The murderer commits the crime from outside the locked room by means of having frozen ice pellets, an icicle or similar, shot through a window or some other opening;
8) The room has been locked from the outside by a string or some other device.

In an imaginative touch Gigi Pandian has invented a series of miracle crimes, each one of which uses one of Dr. Fell's methods. And like Carr she often creates a spooky supernatural atmosphere, with the presence of magic pervading several of the stories.

You have much to look forward to.

—Douglas G. Greene

Table of Contents

1. *The Cambodian Curse*
2. *The Hindi Houdini*
3. *The Haunted Room*
4. *The Library Ghost of Tanglewood Inn*
5. *The Curse of Cloud Castle*
6. *Tempest in a Teapot*
7. *A Dark and Stormy Light*
8. *The Shadow of the River*
9. BONUS NOVELLA: *Fool's Gold*

The Cambodian Curse

A new Jaya Jones novelette appearing for the first time here in this collection.

i.

As I unlocked the door to my office, I had the strongest sensation I wasn't alone. Something was wrong. Out of place.

With the door cracked open, I was greeted by a six-foot statue of Ganesha that towered over me. The elephant-headed sculpture filled nearly a quarter of my tiny campus office, yet since the day the gift had been unexpectedly delivered, it felt like it belonged there.

What didn't belong was the man sitting behind my desk. It was the subtle fragrance of woody-scented cologne that had alerted me to his presence. Dressed in an impeccably tailored dark gray suit with a subdued tie, he was leafing through a tattered copy of the *Journal of World History*. Henry North. A man I never thought I'd see again. And one I'd hoped I wouldn't.

"I'm not going to ask how you got into my locked office," I said, sighing and dropping my red messenger bag onto the desk. "I know better."

"I needed to speak with you privately," he said in his posh English accent.

"You could have simply called."

"You wouldn't have called me back."

"True."

"That landlady of yours is far too inquisitive. Your students, however, are absorbed in their own problems. I thought it best to catch you after class, without prying eyes."

"How did you know I wouldn't go straight home? No, don't answer that either. What do you want, North?"

"You look good, Jaya. I didn't know if you'd be content returning to academia, but you look happy." He stood and offered my own desk chair to me, an otherwise-suave move ruined by the howler monkey decibel squawk of the rusty chair. I suspected that chair had lived in my office since the history department came into existence.

"I'm fine standing." Without high heels, I was a hair under five feet tall. With them, I was still several inches shorter than North.

He sat back down and steepled his hands together. "I need your help."

If I hadn't known him, I would have sworn he was sincere. The expression on his classically handsome face was almost humble. Almost. I should have kicked him out of my office then. But I knew why I didn't. Henry North had once saved my life, at great risk to his own. For some reason that made me think I owed it to him to at least hear him out.

"Don't look so worried," he continued. "I'm not asking you to rob a museum. Not this time. I'm asking you to help me figure out who did."

I must have laughed, because he continued, "Truly, I'm a legitimate businessman now. I help museums and private individuals with art collections assess their security holes."

"Why do you need me?" *Damn.* Why had I said that? "Not that I'm helping."

I expected to see him smirk at my defeat, but he didn't. He frowned. "Things got messy. I can't risk getting close to this. You know I like to stay out of the papers."

"And I don't?"

"No." He smiled. "I don't believe you do. You talk a big game about wanting the quiet life of a history professor. Jaya Anand Jones, the wunderkind professor whose students look up to her and who writes well-respected articles involving heaps of dreary footnotes that lift the veil on little-known historical mysteries. But you don't really want that. You never have. You don't want to be stuck here in this cramped office. You want to be doing more important things than this." He tapped on the journal he'd been reading when I'd walked in. "Your discoveries reach *all of us*, not just a narrow audience of academics. You see through to the bones of truth in local legends and glean what they can tell the world about lost history."

"It's time for you to leave."

"Have you read today's newspaper yet?"

"This is the twenty-first century, North. Who gets the paper?"

He shook his head. "Kids these days..." He trailed off with a mischievous sparkle in his eyes that made him look like a kid himself.

I glared at North and ran a hand self-consciously through my straight, shoulder-length black hair. I might have been a tad touchy about my age, because of how frequently I was mistaken for a student instead of a professor. "I'm in my thirties."

"I know exactly how old you are," he said. "I know your birthday, the dates you received your various—and might I add impressive—degrees, every professor you've ever had, all the places you've lived in your adult life, including when you slept on your brother's couch while finishing your dissertation and the house built on stilts you rented in Cambodia. Don't ever forget how thorough I am."

I'd never forget what he was capable of, but I wasn't going to let him see that he'd shaken me. I didn't look away.

"Look at this morning's *Chronicle*," he continued. "Front page, below the fold. Margery Lexington, owner of the Lexington Museum here in San Francisco, is my client. Or rather, she *was*."

"She fired you? I can't say I'm surprised."

"No. She got herself killed."

He reached into an inside pocket of his jacket and handed me a folded newspaper. "I know you're done with classes and office hours for the day. Read the article. Then meet me for coffee in two hours. Your favorite spot around the corner from your house. The place where all the baristas are required to have a face piercing of some kind."

"I'm not meeting you, North."

"Read the story. That's all I ask."

I did.

I stayed in my office for nearly two hours after North left, reading the article as well as everything I could find online about the dual crimes that were in play: a seemingly impossible murder and the theft of an ancient sculpture.

The stolen piece wasn't only of great historical significance, but was one I knew. By all accounts, it appeared Margery Lexington had been murdered and the valuable piece of history stolen, not by a person—but by a curse.

Which is why, in spite of my better judgment, I found myself on the way to the coffee shop to meet the man who'd once tried to ruin my life before saving it.

ii.

When I walked into Coffee to the People, North was waiting at a two-person table in the window. He sat facing the door and had already ordered me a steaming hot coffee prepared exactly as I liked it. A double espresso with four sugars.

"What did you think?" he asked.

"You could have told me everything in my office two hours ago, but you didn't think I'd believe you."

"The mystery is rather unbelievable, isn't it?"

"That's an understatement. She was your client, so I know you've got more information than the reporters covering the story. If you want my help, you need to tell me the real details—after you tell me why exactly I'm here."

"All things in time."

I downed half my coffee and focused on my breathing. Which, unfortunately, I was terrible at doing. I sometimes wondered if I was the only person of Indian descent who'd been kicked out of multiple yoga classes for disrupting the tranquility.

"If you picked this public spot to make sure I wouldn't strangle you," I said, "terrific job." Though I did consider "accidentally" dumping the rest of my coffee in his lap. I might have too, if it hadn't been so tasty and caffeinated.

He raised his mug in a toast. "To awkward acquaintances. Cheers." He had the audacity to smile as grandly as if we were dear old friends.

What did North want with me? He was a con man, and I was a professor of history who studied the British East India Company. Margery Lexington's museum specialized in Southeast Asian art, and the killer had stolen a valuable Cambodian sculpture. I was familiar with the museum and had once traveled through Cambodia while backpacking through Asia. It was a tenuous connection at best. Why did North think I could help him figure out who had robbed the museum?

"Let's begin at the beginning." He paused, glancing around at the cafe's eclectic clientele. The people in the surrounding tables were a mish-mash of locals. I'd moved into a semi-legal apartment in the attic of a Victorian house in the Haight-Ashbury neighborhood two years before when I'd relocated to San Francisco to teach history.

When North resumed speaking, he lowered his voice. "Let's start with the sculpture that began this series of unfortunate events that led to Margery's death."

"The sculpture," I said, "is the one thing I already know about with certainty. *The Churning Woman* sculpture was the museum's centerpiece, a single section of a larger Khmer bas-relief that depicted a famous scene from a Hindu myth. It's about the Churning of the Ocean of Milk, a tug-of-war between gods and demons for an elixir of immortality. The sandstone sculpture is unique because the characters depicted in the bas-relief battle weren't only the usual ones: a woman warrior was featured prominently too."

North grinned. "Personally, I never understood why the term 'bas-relief' caught on. Couldn't art historians have come up with a clearer term for the common man, like 'flat carving'?" He sighed. "Gold star for doing your homework."

"I expect that's why you gave me a full two hours. But I'd already seen the sculpture. It's well known to anyone interested in Asian feminist history. Scholars are still debating who this mystery woman was—Jayavarman VII's second wife Indradevi or an *apsara* dancer—and it makes that single piece from the full set of carvings even more special." Because of Cambodia's connection to India, I'd come across Queen Indradevi in my research, and her story had always fascinated me. It was the real reason I couldn't say no to

North's invitation. My boyfriend Lane was out of town, otherwise I had no doubt he would have saved me from myself.

"You certainly know how to deflate a fellow's ego. Yet I doubt you know the tragic history of *The Churning Woman*. The Lexington Museum was originally opened by Margery's grandfather, Harold Lexington. It was Harold himself who found *The Churning Woman* and the other six sandstone panels depicting the famous Hindu myth. He discovered the carvings deep in the jungles of Cambodia in the 1920s. But they came at a price. A curse."

"One of the less reputable newspapers reported Margery's grandfather and father were killed by the curse before her." Though I didn't believe in curses, I'd looked up their fates. Both men had indeed died young. I gave an involuntary shudder as I thought of it again.

"The Chronicle story I gave you was much more civilized, wasn't it? They focused on the facts, which I can confirm are accurate. Margery had been receiving death threats in the month leading up to her death. That's why she hired extra security—my own humble firm. Yet in spite of my impeccable precautions, someone broke into Margery's office and killed her in a robbery-gone-wrong. They got away with *The Churning Woman*, the sculpture specifically mentioned in the death threats."

"They weren't exactly death threats."

"Well spotted. The anonymous letters she received weren't straightforward threats—they were worse. The typewritten letters invoked the curse on the Lexington family. The anonymous letter writer claimed to be a Good Samaritan simply warning Margery of her fate. They insisted the curse would be lifted if she returned the museum's Khmer treasure to the temple in Cambodia from which it had been taken, and said that *The Churning Woman* centerpiece was the most important item to return in order to break the curse. One of the letters referred to a 1925 French colonial law that forbids the removal of antiquities from Cambodia. But Harold Lexington had removed the sculptures before that, so there's no real claim."

"Why would a curse be concerned with a colonial law?"

"Exactly. The thief mixed his messages, which indicates to me that it was a hoax, part of his scheme. Maybe he thought if she wasn't frightened by the idea of a curse, at least she'd wonder if there was a legitimate claim that the sculptures didn't belong to her."

"But instead of returning the sculpture to Cambodia, she hired you. Were you her personal bodyguard as well?"

North raised an eyebrow. "Of course not. I'm the brains. She had the museum's security guard, Clay—a man as stupid as a rock, so his name is quite fitting—to escort her from place to place whenever she wasn't with her husband William. She didn't want to be alone in the open."

"She thought being with someone else could save her from a curse?"

"Margery was an intelligent woman. Rationally, she knew the letters must have been a con. Yet underneath, I could see she questioned whether something else was going on."

"I imagine it feels different when your own family has been cursed."

"True," North said. "I was worried too, but for a different reason. It looked to me like a clever thief wanted to bait her into moving the bas-relief to a more secure location, and that's when he'd strike. Easier to steal a large sculpture when it's already in transit. It's a smart plan, actually. One I once employed... but enough of that. I didn't want Margery to act rashly and move it to a bigger museum, something she told me she was considering when she interviewed me. I saw that with small changes, her museum could be *more* secure than a larger one with more resources. As you know, large museums have their own vulnerabilities."

"So she listened to you and kept *The Churning Woman* at the Lexington Museum."

"She did, although she insisted on removing *The Churning Woman* centerpiece panel from the display and putting it in her office. A secure office on the second floor, a room without any windows and one fitted with a safe."

"That's the room—"

"Yes, that's the impossibly sealed room where Margery was killed and the sculpture weighing hundreds of pounds simply vanished."

"Leaving the only possible explanation a supernatural curse," I murmured. "I know you don't believe it. You said you need my help figuring out who robbed the museum. Why do you need me? Isn't that what you and the police are for?"

"Isn't it obvious?"

"Not really. I'm not a detective or a security expert. A poor woman has been killed because your security—"

"There was *nothing* wrong with the security." North spat out the words, and his face grew dark for the first time since I'd seen him that day, making him resemble the man I'd known before. The criminal. But the flash of anger disappeared nearly as quickly as it had emerged, and his voice was calm when he continued. "I don't know *how* exactly it was done yet, but—"

"I'm not a security expert."

"You misunderstand me. That's not what I need from you. *The Churning Woman* was stolen on my watch, and I have to get it back. My security assessment was unimpeachable. This wasn't a flaw in my security. I'm certain of it."

"Then why am I here?" Though as I spoke the question, I knew the answer. North had given it to me as soon as he'd appeared in my office. He mentioned the way I saw the truth in historical legends. And how those truths had led me to lost treasures.

"To find the treasure, my dear girl. I want you to find the missing treasure."

iii.

"It's horrible that Margery Lexington was killed," I said as I stood up to leave, "and I hope her killer is brought to justice, but *The Churning Woman* will turn up soon. At this point, the sculpture is already in transit back to Cambodia. Mystery solved. You don't need me. Only time."

North shook his head. "Sometimes you display a degree of naiveté that surprises me, Jaya. Those threatening letters were a ruse to get her to act foolishly and move the sculpture."

"I know it was a ruse. But a ruse to get the sculpture back to Cambodia. Wasn't that the whole point of the robbery? To get the national treasure back to its people one way or another?"

"Your innocence is rather endearing. This has to be an inside job—and none of the suspects are that altruistic."

I sat back down. "Why do you say that?"

"An inside job is the only way it's remotely possible to have circumvented my security precautions. Margery's husband William is the curator. At first, I didn't think he had it in him to kill his wife, even though he was having an affair. But now my money is on William: if Margery was planning to divorce him over the affair, stealing the sculpture would be a way to ensure he'd get his favorite piece of art from the museum. His mistress Emily also works there, and I wouldn't put it past her. Strange woman, she's doesn't care about people in the least. The security guard, Clay, is useless—Margery swore she wouldn't tell him anything about our new procedures and would only use him as a bodyguard. But with his behemoth shoulders and brooding scowl—which I'm sure he practices in the mirror—she might have revealed more than she meant to. None of the other staff could have had access to the information they needed. It had to have been William, Emily, or Clay, so I was waiting for the police to arrest one of them."

"But now you don't think they will."

"I know the crime can't *actually* be impossible," North said, "but what if nobody can figure out how it was done? Without probable cause, the police won't be able to arrest anyone and seize their possessions."

"Meaning you need to find out how it was done. There are ways to mess with locks—"

"You don't think I know that?" North slammed his mug onto the table. Nobody around us seemed to mind. It wasn't a serene type of cafe. "That didn't happen in this case. I examined the scene myself. But we're getting off track and you're missing the point. I'm not asking you to find the killer. The police are working on that. But compared to murder, the sculpture is a lesser concern to them. That's why I need you to find it."

I should have left right then, but I felt myself frozen in place. The thought of the sculpture being lost forever stopped me from walking away and never looking back. That bas-relief held unsolved mysteries.

"I'm a desperate man, Jaya," North continued. "I can see it on your face, you know you're the only one who can save this piece of history."

I snorted. "You mean save your reputation."

"Tomato, *tomato*. Your ears are turning purple, Jaya. Let me get you another coffee." North sprang up before I could answer.

Though I hated to admit it, North was right. I didn't want to spend all my time confined inside a classroom and office. I looked for missing pieces of history far beyond musty archives for the same reason I'd become a historian in the first place. There's so much about our world we've lost. When people in the past elevated a piece of their history beyond the mundane, there was a story there about what a culture valued. I found those stories and brought them back.

North snapped me out of my reverie by setting an espresso and a croissant sandwich in front of me. The unusual combination of egg, peanut butter, and honey wasn't on the menu, but it was my favorite. I breathed in the heavenly nutty-sweet scent wafting up from the hot sandwich and groaned. I was a creature of habit—and so was North.

"I'm not the first person you asked to help you."

He grinned. "I knew you were so highly intelligent that you'd see through me."

"You can stop the flattery, North."

"But I'm so good at it. And I much prefer it to the heavy-handed measures I used to employ."

I nearly choked on my coffee.

"What?" North said in an innocent voice as he handed me a napkin for the coffee I hadn't yet spilled. "That wasn't a veiled threat. Truly. You don't believe I'm a reformed man?"

"I don't actually care. Your actions are the important thing here. Let me guess who you turned to in the first place to find the sculpture. Contacts in the illicit art world looking for it to pop up there? I don't know how to track down provenance, so I'm sure you also have art historians looking into this."

North laughed. "Of course. You see, it's not that you were an *afterthought*, you must understand. Simply a different angle."

"You want me to find the treasure by looking into the curse."

"That would be lovely, thanks."

"I didn't say I'd do it."

"There will be a finder's fee, of course."

"I don't care."

"You do, even if it's only a little. But let's get beyond crass enticements. You have an impeccable track record for seeing nuggets of truth in legends."

I studied North and ignored the croissant sandwich. I *was* good at parsing out the facts to be found in mythology, but I thought he was missing the most important piece of the mystery: the method of the impossible crime itself.

Even though I had a sense that was key, I didn't argue. Because it wasn't something I could help with. I'd learned from experience that the best way for me to solve a mystery was to approach it from the angle I knew the most about: history. In this case, that meant the curse from the 1920s.

"I suppose it couldn't hurt to look into the history of this supposed curse," I said. "It would be a shame if the piece disappeared into the private viewing lair of a supervillain."

"That's my girl." North held up his hands. "I mean, that's the brilliant historian I've come to respect immensely for her insights—"

"That's a little much."

"It was, wasn't it? I'll leave you to it then. Time's a wasting. I hope to have this sorted by the end of the weekend."

"It's Friday afternoon. It's awfully presumptuous for you to assume I'm free this weekend."

"Aren't you?"

"That's not the point."

"See what you can dig up over the next couple of days. That's all I ask."

iv.

Legend says that the land of Cambodia sprang from the magical union of a local princess and an Indian prince. A majestic prince from a foreign land was sailing through a floating kingdom of water. Intrigued by the newcomer, a brave and beautiful princess rode her boat across the water to greet him. The Indian prince shot an arrow into her boat, pulling her closer. With this show of strength, she agreed to marry him. As a dowry, the princess's father, the king of the water, drank up the water and created the land that became the kingdom of Kambuja.

I always remembered that story, because what kind of fairy tale has a princess frightened into marrying a guy who shot an arrow at her? A dark one, much like the sinister legend that brought me to Margery Lexington's home on Saturday afternoon to talk with her widower, William Edmonton.

It began to rain as I maneuvered into a minuscule parking spot along the side of a jarringly steep street on Russian Hill. The Edwardian-style house Margery and William had shared was within view across the street, and even from my car I could see ornate molding and two small hedges that had been shaped into what looked to be fat guardian lions flanking the entry steps. All of it befitting a couple who ran a museum.

Before I got out of the car, I read my notes again. I didn't want to take up more of the bereaved man's time than I had to. But with the dearth of written information on legends surrounding the curse, I needed him. I'd assumed the museum's materials would mention the curse, as it was much like famous Egyptian curses that capture the imagination of visitors at museums across the world.

Unfortunately, the Lexington Museum's writer went for scholarly over sensational.

As the rain pelted down on the windshield, I reviewed the obituaries of Margery that had been published in local papers since the original news report had come out. In San Francisco she had been known more as a philanthropist than as the owner of the small museum she had inherited from her father. A small, sprightly woman, she appeared in the most recent photos sporting stylishly short dark brown hair, pictured both in ball gowns at local charity galas and in overalls at Earth Day volunteer events in Golden Gate Park. Margery's own family was only modestly wealthy, so she'd initially gotten to know wealthy donors interested in art and Southeast Asian history in hopes of expanding the museum. But she quickly took on a different role, as an advocate and fundraiser herself, raising money in particular for historical preservation and environmental causes.

Though the obituaries briefly mentioned Margery's family history, only one of them went into any depth about her grandfather Harold and the founding of the Lexington Museum. Harold had come to America in 1925 with his young San Franciscan wife Sarah, who was praised for her resourcefulness in weathering the Great Depression, which began shortly after her husband opened his museum and died. Though the text didn't explicitly say he had died because of a curse, it mentioned a history of tragically young deaths in the family.

I looked up from my notes and nearly had a heart attack. A dark figure hovered in front of the car. My phone slipped from my fingers and crashed onto my bare foot. The twinge of pain brought me back to reality, diverting my thoughts from the curse. Which was a good thing, since the figure came closer to the car and rapped on the passenger side window. I briefly considered leaving him out in the rain, before reaching across the seat and unlocking the car door.

"What brings you to my little car?" I asked North as he closed his umbrella and climbed inside.

"I didn't expect you to visit the house of the main suspect alone. I thought you'd be off in a library archive somewhere."

"Libraries don't have information unless that information is written down. This is family history. I needed to talk to someone who knew more about it."

"He could be a murderer."

"I didn't know you cared."

"I need you to find my sculpture."

I swallowed hard, an unpleasant thought forming in my mind. Could North himself have taken the sculpture and killed Margery? But then why would he have involved me? It was a ridiculous idea. Ridiculous. Wasn't it?

"The rain is subsiding," I said, slipping my heels back on. "Let's go."

We ran across the street. Ever the English gentleman, North held his umbrella over my head.

"We're sorry to trouble you," I said when William greeted me at the door. "This shouldn't take long."

I had to crane my neck to look him in the eye. William Edmonton stood a solid six-and-a-half feet tall, with broad shoulders and without a hair on his head. Inquisitive blue-gray eyes observed me as he ushered me inside. In his 60s, he looked more like a retired Olympic athlete than a museum curator. But I doubted I looked like most people expected a professor to look.

"If this will help us figure out what happened to Margery," he said in a strong yet sad voice, "take all the time you need. My sister arrived yesterday, and she's taking care of everything related to the services. She was always much better at that sort of thing."

He took our coats and North's umbrella and led us to a pair of high-backed bar stools next to the high table between the kitchen and living room. The house smelled of cleaning materials and clay. The living room was straight out of a museum, with artfully placed rosewood shelves featuring Southeast Asian sculptures, pottery, and books. The kitchen was more modern family than museum, with well-used, chipped plates and mugs. A bread mixer with flecks of dough on the handle sat on the counter next to a bag of almond flour. Across from us, a large window overlooked the few city blocks before land met the northern part of the Bay. If the fog and rain hadn't obscured the view, we could have seen Alcatraz Island.

"I've already told the police all I know," William said, "and they've gone over the crime scene thoroughly. But Mr. North seemed to think you could help. I didn't realize he'd be joining you today..." He gave North a look that made me wonder if he suspected the man's true character, then turned his attention back to me. "I'm not sure how you can help, but what can I tell you?"

I hesitated and looked out the window at the rain and fog. North had interrupted my thoughts in the car, and I hadn't decided my best approach with William. I needed to know more about the curse, but it wasn't the most rational-sounding thing to bring up.

"I'm sorry," William said. "Where are my manners? Would you two like something to drink?"

"We're fine, thank you," North said.

I shook my head. "That's not why I paused. I was trying to think how best to describe what I need. It's...about the curse."

William's lips tightened.

"Not that I think the curse is real," I added hastily. "That's what's difficult to describe. I'm a historian, and I've seen legends— far-fetched lore involving fairies and ghost stories—that have their basis in fact. By figuring out which parts of a legend are truths that created the myth in the first place, it's possible to uncover real history. In a case like this, it might help us figure out the present."

"Now it's your turn to misunderstand," William said, following my glance to look forlornly out the window at the falling rain. "I didn't make a face because I'm skeptical. I'm afraid the curse is real. It's coming to claim me next."

v.

North had a fit of coughing.

"You think the curse is real?" I squeaked.

William forced a laugh. "I didn't use to. Neither did Margery. Until the letters started coming." He shivered. It was jarring to see such a show of vulnerability in the hulking figure.

"I haven't been able to find much about it," I said as North recovered.

"In spite of our museum and Margery's charity work," William said, "I'm afraid we're not famous enough for our little curse to have its own Wikipedia page. Not until two days ago, at least. You really think this might help?"

"I do."

He nodded. "Margery tried to keep her fears hidden, even from me, but I do know some things beyond what's been reported. First, let me get it out in the open, right out front. Because I don't want you to worry that you're in the house with a murderer. I can only imagine what Mr. North has told you, but I loved my wife."

"William, I don't know what you mean—" North began.

"I'm not a stupid man," William said. "You think I don't know what people are saying? Miss Jones, I want you to understand the truth about me so you'll take seriously what I tell you about the curse. Mr. North, you can feel free to play chaperone from the covered deck behind the house."

North cleared his throat. "Right-o. I can take a hint."

"Nicely done," I said once North had grabbed his coat and stepped into the chilly, damp air.

"I have no patience for that man. I know Margery respected

his skills, but look where that got her." He sighed and rubbed his eyes. After a deep breath, he looked out the window again, speaking to the fog as he continued. "Margery and I had grown apart in recent years. She'd become more interested in philanthropy than scholarship. A worthy cause, certainly, but she enjoyed spending her free time at galas, and I didn't. Our schedules became so different that we moved into different bedrooms. But in spite of what people think, I wasn't having an affair with Emily. Margery knew that. It's true I'd been finding friendly companionship with my co-worker more than with Margery the last couple of years. Emily enjoys going to lectures, she's not so much interested in galas. Not that Margery was superficial. She wanted to do good through her charity work. She even shaved her head earlier this year for a charity fundraiser." He broke off as a boom of thunder sounded.

I took the distraction as an opportunity to steer the conversation back on course. "About the curse..."

"Margery's grandparents were explorers. The grandest of explorers. Her grandmother, Sarah Mann, was from San Francisco, and her grandfather, Harold Lexington, was from a small village in England. They met in Phnom Penh in the early 1920s, both enticed by stories of the French adventurers who'd found ancient Angkorian temples deep in the jungles of Cambodia." The enthusiastic words spilled out of William. As he spoke of the past, his face transformed from one of mourning to that of a little boy recounting an adventure story.

"Sarah's travel companion had fallen ill," he continued, "but unconventional Sarah didn't let that stop her. She went alone to the bar where a group of men had returned from an expedition. She was enthralled by their stories, and even more by Harold himself. They were soon wed and went on several expeditions elsewhere in Indochina before being lured back to Cambodia, in search of a temple that Harold felt he'd been 'so close' to finding on that earlier expedition."

I leaned forward, finding myself caught up in William's

excitement. "He found a lost temple?"

William smiled and shook his head. "He never found it. What he found was the previously buried sculptures from a temple in the Banteay Chhmar complex that a Frenchman had 'discovered.' That's where he found the bas-reliefs that enabled him to open the Lexington Museum."

"Oh." I found myself strangely disappointed.

"Harold did his part surveying the massive temple complex, and there were so many stone carvings that he was able to claim the sculptures he removed for himself, including *The Churning Woman*. This was 1924, right before the law that forbade taking items of historical significance out of the country. Yet a local Khmer guide warned Harold not to take the sculptures. The man had no power..."

"So they ignored him."

William nodded. "Harold wasn't formally trained. He had offers from museums in the U.S. and Europe to purchase the sculptures, but no offers of a curatorship, which is what he coveted. He and Sarah were both shrewd collectors as well as self-taught archaeologists. When they realized they had acquired enough objects and knowledge to open their own small museum, they returned to San Francisco. They opened the Lexington Museum, with *The Churning Woman* bas-relief as the centerpiece. When you got in touch you mentioned you're a historian. Have you seen it?"

"It's phenomenal. I saw the sculpture at your museum, and I saw many like it when traveling in Cambodia." In ancient Cambodian temples, long sections of sandstone panels had been carved in bas-relief to tell epic stories of bravery and battles. After the kingdoms of Angkor fell and their temples were abandoned to the rich jungles that overtook them, trees grew through the formerly glorious stone carvings, causing the stones to break apart until they were often covered by vegetation. Four centuries after being abandoned, the temples—already known to the locals—were 'discovered' by French explorers. And it was the French who wrote romantic accounts of the ruins and began digging them up, rather than the Cambodians who had known about their existence all along.

"So," William continued, "you know how rare it is to have a woman featured so prominently in the battle."

"Do you think it's the king's wife Indradevi?" I asked.

William smiled warmly. "You *are* a historian."

"It's why I agreed to help North, even though I don't always see eye to eye with him. So...was it the queen?"

"I hope we'll find evidence one day that sheds light on that question. The temple complex where Harold unearthed the sculpture is still being excavated."

"Who supposedly cursed Harold?" I asked. "The guide you mentioned? What was the curse?"

"Margery never took it seriously, so she didn't learn the details. The follies of youth...She tried to distance herself from it. I'm sorry to say I encouraged this as well. Even her grandparents didn't take it seriously at first. It was only after Sarah gave birth to a child and the museum opened that Harold died of malaria. That's when Sarah began to rant and rave about the curse waiting to strike just when they were on the brink of happiness."

"That's how malaria works," I said. "It takes its time and comes back."

"I know. That's what we thought at first. But Sarah had been a rational woman until that point." He held up his hands to put off my objections. "There's more. Sarah's child, Margery's father, died soon after his fortieth birthday, shortly after he'd taken over the museum. Margery never talked about it. She didn't like to speak of it. The only thing she told me was that it was traumatic to have him die of a suspected hereditary heart condition. I have a feeling, now, that she pushed it from her mind because she suspected there was something to the curse, but she didn't want to admit it could really be true. Then, when Margery started receiving threatening letters mentioning the curse, it got to her much more than I expected. It was only then that she admitted the mysterious circumstances surrounding her father's death—there was no heart condition, hereditary or otherwise. He was in perfect health before his death. I realized, then, that a part of her had always believed in the curse. That's why she'd never talked about it."

"Her father and grandfather didn't receive the letters, did they?"

"Not that I'm aware of. But there are other similarities. They all died young. And Margery's philanthropy was making her happy, just as her father and grandfather found happiness shortly before their deaths. Though she and I had grown apart, I believe she was doing what she loved. Her true calling. Can't you see the pattern? Each of them found happiness before they died young. I can see the skepticism in your face, but surely you must admit there's a pattern."

"Perhaps if I saw the letters," I said diplomatically. His "pattern" was so weak I wouldn't even call it that. But his wife had been murdered in a mysterious way, which was enough to forgive the irrationality.

William brought me photocopies of the letters. They had been typed on a typewriter, and each conveyed a slightly different threat, referencing the colonial law, the importance of the sculpture, and the curse itself. There were no specific details about where the thief wanted the sculpture returned, only to the Cambodian people.

I froze when I saw the last letter in the small stack. It wasn't a photocopy. This was an original. And it wasn't addressed to Margery.

I gasped. "This one is addressed to you." This letter was only one line. *Return* The Churning Woman *to the Cambodian people, or the curse will strike again.*

"The letter arrived in today's mail shortly before you came," he said, swallowing hard. "Our murderous 'Good Samaritan' appears to believe I'm in possession of *The Churning Woman*."

vi.

"That doesn't make any sense," I murmured. "There are *two* thieves working independently? And one got there first?"

"I don't know what's going on," William said, "but I hope this one is a copycat, someone with a sick sense of humor who read about Margery and the theft. We'll see what the police think."

"You haven't told them yet?"

"I'm on my way there as soon as we're done," he said. "Unless there's anything else, we can collect Mr. North from the back porch."

"I'm sorry to have kept you," I said, "and to have wasted your time. I thought you'd know more details about the original curse."

"I should have asked more questions of Margery, Emily thought so, too. But it was so painful for her that I hated to press."

I lifted my damp jacket from the coat rack and turned to examine an old photograph hanging next to it on the wall. William and Margery as a young couple at The Met in New York, pictured with the museum's mascot William the Hippopotamus, the iconic Egyptian ceramic figurine painted with a bright blue glaze. Seeing the affectionate look on his face in the photograph, I couldn't imagine William killing Margery. But time changes people.

"I love that photo," William said, his painful expression lightening. "That little blue hippo is how Margery and I met. I'm named after William. That's why the hippopotamus is our emblem. You might have noticed the hippo topiaries in front of the house."

So that's what those bushes were meant to be.

"In the backyard," William continued, "we had a large stone hippopotamus bench built into the porch. We used to spend a lot of time out there together, looking at our view...We fell out of the habit after an earthquake cracked the foundation under the bench. But Margery got it fixed recently. I'd hoped that her interest in spending more time with our stone bench William meant she and I might become close again as well..."

"That's really how you got your name?"

"My father was a museum curator originally from New York. As a boy he spent countless hours at the museum, and he adored William. I was his first child, so he named me William, after the hippo. It was my fate to follow in his footsteps and essentially live in a museum."

"So you know better than most people about how museum security works."

"I was wondering if you were going to ask about that. I do, and I wasn't able to help the police figure out how someone broke in. I know Henry North suspects me of killing my wife. Yes, I love *The Churning Woman*. It's well known that it's my favorite piece in the museum. But even if Margery was going to file for divorce—which she wasn't—I don't want the sculpture for myself. I want it for the world. Now it's gone. And I have no idea how it miraculously vanished from Margery's office. Or why the letter-writer now thinks I have it."

"I'm sure the police will find someone messed with the security cameras or something."

William paused and gave me a strange look. "Didn't North tell you? I was in the museum when it happened. I was near Margery's office. I would have seen and heard if anyone went by. Nobody did."

William walked down the hallway to retrieve North, and I stared in stunned silence at his back.

"Hippopotamus got your tongue?" North asked once we were back inside the car. "You're unusually quiet. Not like you at all. Please tell me you had a brilliant revelation while interviewing William. That will make it worth my while when I catch the death of cold from being stranded outside on that frigid concrete porch."

"I know less than I did going in," I said, starting the car.

"Follow him." North pointed at the driveway where William was backing out, then turned up the heat. "What did you say to him? Whatever it was, nicely done. He could be checking on his spoils."

"We're not following him. He's going to the police station."

"To turn himself in? Even better. Why didn't you tell me how well it went?"

"He's going to the police to show them the threatening letter he received in the mail today."

North scoffed. "Right."

"I'm serious. He showed it to me."

North swore. "Another ruse? It must be a desperate attempt to cast suspicion away from himself."

As it turned out, that was exactly how the police saw it. William was arrested the following day.

The police had noticed a more prominent watermark on this paper than the others, and upon searching William's home, found the typewriter that had been used to write the threatening letters, as well as the paper on which they'd been typed. All of the letters had come from William's own typewriter.

Instead of putting my mind at ease, I had a nagging feeling something was missing. Something I couldn't yet grasp was tugging at the edges of my consciousness, telling me William hadn't killed his wife. Telling me that the true solution was still to be found—in the curse.

vii.

I learned through North—God knew where he got his information, for it wasn't reported to the press—that William insisted someone else must have broken into his home and used the typewriter.

On that foggy Sunday morning, North relayed this information to me as we sat directly across from the Lexington Museum. The museum was located in North Beach, the Bohemian-cum-touristy neighborhood that could no longer be considered Italian, though some of the city's oldest and best Italian restaurants still lined Columbus and Broadway streets. We had the cafe's prime sidewalk spot. On the corner of two streets, it was the perfect location for people-watching, and other cafe patrons glanced covetously at our spot as they looked around with their cappuccinos.

I didn't think North had lucked into the table. Henry North was a man who thought of all the angles and prepared for every possible situation. There was a time he'd wanted a table with a certain vantage point for a heist and wasn't sure who would be sitting there, so he'd obtained passes to a Paris amusement park, as well as tickets to an opera and a sultry dance show, plus dinner reservations at a restaurant impossible for mere mortals to secure, and most likely other contingencies. I briefly wondered what the lucky tourists or locals who'd had this particular location moments before had gotten out of the deal. Hopefully something better than having North tell them their car was being towed.

"Sorry you didn't get to delve more into the curse before they caught William," North said. "Regardless of how much you protested, I knew the challenge had you hooked."

"The curse is a lost cause now anyway. Did you see the dozens of online sites that sprang up after Margery's murder? They're supposedly discussions of 'inside information' about the curse, but it's all fake information that was written in the last three days. The curse is now a full-blown legend, 99 percent of it false. How is a historian supposed to do her job in the twenty-first century?"

"Which is why you want to see the records inside the museum."

"The sculpture is still missing."

Our original plan had been to meet at the museum itself, but it was still closed to the public as a crime scene. No police tape lined the museum's modest facade. Instead, a prominent CLOSED sign had been hung on the entrance's double doors. The museum was smaller than I'd remembered, similar in size to the historical City Lights Bookstore down the street.

"Life was easier when I didn't have to work *with* the police," North said. "It's an affront to my dignity that they're keeping the museum's security consultant locked out of the museum."

"Someone's inside, though," I said, pointing at the second-floor windows. "Is that a flashlight beam?"

North swore and jumped up. I swung my red messenger bag across my chest and ran across the street ahead of him.

"I don't see it anymore," I said, standing at the front of the building. "Maybe it was a reflection from a passing car? It's foggy enough that some people are using headlights." Though as I spoke the words, I didn't believe them myself. There had definitely been a moving light inside the museum.

"No," he said with a firm shake of his head. "Come on. This way."

We hurried along the street past an antique store and an art gallery, until we came to a narrow alley, which led us to the delivery area at the rear of the businesses.

"Where's their car?" he murmured as he extracted his cell phone. He turned away from me and spoke quietly, so I couldn't hear his conversation. When he turned back less than a minute later, his face was red. "It's not the police inside."

"One of the staff members, then," I said with more conviction than I felt. Those flickering lights...

North shook his head and stared at the rear door. "According to the police, nobody is supposed to be inside the museum yet."

"Where should we wait?" I asked.

"Wait for who?"

"The police."

"That beautiful naïveté of yours surfaces again. The police have arrested their killer. They have more important crimes to worry about than a museum staffer who's crossed a police line."

"Nobody is coming? But what if William had an accomplice? Or if he didn't do it?"

North entered a string of numbers into a keypad next to the back door. The lock clicked, and with a smile, he pulled the door open. "After you."

viii.

"This is a terrible idea," I whispered to North as we crept through the museum's back hallway using my cell phone's flashlight. The words were barely out of my mouth before I stumbled over one of the storage boxes stacked against the wall.

"You're right," North said in a regularly modulated voice, clicking on a light switch. "First rule of thievery—or is it the seventeenth? I can't recall—is that it's best to act like you belong somewhere. Nobody pays attention to lights going on in a house or a business. But they *do* pay attention to suspicious flashlight beams, like the flickering light you saw. If these lights had been on the whole time, you wouldn't have noticed anything suspicious. Why is your face scrunched up, Jaya? You're the one who wanted to get inside the museum to solve the mystery of the missing sculpture."

"Is it a crime to want to see an important piece of history saved?"

"Yes. In this case I think it is, since it involves breaking into a museum."

We reached another locked door. North entered a code into another keypad, and also took out a strangely shaped key and inserted it into a physical lock.

"That's a lot of security," I said as we stepped into the portion of the museum open to the public.

"There are cameras, too," North said, pointing upward at details in the molding that looked nothing like cameras to me. "But don't worry. I'll delete the files once we're done here."

"Couldn't the killer have done that too?"

"You mean William? Theoretically possible," North said grudgingly, "though highly improbable. But that wasn't the problem in this case. That's not what hap—" he broke off as the lights flickered.

My breath caught. The lights flickered right as we passed the empty space that had once contained *The Churning Woman*.

"Faulty wiring," I said. "That must be what's going on."

"I wonder...I'll be right back. Don't worry. I'm not going far."

While I waited for North to return, I looked at the other sculptures in the room. Many of the intricate sandstone carvings were behind glass cases, but the largest pieces remained in the open so visitors could experience them more intimately. That included the rest of the panels from the allegory of the Churning of the Ocean of Milk—now missing *The Churning Woman* centerpiece. I thought back on the curse. To someone already on edge, flickering lights inside the museum could make it feel haunted. Had that happened the night of the murder? Had the culprit been trying to scare Margery? And if so, to what end? Was there more than one perpetrator? Was that why someone believed William had the missing sculpture? And why bring up the French colonial law if they wished to scare her with a curse?

Harold Lexington claimed he had removed sculptures from Cambodia in 1924 before it was forbidden to do so. But he didn't arrive in San Francisco until 1925, and he'd set up his museum years later. I wondered...Was the official timing a lie? Or was it simply more misdirection?

"Boo," a voice next to my ear said. Instinctively, I stepped on his foot with my heel—before realizing it was North. Still, I wasn't going to apologize to someone who'd once kidnapped me.

North proceeded to swear colorfully for a full minute before saying, "That's what I get for solving this mystery."

"You did?"

"Well, not exactly. But I did discover we're alone inside the museum. There's no intruder. There's a timer set to make the lights flicker."

"To scare Margery into believing the curse," I said.

"Or at least throw her off balance. Bloody effective. I'm not above saying my heart skipped a beat when we walked past the spot where the cursed sculpture once sat."

"Didn't you notice it before?"

North shook his head. "William must have set it up to go off at times only the two of them were working late."

"It's not late right now," I pointed out. "And William was worried too."

"Jaya, the man killed his wife. He was acting. He must have been the one who fiddled with the lighting. He probably changed the settings to confuse things."

"Maybe. What were you telling me before the lights flickered? About the camera footage."

"Right. The camera footage wasn't deleted the night of the theft and murder. And it wasn't tampered with in any way. The cameras were on, and after everyone else left for the night, the footage showed Margery going into her office. She left the door open. A bit later, William also returned to the museum to do some work in his own smaller office. He didn't go anywhere near hers, but the hallway camera showed Margery's door closing. Nobody else went near it. Neither the sculpture nor Margery ever left her office. Yet the door had to be forced open by the police after William supposedly heard her cry out. It has to be a trick that enabled him to have that alibi, though I can't figure it out. And no, there are no secret passageways. The only secret room is the large safe in her office where the centerpiece sculpture was stored before it disappeared."

"There are no cameras inside either office?" I asked.

"People need a modicum of privacy."

"Can you take me there?"

The stairs creaked under our feet as we ascended the narrow, winding staircase leading to the second-floor offices. The only other way upstairs was a freight elevator twice as wide as I was tall, which was used to move the sculpture into the safe in Margery's office.

North had keys to all the rooms, and he explained that the multiplicity of keys was why the private offices had dead bolts, so the occupants could lock the door from the inside.

While I looked through William and Emily's offices, North went across the hall to Margery's. I found references to the sculpture in each of their files, as it had been both the centerpiece of the museum and also clearly William's favorite. It was also much beloved by Emily, and I wondered if William was telling the truth, if they were really just good friends. William had mentioned something at his house: Emily was interested in the curse as well.

"What are you doing, North?" I called down the hall. When he didn't answer, I was again struck by the niggling thought that North himself might be involved in the theft. But if so, why would he have involved me? Could there be something else he was looking for?

I ducked under the crime scene tape and entered Margery's office. "Earth to North."

"It makes no bloody sense," he murmured.

"How William did it?"

North nodded, but his eyes remained fixed on the door I'd walked through.

"I thought you didn't care how it was done, as long as you got the sculpture back," I said.

"How am I going to prevent this from happening in the future if I don't understand how a sculpture weighing hundreds of pounds disappeared, not only from a secure safe, but also a sealed room?"

ix.

"Now that we're in the room where the crime took place, show me what happened," I said.

North toyed with his collar as he glanced nervously around the room. "Since Margery and William had grown apart lately, they didn't travel to the museum together. Margery was working alone in her office in the evening after the museum had closed. She knew my security was good, and she wasn't counting on one of the three other people who could get inside—William, Emily, and Clay—killing her."

"She was working here in this second-floor office?"

North pointed to the corner. "That's where they found her. She'd been hit with a heavy bronze statue she kept on her desk."

"You said William heard it happen?"

"Yes. Margery was here working late when William arrived to do some work on his own. The security cameras confirm this timeline."

"Why were they both working so late?"

"With *The Churning Woman* out of sight, they were trying to come up with what to feature instead, so everyone was working overtime. William says he saw the light on in her office, through the open doorway, but that he didn't go inside to say hello. Again, the cameras confirm this. A few seconds later, the cameras also show Margery's door closing. The office doors swing inward, so the cameras didn't show if it was Margery or her killer who closed the door shortly after William's arrival."

"But later," I said, "there was nobody aside from Margery in the room."

North nodded. "By the time the police arrived, yes. William says he heard Margery cry out, so he rushed from his office. But keep in mind, the cameras don't record sound. William tried to get in, but the door was bolted from the inside. When Margery didn't respond, he called 911. They broke down the door and found her inside. Alone. Dead. With the safe wide open, and the sculpture gone."

"There aren't any windows in here."

"No. The only windows are in the museum section of the building. So what do you think?"

"I think I need some lunch. Alone."

As it happened, I didn't end up eating lunch by myself. My best friend Sanjay was in town between performances and agreed to meet me for lunch at a Cambodian restaurant in the Mission district. A successful stage magician who performed as The Hindi Houdini, Sanjay had a big ego but an even bigger heart. There was a time when I'd briefly wondered if we might become more than friends, but it wasn't in the cards. I was in love with another man, and as someone I saw several times a week and argued with just as often, Sanjay felt even more like a brother to me than my brother Mahilan.

Since he was a magician, Sanjay had an insightful way of analyzing seemingly impossible situations. He thought about misdirection for most of his waking hours. But in this case, after I told him everything I knew over our lunch of shredded mango salad and fish amok stew, he sat back and shook his head.

"I don't see how it's possible," he said.

"That's not what you were supposed to say. I hoped you were wearing your bowler hat through our whole meal because you were going to pull a miniature sculpture out from under it, or something that would shed light on the problem at hand."

"Sadly, no." He raised the hat and grimaced before quickly putting it back in place. His thick head of black hair was marred by a distressingly large strip of gauze.

I gasped. The bandage began above his left ear and stretched more than three inches.

"Bad timing on a new illusion," he said. "Eight stitches."

"Are you okay? When did it happen? Why didn't you call me?"

He grinned at me. "It was down in LA. And I'm OK. I'm mostly concerned with my hair."

My tension eased and I laughed. Of course. Would his fan club, the Hindi Houdini Heartbreakers, still love him without his gorgeous hair? I expected they'd love the chance to give him some TLC.

"What?" he said. "This is my livelihood here. I have to look my best. I'm going to have to perform in my turban until this heals, which rules out any of the illusions that need my magic bowler hat."

"Are you on pain medication? Maybe that's why you can't see any way out of this impossible setup."

"Nope. If there are truly no secret exits from Margery Lexington's office and the videotapes haven't been tampered with, this Cambodian curse looks a lot like it's the only explanation. Which of course I don't believe. Which leaves..."

I leaned across the table. "You have an idea?"

The waitress chose that moment to bring us coffees and pumpkin coconut pudding for dessert—which we hadn't requested.

"On the house," she said, smiling shyly at Sanjay. She was cute. I wondered if he'd slip her one of his cards before we left.

"Your idea?" I prompted again. My eyes didn't leave Sanjay's as I spooned sugar into my coffee. Which was a problem, since it turned out to be a spicy bird-chili salt. I took a sip and shuddered. That flavor combination was too strange even for me.

"The videotapes might have recorded a true situation, but what if the *timing* is off? What if that happened another night? That must be it."

I shook my head. "I thought of that. The security expert confirmed the videotapes weren't tampered with. Plus it shows everything that happened."

"The security expert? Why are you working with a security expert? This puzzle was so interesting that I didn't even ask you why you're working on it."

"Because of the missing piece of history."

"You read about it and offered your services?"

"Not exactly," I mumbled.

Sanjay sniffed the pudding. He was a notoriously unadventurous eater. "What aren't you telling me, Jaya?"

"You should leave the waitress your number."

"How do you know I didn't already?" He grinned and deftly flipped his playing card size business card between each of his fingers. "But you're the one using misdirection now. Changing the subject. I don't know why, but don't you have a real job with lectures or something to prepare for?"

He was right. Sanjay was annoying that way.

I left Sanjay to flirt with the waitress and went to my campus office to prepare for the following week's lectures. Since Lane was traveling abroad for work, I should have been making better use of my time than solving a problem for Henry North. But I needed to be at peace with the fate of the unique Cambodian sculpture. I expected that William, if he was indeed guilty, would strike a deal with the prosecutors to get a reduced sentence if he revealed where he'd hidden it.

Yet try as I might, I couldn't focus. The curse hoax and William's guilt didn't fit together. I was missing something.

The next day, I learned my suspicions were right. William was released on bail—and as soon as he arrived at home, someone tried to kill him.

X.

William had been poisoned. He survived the attempt on his life but was barely hanging on.

North asked me to meet him at the hospital where he was keeping vigil with William's sister as well as his co-worker Emily. I declined the invitation. I told myself I was done sticking my nose into the murderous mess of the Lexington Museum. I hoped to see the historical sculpture returned, but no more playing detective for me.

If only life were that easy.

When I let myself into my office on Monday morning, North was waiting for me inside. Admitting defeat, I taped a message to my door saying office hours would begin fifteen minutes late.

"I suppose I should be brief," North said, "if fifteen minutes is all I've got. You were right that it's the mistress after all. Not the husband."

"I never said that. I just said I wasn't convinced it was William."

"Potato, *potato*."

"Emily's been arrested? And she wasn't his mistress."

"Whatever she is to him, she hasn't been arrested yet. But William was poisoned by his favorite treat: sugar-free almond flour cookies made with a pungent dried fruit imported from Cambodia that masked the flavor of the poison. Emily baked the cookies— supposedly to celebrate his release from jail—but he didn't die quickly enough and called 911, so she wasn't able to dispose of the evidence."

"That's awful," I said. "But since I don't know anything about poison, and I doubt this is a social visit, I take it *The Churning Woman* is still missing and that's why you're here?"

A knock on the door interrupted us, so I didn't get to hear whatever excuse North would come up with. I opened the door and let the student know I'd be a few more minutes.

"What did that young ruffian say to you?" North asked as I closed the door. "You're as white as a sheet."

I leaned my back against the door, my mind racing. "It wasn't what he said. It was the interruption itself." I thought about everything I'd learned over the last three days. "The office door being closed...The salt at the restaurant not being the ingredient I thought it was...Margery supposedly shaving her head for charity..."

"You've solved it," North whispered.

"Maybe." My gaze snapped to North. "I need you to find out two things for me." I wrote a note on a slip of paper and handed it to him. "Call me when you find out the answers."

He frowned. "Medical records? How am I supposed to find this out? The first is most definitely confidential."

"When has that ever stopped you before?"

"True."

As I wrapped up office hours two hours later, North was waiting outside my door.

"You were right," he said. "She had stage four melanoma. And it wasn't the force of the bronze statue hitting her that killed her; she overdosed on morphine. How did you know? And why does it matter?"

"The only solution that made sense was farfetched, unless one final criterion was met. That wasn't the main reason Margery Lexington killed herself, but—"

"Killed herself?"

I nodded. "That's how the impossible crime was done."

"You're forgetting that someone tried to kill William *today*. Unless she rose from the grave—"

"I can explain that too. Let me start at the beginning. Margery and William had already drifted apart. The newspaper stories backed up William's account that she was the philanthropist who was part of San Francisco society, whereas William was the scholar who kept his head down and attended to the museum. Reading between the lines of what William said and those photographs in the paper, she was concerned with being important. She was front and center in photos at galas and at volunteer photo-ops. She wasn't the helpless victim she pretended to be when she hired you last month."

"I didn't exactly say that," North protested.

"She told you how fearful she was of the letters. Of the curse. One thing I should have realized earlier, when I spoke to William, was that *there was no curse* until Margery invented it last month."

"Of course there was a curse," North snapped.

"Was there? Tell me, why exactly do we think so?"

"Her grandmother Sarah wrote of it. That's documented. Isn't that what you historians care about? Historical documentation?"

"What the accounts from Margery's grandparents *actually* say," I said, "was that they were 'warned.' They were warned by an understandably angry person whose heritage they were stealing."

"Margery said it was a curse, not a warning," North began, then swore. "I answered my own question, didn't I?"

"I'm afraid so. Everything we know about the 'curse' is from what Margery told people this month. She planted the seed with her husband after she started receiving the threatening letters—which of course she sent to herself. Only then did she tell him the details of her grandfather's death—details she had previously claimed not to know, but now she 'confessed' to William she'd held back because her grandmother had been afraid of a curse. Margery had also never told William the details of how her father died, probably because it was painful, so she used that as an opportunity to invent 'mysterious circumstances.'"

North swore.

"There were no online references to the curse before she died,"

I continued. "Not one. Just as there was no reference to the curse in the museum's materials. I thought it was because they were interested in facts more than publicity, but it's because it *never existed*."

"She hated him," North said. "She hated William for making her feel superficial, and for leaving her emotionally for Emily. And William and Emily both loved that sculpture..."

"And she was dying," I said. "She didn't tell anyone about the cancer, instead saying she shaved her head for a cancer charity. She and her husband had already drifted apart and were living separate lives, so the charade wasn't difficult. Angry and alone, she thought up the idea to frame William for her inevitable death. And if he didn't get arrested, the next time he baked his favorite dessert, he'd die. She must have known it was a risk. Even if both of those parts of her plan failed, then at least as a free man he wouldn't have his prized possession that he and his mistress both adored."

"But how did she kill him from beyond the grave?"

"She'd already planted the poison."

"She wasn't a monster who would have someone else die accidentally," North said. "Hating your spouse enough to kill them is one thing, but leaving poison for any random person to die? I can't see it."

"I can't either," I said. "William's favorite cookies are homemade, and you pointed out the unusual ingredient used in them. I saw the makings for them on the counter, and I can't imagine anyone else liking that recipe. Margery knew he was the only person who would be poisoned."

"But why the impossible crime? If she wanted to frame William in the first place, which she did so well in so many other ways, why make it seem like he *couldn't* have done it?"

"I don't think she meant to have it look impossible. Remember she was working alone at the museum. She'd already removed the sculpture from her safe. She was planning on killing herself with a morphine overdose, making it look like someone was forcing her to open the safe and accidentally gave her too much of the relaxing drug. She was going to leave both the door to the safe and her office open—"

"When William unexpectedly showed up at the museum," North said. "That's why she had to close her door and lock herself in, because she'd already started her plan."

"She had to think fast. She injected herself with the rest of the drug, then cried out and toppled a heavy sculpture so it would make noise and look like someone had hit her with it."

"And here I was thinking I was the king of contingency plans," North murmured. "But Margery has me beaten. Killing herself and framing William. Or in case he wasn't sent to jail she'd kill him from beyond the grave. Or at the very least she'd make sure he didn't get to enjoy his favorite sculpture that he and his mistress loved. Bloody brilliant."

"She had a fourth plan too," I said.

North raised an eyebrow.

"Remember the 1925 French colonial law mentioned in the letters? If we find the bas-relief sculpture, what do you want to bet it's hidden with information from her grandfather proving it didn't leave Cambodia until 1925. Or at the very least her own research that calls into question the timing. William won't get to keep the sculpture regardless."

"I'm sorry you won't get your well-deserved finder's fee, Jaya, since even though you solved the mystery, the sculpture is lost forever."

"Why do you say that?"

North stared at me. "You know where it is?"

"I think I do. It's somewhere only Margery could have hidden it. It's obvious, when you think about it. But nobody was looking there. It's a spot that only the murder victim herself would think of."

I learned that William woke up the following day, with Emily at his side, cleared of all charges. The police found the contractor

Margery had hired to "fix" the earthquake-damaged back porch. The man, speaking through a translator, confirmed he'd been asked to bury an old slab of sandstone for sentimental purposes, and had been given a hefty tip to post a letter for Margery on a specific date.

The police unearthed *The Churning Woman* sculpture, hidden underneath the renovation of the cracked back porch, the renovation that William had thought Margery wanted because of their beloved hippopotamus bench. The bas-relief was wrapped in plastic along with documentation about its 1925 passage to America, and it hadn't fared too badly underneath the back porch bench of William the Hippopotamus—directly under his rump.

The Hindi Houdini

This Sanjay Rai short story originally appeared in Fish Nets: The Second Guppy Anthology, *edited by Ramona DeFelice Long and published by Wildside Press in 2013. The story marked Sanjay's first appearance as a lead character, and was nominated for both Agatha and Macavity awards.*

The young man in a pristine bowler hat attempted the futile exercise of extricating himself from the twenty-foot fish net that had fallen onto the stage.

The netting was heavier than he'd imagined, causing him to fall to his knees when it dropped. He lifted the knotted rope pressing against his shoulders, shifting his hat in the process. A rose petal emerged from beneath the rim and fluttered to the floor.

"The net isn't supposed to drop until I reach the trunk," he said in a raised voice, ceasing his squirming and readjusting the bowler. "Markus, can you get this thing off of me?"

Sanjay Rai, a.k.a The Hindi Houdini, was practicing for his magic show at the Cave Dweller Winery in California's Napa Valley. It was his first day setting up for his series of shows that would run for the summer tourist season. In his late twenties, Sanjay had already developed quite a following. He liked to think of himself as a magician and escape artist for the twenty-first century with the sensibilities of previous ones. He performed in a tuxedo, alternating between a bowler hat and a turban. Either one could hold what he needed for his sleight-of-hand.

"Sorry!" a voice called out from above the stage. After several seconds of shuffling, a wiry stagehand appeared. An oversized dress shirt and jeans hung loosely over his thin frame.

"This net," Sanjay said from beneath his confines, "is way too heavy."

"You're the one who bought it," Markus said.

"And you're the one who dropped it *on my head* instead of on the trunk."

"Let me get Wallace to help me get you out of there."

"I think Lizette is backstage," Sanjay began, but Markus had already left the theater by a stage door.

Sanjay shifted his bowler hat again, making sure it was firmly in place over his thick black hair. The netting bore into his neck and shoulders, but his hat was an important prop. If he removed it now, Markus, Lizette, or Wallace might learn his secrets. And that would never do.

"Got him!" Markus called out from the back row of the theater. The theater's manager, Wallace, looked worse than the last time Sanjay saw him. A glass of red wine swayed in his hand as he tottered down the aisle. It was only five o'clock, but it was obvious Wallace had already had a few. A theater on the grounds of a winery was probably not the best place for him to work. His handsome face would be permanently ruddy within a few years at this rate.

"I'm sure Markus can handle this on his own," Sanjay said, eyeing Wallace's glazed eyes.

"Ha!" Wallace barked. "Technical difficulties, eh, Houdini?"

Sanjay hated it when Wallace called him Houdini. Coming from most people, it was a sign of respect. Not with Wallace. There was a mocking lilt in his voice as he said it. Sanjay wished the pleasant Lizette had been helping instead.

Wallace set his wine glass on the edge of the stage and heaved himself up to help Markus. He wasn't a large man, but climbing onto the stage winded him. Sanjay held his hat firmly as the two men lifted the netting. A button on the cuff of Markus's long sleeve caught on one of the knots and the net dropped back down. At least

Sanjay wasn't wearing one of his many tuxedos. He wasn't used to working with this particular rope, so he didn't know what its effect would be on fabric. He could have freed himself without dislodging his hat if he needed to—a Swiss Army knife was one of the items concealed on his body—but he hadn't wanted to damage the important new prop.

In spite of a tipsy theater manager and a stagehand in an ill-fitting dress shirt, Sanjay was freed less than a minute later.

"I'll get this back in place," Markus said.

Wallace scooped up his glass of wine and retreated, chuckling to himself. "I'll be in my office for the next hour," he called over his shoulder, "if there are any more magical mishaps."

"You should have asked Lizette to help," Sanjay said, brushing off his knees.

"Did I hear my name?" Lizette's curly auburn hair shone in the stage lights as she stepped from backstage carrying a box of plastic musical instruments for the show.

"Oh!" she cried out, spotting the net. "Isn't that supposed to fall onto the trunk?"

"I know!" Markus snapped. "I screwed up. I get it."

Sanjay had enjoyed working with the married couple much more the previous season—before Lizette had an affair with Wallace. As far as he knew, the affair had been short-lived, but it still made things awkward. The magician hoped they'd be able to focus enough to help him prepare for his show next week. The Saturday night opening performance was already sold out. Even more importantly, Jaya would be there. He'd only met her recently, but he could tell she was something special. Then again, Markus had probably thought the same of Lizette before he learned she was sneaking off to sleep with Wallace rather than scrapbooking with a girlfriend as she claimed.

Markus struggled to get the net back in place above the stage. Sanjay's on-stage magician's assistant would arrive the next night for several days of proper dress rehearsals. Usually this first day of initial setup was a relaxing one. Usually.

"Ready?" Sanjay asked.

"I want to make sure I don't drop the net early again," Markus answered from the cat-walk above. "I've got a question for Wallace about the levers before we start." He pulled out his cell phone.

"He's not answering," Markus said after a few moments. "Never mind. I'm sure it's fine. Um. Yeah. Pretty sure."

"You don't sound too sure."

"It's fine, Sanjay. Don't worry. We got the net off you before, we can do it again."

Sanjay couldn't imagine anything he'd like less. "Can you find Wallace?"

"I don't want to lose sight of this lever."

Sanjay sighed. "Let me see if I can find him."

As Sanjay walked around the side of the theater to the winery's administrative offices, he attempted to push thoughts from his mind about what the rest of this season would be like. Markus hadn't always been so absent-minded, but clearly the affair had gotten to him.

Sanjay's knock on Wallace's office door was met with silence. He glanced at his watch and knocked again. Less than thirty minutes had passed, and Wallace had said he'd be there for at least an hour. He was probably drunk enough to forget what he'd said. Sanjay tried the door to the office—locked—before heading back to the theater.

"He's already gone home," Sanjay reported.

"That's odd." Markus tied up a rope he'd been holding and climbed down. "Wallace never goes home this early."

"Well, he did tonight. Have you noticed how much he's been drinking lately? He locked the door but forgot to turn off the light of his office, too."

"What?"

"The light was on under the door," Sanjay said.

Markus's face darkened. He cleared his throat. "He locks his door when he's inside and doesn't want to be disturbed." He hurried outside to the winery complex adjoining the theater, Sanjay following on his heels.

Sanjay wasn't sure of the big deal. They all knew Wallace would lock his door since he dealt with the money from the theater.

"Wallace!" Markus shouted, pounding on the door. "Is Lizette in there with you?"

No answer. Markus shook the door handle. The door rattled but didn't give.

"You can open it," Markus said, pointing his finger at Sanjay.

"You mean break in?"

"I know you can do it. I've seen your tricks."

"Illusions," Sanjay corrected him.

"Can you open it or not?"

"I really don't think I should—"

"Oh." Markus crossed his arms. "Your tricks are just tricks then. No skill involved. I get it. I always suspected as much."

"Of course I can do it," Sanjay snapped. He ran his hand across his forehead. Or so it would appear to any observer. In reality, two fingertips brushed under the edge of his bowler hat and emerged with a thin lock pick. He knelt down and got to work.

A bead of sweat covered Sanjay's brow before the lock clicked open five minutes later. It was a challenging lock. A bolt. Markus's heavy breathing and pacing behind him wasn't helping. Neither was the fact that the indiscrete couple inside was sure to hear what was going on.

Sanjay pushed open the door. He wasn't looking forward to finding Lizette inside with Wallace. Sanjay straightened up and looked inside. His body relaxed. Lizette wasn't in the office. Neither was Wallace. He must have left early after all and simply forgotten to turn off the light.

"That's where you two went," a light voice said from behind. Lizette.

"On a wild goose chase," Sanjay said—right before Markus gasped. That's when Sanjay spotted an outstretched arm on the floor behind the office desk.

Markus rushed forward, Sanjay and Lizette close behind.

"Oh, God," Markus said, kneeling beside Wallace's prostrate body. He leaned his head over Wallace's chest.

A broken wine glass lay on the carpet next to his body; the red wine forming what looked eerily like a pool of blood.

"He's not breathing." Markus shook his head slowly as he raised himself up.

Lizette's scream pierced the air. She raised a shaking hand and pointed at the red liquid on Markus's hands. It was too thick to be red wine.

Sanjay moved closer to Wallace's body. He saw why Wallace wasn't breathing: a dark pool of blood was visible next to Wallace's neck. A pair of sharp scissors with pink handles lay on the floor next to his body.

Nobody moved. Time and motion took on a sticky quality. After what felt like hours to Sanjay but was probably no more than five or ten seconds, Lizette screamed again. The shrill sound made Sanjay's body shake.

"Don't you see?" She cried out. "The scissors. How did they—?"

"Shut up!" Markus yelled. The scream had broken the spell for all of them. His eyes darted around the room.

"There's no one here," Sanjay said. His voice was steady in spite of his nerves shaking inside. As a stage performer, he was used to putting forth a confident voice no matter how he felt inside. "We've got to call the police."

Lizette nodded. She reached for the phone on the desk.

Sanjay held out his arm to stop her. "Not from here," he said. "Evidence."

Lizette shuddered. "My phone is in my purse. It's backstage." She left without looking back at the scene.

Sanjay let out a long breath and walked to the doorway. He frowned as he looked at the lock he'd picked. He began pacing slowly in the small area at the front of the office, his eyes scanning the walls of the room. He knew there was nobody hiding in the room, but there was something wrong with the scene.

"I can't believe she killed him," Markus said under his breath.

"What?" Sanjay stopped pacing. "Lizette didn't kill anyone."

"I don't want to believe it, either. But those are her scissors she uses to make scrap books. And you and I were together all evening after we saw Wallace alive and well."

"She couldn't have done it," Sanjay insisted.

"Until a few months ago I would have believed you. But after she had an affair...I just don't know what to believe anymore."

"No," Sanjay said. "I mean I don't see how she could actually have done it—how *anyone* could have done it. This type of lock doesn't automatically lock from behind."

"What are you talking about?"

"The lock on the office door—" Sanjay lowered his voice. "The one you had me pick. It was a *bolt*. That's why it took me so long. It wouldn't lock if someone killed him and slipped out of the room. And there isn't a window in the office. I don't see how anyone could have done it."

"That doesn't make any sense."

"No," Sanjay said. "It doesn't."

A hush fell over the room for the second time that evening. Sanjay stood without touching anything, twirling his bowler hat in his hands as they waited for the police. He knew he should be thinking about the tragedy of the murder, but honestly, he'd never liked Wallace. Wallace was a crass womanizer who'd gotten the job as theater manager because of family connections in the community. Instead of murder, Sanjay's mind drifted back to the illusion he was creating with the fish net.

The fish net was a new addition to one of his mainstay illusions. He was to escape from a trunk that was secured by chains, which he'd done before, and he was adding a fish net covering the entire trunk to make the escape appear impossible.

What had gone wrong earlier that day with the timing of the net drop? The theater was a relatively new building, and in spite of Wallace's incompetence as a manager, it was well kept. There shouldn't have been anything wrong with the equipment. There was only one possible conclusion: the timing problem had to have been simple human error.

Sanjay mulled over the phrase in his mind: simple human error. He was no longer sure if he was thinking about the illusion or the murder. There was something off about both. As if they were both an illusion.

"Markus," Sanjay said. "What had you wanted to ask Wallace about the levers?"

"What?"

"You said you needed to ask him something. That's why we went to look for him. What did you want to ask him?"

"How can you think about your trick—"

"Illusion," Sanjay said automatically.

"It was nothing. He mentioned a change I'd forgotten about." Markus tugged at his sleeves, avoiding Sanjay's gaze. He'd been able to wipe the blood off his hands with tissue, but bloody spots covered the edge of his right sleeve.

Sanjay took a sharp intake of breath just as Lizette returned to the office. He watched her red-rimmed eyes as the pieces clicked into place in his mind.

"They're on their way," Lizette said weakly.

"Lizette," Sanjay said, his heart speeding up. "Did you see any blood on the carpet when we entered the room?"

"I did," she said, "but I thought it was wine."

"There was a pool of wine," Sanjay said slowly. He placed his hat back on his head, thinking hard as he ran his fingers along its crisp rim. "But did you notice *two* pools of red when we walked in?"

"No." Lizette sniffled. "Just one."

"Me, too," Sanjay said. "It was only the wine at first. Not blood. Because we had the timing wrong."

"The timing?"

Sanjay's heart was pounding in his chest now. He hoped his voice didn't betray him. Unlike the stage, this was real life—and he was standing in a room with a murderer.

"Wallace locked himself into his room," Sanjay said, "as he usually did, and passed out from a drug that had been put into his wine. Markus was adamant I get him into this office—*before Wallace woke up.*"

"That's ridiculous," Markus said. "I was with you all evening."

"Except for when you went to get Wallace that first time, when he returned with a glass of wine and was already walking unsteadily. You needed me as your alibi. You knew he always locked his office door—and you knew I know how to pick a lock. You could be with me all evening setting up, and then have us discover the body together. You weren't counting on the fact that the lock of the office was one that couldn't be locked automatically when someone left the office. You wanted to implicate Lizette, using her scissors, and knowing you had a better alibi than her. You had to do it, because you were the one with the motive."

"My scissors," Lizette said, her voice breaking. "You mean Markus—"

"But you said it yourself, I was with you!" Markus said to Sanjay. "I *do* have an alibi."

"Except for the fact that Wallace wasn't dead before we walked into that room," Sanjay said. "Only drugged. That's why he was acting so sluggish when he came into the theater. The drug was already in his wine. When you rushed over to him just now to supposedly check if he was breathing, *that's* when you stuck the scissors in his neck. You could easily hide scissors in your hand under that ridiculously long-sleeved shirt—with your alibi standing right here next to you."

"I got blood on my hands when I was trying to save him," Markus said, his voice quivering.

"Then I suppose there won't be traces of a knockout drug in his system?"

Markus didn't respond.

"You pushed my buttons just right, too," Sanjay said, shaking his head. "Egging me on so I'd go looking for Wallace, and so I'd prove I could unlock this door."

"Markus?" Lizette whispered. "How could you?"

Markus's eyes narrowed as he faced Lizette. "How could I? *You're* the one who did this. Did you think I'd let you get away with the affair? That I'd let *either of you* get away with it?"

Before Sanjay realized what was happening, Markus lunged toward Wallace's body. He was going for the razor-sharp scissors.

Standing in the doorway, Sanjay knew he wouldn't have time to reach Markus before he grabbed the scissors. But there was something else he could do. He lifted the hat from his head and flung it at Markus, spinning it like a Frisbee. He aimed for Markus's head. The throw almost succeeded. It hit his neck.

Sanjay cringed as Markus cried out. Pushed off balance, Markus fell across Wallace's desk. Sanjay ran forward and snatched up his hat. He quickly pulled a piece of rope from inside the hat and bound Markus's hands behind his back.

"What the hell?" Markus asked in a daze, blinking furiously. "What hit me?"

Sanjay finished tying the knot—more tightly than was strictly necessary—and stood back to look at his handiwork. He picked up his hat and knocked his knuckles on the rim of his specially constructed hat. His fingers rapped as loudly as if he'd knocked on a door. "I knew there was a reason I never wanted you to know the secrets of my illusions."

Markus groaned.

Sanjay lifted his steel-rimmed magician's hat onto his head.

The Haunted Room

This Jaya Jones short story originally appeared in Murder at the Beach, *the 2014 Bouchercon Anthology, edited by Dana Cameron and published by Down & Out Books.*

"There's no such thing as ghosts," I said.

I believed what I said. At the time. But what Nadia was about to tell me made me question what I thought I knew.

"Jaya," my landlady said to me with a shake of her head. "Though your experience in Scotland had a rational explanation, that does not mean it is always so."

I eyed Nadia skeptically. "I didn't know you were superstitious."

We were sitting together on a park bench across the street from the "haunted" house Nadia had brought me to see, a San Francisco mansion from the post-Gold Rush boom in the late 1800s. Because I'd recently solved a mystery that involved folklore and a legendary Scottish fairy, Nadia wanted to tell me about her own unsolved mystery.

Nadia shrugged. "There are more things in heaven and earth, Horatio, than are dreamt of in your philosophy."

Nadia had come to California from Russia as a young woman and had lived in San Francisco for decades. She spoke perfect English, but with a strong accent. And she loved being dramatic. Which included quoting Shakespeare.

"Your ghost story has to have a rational explanation," I insisted. A swath of fog descended around us as I spoke, making my statement less convincing. I shook off the feeling. It was summer in San Francisco. Chilly weather was to be expected, especially on the hilltop that gave the Pacific Heights neighborhood its name.

After leaving India as a child, I grew up in the Bay Area, but on the other side of the bay. My father raised my brother and me in Berkeley, which, while only ten miles from San Francisco, has a completely different climate. After spending my childhood in scorching Goa and sunny Berkeley, I still wasn't used to San Francisco weather.

"I will tell you the whole story," Nadia said, wrapping her black stole more closely around her elegant shoulders. "You can be the judge of whether or not you believe it."

I nodded, not taking my eyes from the building. A gust of wind blew my bob of thick black hair around my face.

"It was in October," Nadia continued, "nearly two years ago, before you moved here for your teaching job. I have always thought of Halloween as a holiday for children, but Jack made it sound exciting. Plus, the profits from this haunted house go to charity."

"I remember hearing about this place." It sounded like the kind of thing Nadia's on-again off-again paramour would like.

"It is still a popular attraction," Nadia said, "but I will *never again* step inside. Not after what happened there." She shivered as she looked at the dark windows of the house.

The effect was contagious. Nadia was not a woman who scared easily. The haunted house was in a part of the city I rarely passed by, and based on Nadia's reaction to it, I found myself wondering if this imposing Victorian structure had unconsciously caused me to avoid the neighborhood, in spite of its gorgeous views of bridges and beaches. This house was one of the oldest in the area, having survived the Great Earthquake of 1906.

"I wore a gown from that thrift store Aunt Cora's Closet down the street," she continued. "Cream-colored satin, reminiscent of Countess Volkonskaya. A brocade, matching satin gloves, and a crimson silk hat."

That was more like Nadia. She noticed my amused reaction

and shrugged.

"Even though the holiday is childish," she said, leaning forward conspiratorially, "if one chooses to participate, one should do so in the spirit of the occasion. Jack did not mind my smoking that evening—I was playing the part of a countess, you see, with an elegant cigarette holder—"

"Nadia," I cut in.

"Yes, yes. You young people are so impatient. You must allow an old woman an excuse to ramble."

I had never learned Nadia's exact age. She looked like she was barely old enough to have retired, but I had a suspicion she wore her years well and might have been much older. And I wasn't so young. I'd recently turned thirty. I've been told I look younger, which I attribute to the fact that I'm only five feet tall. It's an image I've had to fight against. As an assistant professor of history, it's rather embarrassing to be mistaken for a college student.

"Jack said it would be a romantic evening to go to a haunted house." Nadia continued, "There was a full moon that night. He said we could go on a moonlit walk afterward."

"So you went to the haunted house and it was *spooky*?"

Nadia ignored my sarcastic remark. "You will not be able to dispute what I experienced. After waiting in line, we were placed into groups to walk through the rooms of the house. The darkness was nearly complete. The brightest lights were the dim EXIT signs above the doors. Only the light of electric candle chandeliers lit up the displays—dry ice around tombstones in a cemetery room, animated skeletons in caskets in a morgue room, mannequin figures masked with beaked bird masks in a plague room. It was the plague room where it occurred."

Nadia paused, and in spite of myself I waited in rapt anticipation for what she would say next.

"This room, it was not like the others. As soon as I entered, I knew this. A strong sensation of cold washed over us. You may be aware that cold spots in a house can indicate the presence of a ghost."

I was tempted to think Nadia was re-imagining the past, since she had a dramatic personality. A more rational explanation was that cold air was piped into the room for exactly the effect Nadia described.

"One of the plague figures in this cold room was not a mannequin, but a teenage boy working at the haunted house. He was very still at first—then reached out and grabbed a woman in front of me. I was not frightened, but it was a shock, you understand. That is why I dropped what I was holding in my hands: my gloves—which I had taken off in the heat of the stifling rooms— and a large ring that slipped off when I removed the gloves. It was not a ring that was especially valuable, but it was meaningful to me. Blue sapphire costume jewelry. As soon as my gloves and ring fell, I alerted Jack. He found a light switch hidden next to the exit door. The other six visitors in the room complained of ruining the atmosphere, but they did not stop him. My gloves were where they had fallen, *but the ring was gone.*"

"It must have rolled away," I said.

"Jaya, do you think us stupid? We searched everywhere. The others moved on, but Jack and I searched the entire room. The ring was gone. And before you say that one of the others must have stolen it, remember this was *not* a valuable ring. Nor did it look like one. Even if someone had thought it to be valuable, none of the people we were with crouched down to the ground. They did not have an opportunity to pick it up.

"It was then," she continued, "that I learned the history of this haunted room. There was a crime committed there almost three-quarters of a century ago. A crime that was never solved. Because it was committed by a ghost—a ghost who is still there."

As if on cue, a light rain began to fall.

"Come on," I said, "let's get out of here."

Nadia lingered a moment longer before following.

"Tell me the rest of the story," I said, ducking into the awning of a nearby café as the rain began falling harder.

We grabbed a table at the front of the café. With the rain

pelting against the window, I ordered hot coffee and a piece of the thick, gooey apple pie I saw another patron eating. There was sure to be enough butter and sugar in that pie to solve any problem.

"The house," Nadia said, "was built by a man with money from the Gold Rush. Several workmen died during its construction, which explains the ghost."

"Naturally."

"You mock me, but you should not. In the early 1900s, he lavishly entertained many wealthy people who would visit. On this famous visit, a portly scholar was visiting from his East Coast university. They shared a good meal with wine, and the owner saw his guest to his bedchamber. It was no ordinary night. The scholar locked himself into the room and put a chair under the door handle. You see, he was traveling with something very valuable to the academic community. This is why he wished to stay with his friend rather than at a hotel. But his precautions were for naught.

"The good professor reported a strange, ghostly noise shortly after lying down to sleep. He would not have thought much of it, for his girth made most beds squeak with all manner of sounds under his weight, except that this noise came from *the other side* of the room."

I had to hand it to Nadia. She was a great storyteller. "You sound like you were there," I said.

"After I experienced it myself, I read a history book. May I continue?"

I nodded and took a sip of the coffee that had been set in front of me without my noticing.

"When the scholar rose from the bed," Nadia said, "he saw that the historical scroll he had discovered was *gone*."

"That sounds like a strange thing for a ghost to steal," I commented.

"It was the reason he was visiting San Francisco. The ghost must have sensed its importance and wished to be malicious."

"Or someone in the house stole it because it was valuable."

"The room," Nadia said with a raised eyebrow, "and the *whole house* was searched. But that was unnecessary since he had secured his room *from the inside*."

"There must have been a false panel in the room."

"The room was carefully inspected by a police officer, and then a private detective. There were no false panels. Even if you do not believe that, you must believe what has happened in the decades since then. The man who owned the house was long dead when Alan Marcus bought the house and opened it up for a Halloween charity.

"Yet," she continued, "whenever people go into that room...*something disappears*. It began with children's toys. The ghost stole marbles from a child. This was decades ago when marbles were popular. The ghost has continued to steal, most frequently from children. It can only be a matter of time before the ghost takes not only crayons, but a *child*."

This time my shiver wasn't from the cold. I didn't feel nearly as warm and cozy as I should have sitting across from Nadia with a steaming coffee in my hands.

"I know that expression of yours," Nadia said. "I have convinced you."

"You've got me curious. I admit that much."

Two hours later, I sat surrounded by books and printouts from the newspaper archive at the library. As a professor of history, piecing through history is what I do, and I do it well. Absorbed in research, I was in my element—but I failed to come up with answers. Instead, I was more intrigued than ever. Much like Sarah Winchester's desire to build new rooms onto her sprawling San Jose mansion until she died, the wealthy man who built this house wanted to renovate his home until his death. Unfortunately, he didn't care much for the safety of his workers. At least two men had died in construction accidents while working on the house.

I didn't blame Nadia and countless others for assigning supernatural significance to the events that had taken place in the mansion. Though Nadia had exaggerated—it wasn't every time someone entered the haunted room that something went missing—the disappearances had happened enough times that something was going on.

Had the new owner Alan Marcus figured out the secret of the room and decided to use it to rob people? Initially that seemed like the easiest explanation, but none of the facts supported it. Not only was Mr. Marcus a wealthy man with no financial troubles, but the things that went missing were very rarely valuable.

Another strike against that theory: when I called Mr. Marcus, the retired gentleman wasn't the slightest bit evasive. He said he'd be happy to meet with us and show us the peculiar room.

On my way downstairs to tell Nadia of my plan to visit the inside of the house, I ran into my neighbor, Miles, a poet who was stopping by to invite me to a poetry open mic night that evening. When I told him what I was busy doing, he asked if he could come.

"I thought you had to practice reciting your poem," I said.

"You're going *now*?" he asked. "Aren't you supposed to be working on a course syllabus or something?"

"Don't remind me."

I wished Miles good luck preparing for his poetry reading, then found Nadia, who wasn't any more helpful. True to her word, she refused to go back to the house. Was I the only one who cared about the baffling mystery of the haunted room?

"What if we could get your ring back?" I said.

"Tempting," Nadia said. "Very tempting."

That's how I found myself heading back to the mansion with Nadia that afternoon. At least the rain had let up.

"I've been thinking," I said as we approached the house. "What if Mr. Marcus wanted to throw the police off the scent by stealing seemingly random items to disguise the theft of a few valuable ones?"

"You found a historic treasure, Jaya, and now you think you are an expert at all types of crime-solving?"

Nadia's sarcasm be damned, I was feeling quite pleased with

my deductive abilities until Mr. Marcus opened the door. I liked him at once. The octogenarian greeted us with a hearty handshake and a mischievous smile as he asked us if we were going to be the ones to solve his mystery. Most importantly, he also offered us coffee and cookies before we got to work. A man after my own heart.

He explained that he only used part of the house during most of the year. The haunted house section wasn't currently in use, its sparse furniture covered in sheets for ten months of the year. "After my wife passed away," he said, "I no longer entertained. There wasn't much point in keeping up the whole house."

I ate several cookies while listening to stories about his wife, who threw a wicked party in her day. Nadia sat stiffly, barely touching her coffee. I, on the other hand, was quite comfortable. Mr. Marcus kept the heat turned up, leaving me contentedly cozy on the plush couch. If it hadn't been for my curiosity, I would have been happy to spend the afternoon looking out the sweeping bay windows with views of the Golden Gate Bridge.

Once I declared I couldn't possibly eat another cookie, Mr. Marcus led us across the sprawling house to the room. We walked on beautiful Persian rugs in the hallways and passed original oil paintings that looked vaguely familiar, plus a series of impressionist paintings of San Francisco beaches. The perspective of the scenes suggested they might have been painted from the main room of the house, long before the city had grown up around it.

Inside the supposedly haunted room, Mr. Marcus tossed the sheets aside and stood back, letting me have a closer look. The thick floorboards creaked beneath my feet.

I had learned a thing or two about false panels from my best friend, Sanjay. He's a magician, so I would have called him except I knew he was out of town preparing for a show. Even though he didn't trust me with all his secrets, I had a good understanding of how many of his illusions worked. The same principles stage magicians used could be applied to situations like this. But that knowledge wasn't helping me here. I was fairly confident I wasn't missing any secret panels. But I had to be missing *something*.

"Intriguing, isn't it?" Mr. Marcus said. "The unsolved theft was one of the reasons that initially drew me to this place. My wife was a history buff. She loved the idea of living in a piece of history."

"So you two looked into the construction of the room."

"Oh yes," he said, "most certainly. But we never found any hidden entrances to the room."

"The walls—" I began.

"That," Mr. Marcus said, "is the strangest part. Even if we missed a false panel, there's no extra space between these walls. An electrician did some poking around years ago. There's nothing there—and no room for anything to be hidden."

After eating another cookie—it would have been rude to turn down his hospitality—Nadia and I departed, and I headed back to the library. This time I paid attention not to the sensationalism surrounding the original crime or the construction of the house, but to the pictures of the room itself.

The layout of the room struck me as strange in the original historical photos. The nightstand had been placed across the room from the bed. That was odd...

I stepped outside and pulled out my cell phone.

"Mr. Marcus," I said, "I know you checked the walls, but did you ever check the floor for any false panels?"

"We certainly did. The floorboards were all connected to each other. There were no false panels there either."

"But did you check *the space* underneath the floor?"

There was silence on the other end of the line.

"You know," he said, "I don't believe we did. But without a teleportation device, I don't see how anything could have fallen through that solid floor."

"Do you mind if I come back? I promise it won't take long."

This time I returned to the mansion with extra backup. Not

because I was afraid of a ghost, but because I needed to replicate the girth of the man who had once stayed there and been robbed of his valuable discovery.

Nadia pursed her lips when I insisted on grabbing Miles from the poetry open mic night that was wrapping up at a coffee house in our neighborhood, but she said nothing. She didn't like Miles, but she was at least as curious as I was.

Twenty minutes later, the three of us piled into the corner of the room where the bed once stood.

"Mr. Marcus, we need you, too, if this is going to work."

As he crossed the room and stepped within a foot of me, Miles, and Nadia, the floor began to shift.

It wasn't the movement of a single floorboard; the whole floor was subtly tilting. The floor was ever-so-slightly pivoting around a fulcrum in the center of the room. The tilt of the floor around the central hinge resulted in the edges of the wooden flooring being lower than the bottom of the wall. It was only a couple of inches—a small enough shift that in the dark it would have felt like stepping on a loose floorboard—but it was enough for anything small and circular to slip out of the room to the space beneath the floor.

I took a pen out of my bag and dropped it. It rolled away and disappeared into the darkness.

Everyone began to move at once.

"Stop!" I said. "If any of us moves from this spot, the floor will go back to normal. "It was only because we have enough weight here that it activated the mechanism that was put in place to rob the professor who stayed here."

"Ingenious!" Mr. Marcus said, clapping his hands together. "Ingenious, but nasty. He altered this room and set it up to rob his friend."

"Let me see if I can see what's going on under there." Without moving away from the others, I crouched down on the floor and pulled a flashlight and a magnifying glass from my messenger bag.

Sure enough, I could see an assortment of dusty items, mostly children's toys like matchbox cars—anything that *rolled*.

In the midst of the treasures, my flashlight shone across a blue stone ring. Nadia had said it was a piece of blue sapphire costume jewelry she'd lost.

"Miles," I said. "Can I borrow a pen?" He handed me a pen, and I used it to snag the large ring in the midst of the hidden treasures. Standing up, I handed Miles his pen and Nadia her ring.

"After all this time," Nadia said, shaking her head. "Thank you, Jaya."

"You can all move now if you want to," I said. "I've seen what I needed to. Nobody has been stealing things in this house—not a ghost, not even a person. At least not for around eighty years. It was this mechanism."

I stepped away from the group. The floor slowly straightened out from its central pivot point. Because the floorboards were thick and uneven in this section of the old house, the small amount of space between the floorboards in the center of the room hadn't raised any suspicions.

"A hinge," Nadia murmured.

"I'm *so* writing a poem about this," Miles said, scribbling a few lines in his beaten-up notebook he kept in the pocket of his cargo pants. "A theft from long ago," he murmured to himself, "high above the Pacific Ocean's beaches where the wind doth blow...Jaya Jones is the insightful professor, who's more than a good guesser..."

"Only when all the forces align," I said, ignoring the clunky rhymes of Miles' poem, "does something go missing. The floor was rigged to steal one particular thing—a valuable scroll from a very large man. The thief who owned this house was able to set things up with precision for that one-time event. He got his 'friend' inebriated and saw him to bed with his valued possession safely in the corner of a room locked from the inside, with the bedside table and lamp across the room from the bed. When the large man went to bed, it would necessarily be dark. He would feel himself lower down into what he thought was an uneven mattress but wouldn't see the shift in the floor."

"When I opened my haunted house," Mr. Marcus said,

grinning excitedly, "people would huddle closely together because they were having fun being frightened. Acting as a group, they replicated the weight necessary to activate the lever. That's when the disappearances began."

"Exactly," I said. "In the darkness and commotion, people felt that something was happening, but couldn't identify exactly what it was. They were already discombobulated from walking through dark rooms that played with their senses. And as soon as they moved to turn on the lights, the floor was again completely flat. It was *the house itself* collecting treasures all these years."

"What a wonderful haunted house!" Nadia said. "I cannot wait until next Halloween."

The Library Ghost of Tanglewood Inn

This Jaya Jones novelette was originally published by Henery Press in 2017 and won the Agatha Award for Best Short Story.

i.

"I can't believe you forced me to get into that stifling sardine can on the most crowded travel day of the year, Jaya." Tamarind dropped her plaid backpack at her feet. The overstuffed bag fell onto its side, hiding her purple combat boots.

A few minutes before, we'd stepped off an oversold flight we'd barely squeezed on to. Yet we were still over a thousand miles from home. We'd left Japan en route to San Francisco via a tangle of connections because of our last-minute booking, and weather conditions diverted us to Denver—where all planes were now grounded due to a snow storm.

Which is how we found ourselves stuck in a line that snaked for miles—or at least far too many slyly hidden twists and turns—to reach an airport counter where we hoped to find out our fate. The only reason I'd agreed to fly on one of the most crowded travel days of the year was the anticipation of what was waiting for us on the other end. It now seemed unlikely I'd make it in time.

A man in line next to us cleared his throat. He was already dressed for the weather outside in a parka, wool hat, and infinity scarf, and carried ear muffs in a gloved hand. Everything he wore was a shade of gray. If he got lost in the snow outside, it occurred to me that no one would ever find him. I bit my lip to stop myself from laughing. I must have been giddy from lack of sleep. After the week I'd had chasing a murderous ninja, tracking down a missing trading ship from two centuries ago that nobody else thought existed, and helping with a magic show based on an impossible illusion, my imagination was running wild. But the past week was behind me. Why was I still on edge?

"The Sunday after Thanksgiving isn't actually the most crowded travel day of the year," the man said, smiling at Tamarind. At least I imagined he was smiling based on the cheerful tone of his voice. It was hard to see much beneath the hat and scarf except for youthful dark brown eyes and light brown skin. "That's only a myth."

Tamarind scowled at him and his face reddened.

"Sorry about my friend," I said. "Long day."

"For us, too," he said.

Tamarind and I exchanged a glance as the line inched forward. Was he referring to his suitcase? I looked around the line, filled with frustrated travelers of all ilk. In our immediate area were parents with slumped shoulders carrying young children and pushing precariously stacked baggage carts, older kids playing a game of hide and seek around baggage claim, college students in sweats with their eyes glued to their smartphones. Our gray snowman wasn't traveling with any of them.

He laughed. "I'm not as eccentric as I look. I'm not used to snow so I bought all this in one of the shops in the airport while my boss got in line. But now I can't find him and he's not answering his phone. He's—"

"There you are, Kenny. Why are you in this ridiculous line?"

The speaker wasn't traditionally handsome, but he had presence far beyond his looks and stature. With his long black hair, pale skin, and a stride that caused the sea of people to part, he looked like a haunted anti-hero who'd stepped out of a vampire television show. Like his companion, he was already dressed for the storm. And he must have ventured outside. Clumps of snow dotted his stylish, Victorianesque black coat.

"Honestly, sometimes I don't know why I employ you," the newcomer continued. "I found us a taxi and a hotel with rooms available."

"Shut. Up." Tamarind said. "I thought the local hotels were already booked up and we'd be stuck in purgatory for the night. How'd you beat the system? And by the way, that vintage coat is to die for."

He grinned at her and eyed her purple combat boots. "Nice boots. I have my ways. Feel like escaping purgatory? There's room if you two want to come."

"Thanks, but we're fine," I said.

"We're *not* fine," Tamarind said. "Jaya, for the love of all that's good and holy, please remember that not everything is a murderous plot."

Kenny choked. His vampiric boss laughed. "Don't worry," he said. "There's a chaperone in the taxi."

I slipped on my jacket, hefted my travel pack onto my shoulders, and followed Kenny's boss past another line of angry passengers. Tamarind was right. No flights were leaving that night, and I didn't want to spend the night at the airport. I was overly suspicious of everything these days.

"Why does he look so familiar?" Tamarind whispered. "Maybe you were right about being cautious. Do you think he's hypnotized us and we're following him into a cult?"

"You watch too many B movies."

"Of course I do. They're awesome."

Our benefactor, who did look vaguely familiar, led us past an outdoor line of shivering people boarding the last shuttle buses to take stranded travelers to local hotels. The area was nominally shielded from the elements, but the snow was blowing sideways. I'd spent the first eight years of my life in Goa, India, and grew up in California after that. I wasn't prepared on any level for a Colorado snowstorm. I pulled my completely inadequate jacket more tightly around me, wishing I'd brought something warmer like Kenny or was at least wearing more practical shoes than my heels.

I bumped into Tamarind as our group came to an abrupt stop in front of a taxi so large that an automated step descended when the driver opened the back door of the SUV. I hesitated when I didn't see other people inside.

"What are you standing around for?" a woman's voice with a faint Irish accent called from the back seat. "Shut the car door already if you're not getting in. It's colder than Finnegan's feet the day they buried him."

I stepped forward and saw a woman with a bountiful bun of silver hair on top of her head sitting in the back row of seats. She looked up from her knitting and nodded at me, not missing a beat with her stitching.

The driver took my bag, in spite of being only a couple of inches taller than my five-foot frame. Underneath her driver's cap, tendrils of curly auburn hair had blown loose in the wind and encircled her petite face. My mind at ease, I climbed into the heated car.

"Simon was kind enough to offer me a ride after I stopped him for an autograph," the knitting passenger said. "Are you fans as well?"

I felt my cheeks flushing as I brushed snow out of my hair. *Was* Kenny's boss an actor on a vampire TV show?

"I didn't have a chance to introduce myself earlier," said our host from the front seat. "I'm Simon. Simon Quinn."

I groaned to myself. That's why he'd looked familiar. He was the famous author. Or rather, the *infamous* author. What had we gotten ourselves into?

"Buckle up," the driver said, tossing her cap aside. "The roads are killer out there tonight."

ii.

Outside the windows, flurries of white interrupted the bleak darkness. If anything could bond our motley crew of passengers, it was surviving the zero visibility conditions.

Thanks to our driver, whose nametag on the dashboard identified her as Ivy, the road barely felt like the obstacle course that it was. She navigated two unexpected snow drifts and a fallen tree branch with the footwork of a race car driver, all the while chatting with Simon about his books.

"Is it true you based the character Stetson Quick on your own experience being wrongly accused of murder?" Ivy asked.

"You've no idea what it feels like to lose someone you love in such a brutal way," Simon said. A reflection of his forlorn face flashed in the side window. "You think it can't possibly get any worse, but when the police think you're the one who did it...It's why I found myself compelled to write *To the Quick* while awaiting trial."

Simon Quinn had made a name for himself writing literary thrillers about a reluctant hero—a man who'd been wrongly convicted of murder, and after escaping from prison, lived in the shadows while traveling the country and helping others who'd been wrongly accused. Simon's books weren't my cup of tea, but millions loved them. Of the people who didn't, many objected not to the content of the books, but the character of the author.

"Didn't you care that her family thought you were exploiting the situation?" Tamarind asked.

In the window's reflection, I caught a flash of annoyance flicker across Simon's face. He quickly covered the expression as he swept aside his black hair. He couldn't have been older than his early thirties, but his face bore the deep lines of worry of someone much older.

"Simon's work has always been about redemption," Kenny said. "He's given so many people hope that it's unfair to—"

"It's all right, Kenny," Simon said. "It's true that her family wished I hadn't used facts so closely related to the case in the novel, but it's what was so therapeutic, not just for me, but for everyone following the trial. As Kenny said, the pain of a few resulted in redemption for many."

"They're brilliant books," the Irishwoman said, not looking up from her knitting.

"Exploitative is what they are," Tamarind murmured loudly enough for only me to hear, but I saw Kenny's posture stiffen.

Tamarind fell uncharacteristically silent after grumbling, "Why didn't I listen to you when I had the chance?" She crossed her arms and popped on headphones, giving a spot-on impression of a sulking teen. It made her look closer to sixteen than her true age of twenty-six.

If Tamarind hadn't been one of my closest friends, I would have thought she was nervous about the snowstorm. But I knew she couldn't stand manipulative people. She worked as a librarian at a public university even after being offered more lucrative jobs, because she wanted to help people directly. I didn't know if it was true that Simon had strangled his college sweetheart ten years ago, but he'd leveraged being acquitted for murder into fame and fortune as a bestselling author.

While Ivy asked Simon more about his books, I became immediately enamored with my knitting seatmate Dorothy, who insisted I call her Dot. She'd been a high school history teacher in both Ireland and the US—a far more difficult job than my own job of history professor. Aside from a few of the students in my Intro to World History course that satisfied a graduation requirement, my students wanted to be in my classes. They were bright, curious, and at an age where they were convinced they could save the world. My best students believed me when I told them the old adage: *Those who don't know history are doomed to repeat it.* They took the saying to heart, and I didn't doubt they'd make a difference far beyond the classroom.

Dot felt the same about her students. A retired widow, she was now a volunteer tutor for low-income students in Albuquerque, where she was trying to return after spending Thanksgiving with her daughter's family in Colorado.

"My daughter's *manky* husband dropped me off at the airport before making sure my flight wasn't grounded," Dot said with a shake of her head. "Young men these days. No offense, Kenneth. You seem to be on the right path. It must be an honor to work with Simon."

Was it my imagination, or did her words have the distinct ring of sarcasm?

"It is," Kenny said. "I've learned so much this year as his research assistant. I've—"

All conversation broke off as the car swerved abruptly. My seatbelt caught with the sudden shift in movement, and Tamarind grabbed my arm.

"Sorry," Ivy said, maneuvering around a car crash on the side of the road.

"Nice reflexes," Kenny said.

Ivy beamed. "When I was younger, I dreamed of becoming a NASCAR driver." Even in the reflection of the rearview mirror, she glowed with that adventurous spirit.

After twenty minutes the SUV came to a stop and Ivy turned off the engine. It had taken longer than I'd thought it would to reach a hotel. Assuming that's where we were. I still couldn't see anything.

"Kenny," Simon said, "take care of this."

"Right," Kenny said, passing a credit card to Ivy.

"Bloody hell," Simon exclaimed as he opened his door. "Where are we?"

"What an affectation," Tamarind whispered. "He's not British.

He's not even Australian. He's originally from here in Denver." She rolled her eyes.

"The other hotels are full," Ivy said to Simon. "I knew this one would have room because it's further out and up on this hill that most drivers won't brave in a snowstorm. You should all count yourselves lucky you aren't sleeping on the floor at the airport." The last of her words were lost on Simon as he slammed the door behind him and trudged through the snow toward the hotel without a glance back at us.

"I, for one, am thrilled not to be sleeping on the airport floor," I said.

Kenny had already slipped his credit card back into his wallet, but he wasn't moving.

"Um, Kenny," Tamarind said, "could you move so we can get out?"

"Sorry." He looked up from his phone, a not-sorry grin on his face. "I was looking up the hotel. It's perfect. Absolutely perfect. I need to tell Simon." He jumped out, but to his credit, instead of chasing after Simon he stood at our door along with Ivy to help the rest of us navigate safely to the icy ground.

"Those two are a strange pair," Dot said, once Kenny was out of earshot.

The snow was still blowing sideways, but outside the car I was able to see the outlines of a hotel. It looked more like a Victorian mansion than a modern hotel. Two turrets flanked the sides of the three-story building. A curtain fluttered in the high window of the left turret. Was someone watching our arrival? I was half blinded by the snow and darkness, so I couldn't see whoever was standing in the window.

More interesting than an inquisitive observer and old-fashioned architecture was the gnarled tree that stood in front of the hotel. "Stood" is perhaps the wrong word to describe it. Its thick trunk twisted around itself, and it had grown not toward the sky but hunched over as if protecting the hotel from an invisible foe. Past the tree, the entryway beckoned. A wrought iron sign above the jade green double door read TANGLEWOOD INN.

I picked up my bag and walked to the entrance of the Tanglewood Inn.

iii.

A lone woman greeted us at the front desk of the hotel, which was decorated with paper cutouts of smiling cartoon turkeys holding a banner that said HAPPY THANKSGIVING. Her thick black hair was so long that it disappeared behind the counter. She held a phone in her hand and wore a frown on her face.

"I'm surprised you made it," she said, hanging up a landline phone at the counter. "The storm is getting worse, so they're not routing any more people this far."

She introduced herself as the owner, Rosalyn, checked us in, and showed us to our rooms. I was given the tower room. The one where I could have sworn I'd seen the curtains move.

"I hope everything is to your liking," Rosalyn said. "Our maid left before the storm picked up, but I'll do what I can to get you anything you need."

"Your staff isn't here?" I asked. "I thought I saw someone in the window when we arrived."

Rosalyn shook her head. "The guests who were here for Thanksgiving left this morning. Both the maid and chef left for the day. But don't worry. I have plenty of leftovers. I know it's late, but I bet you're hungry. I'll bring snacks to the library."

Kenny and I were the first to arrive in the library, which served as the hotel's common room. The grandfather clock near the fireplace struck ten o'clock just as we entered.

Now that he was out of his bulky snow gear, I got my first good look at Kenny. Dressed in jeans and a bright white dress shirt, with an inquisitive expression on his face, he reminded me of my brightest college students. He couldn't have been much older than them.

"Why did you say this place was perfect?" I asked him as I surveyed the room.

Although the hearth held a cozy fire, the best word to describe the room was spooky. A fierce gargoyle glowered at us from the high mantle above the fireplace. Heavy burgundy drapes covered the windows, and I could hear the wind whistling wildly outside. The walls were lined with built-in bookcases that were filled with books so old they looked antique. The towering wood-paneled grandfather clock was big enough for kids to hide inside.

But none of that was what made the library feel like it belonged in a haunted house. It was the ornate candelabra hanging above a central oak table, with faux candles held in the mouths of pewter serpents that looked as if they were waiting for a séance to take place on the table beneath. Like the image of the hotel from the outside, the inside looked like it was frozen in time from over a century ago.

"You didn't look this place up when we arrived?" Kenny asked.

As a historian, I had a complicated relationship with the internet. While helpful for finding good restaurants, when it came to history it led me on the wrong path more often than not. I shook my head.

"Simon hired me as his research assistant because of my location scouting experience," he said. "I'm always on the lookout for good settings."

"He likes creepy settings that he acts like he hates?" I watched the shadows dancing across the bookshelves as the fire crackled.

"He likes places with a good story."

Rosalyn stepped into the room carrying a heavy tray as expertly as the best servers I'd known when I'd been a waitress.

"This place has a great story," she said. "That is, if you like ghost stories. The Tanglewood Inn is supposedly haunted."

Kenny's eyes lit up. "So it's true. Maybe Simon will set his next book here. The desolate setting is fantastic."

"I wondered if he was that famous author," Rosalyn said as she set the tray on the séance table. "The fridge is filled with Thanksgiving leftovers, so help yourself to as much as you'd like." She unloaded bowls of shredded turkey stewed in cranberry sauce, mashed potatoes with cranberries on top, and sweet potato pie with cranberry compote. "I hope you like cranberries. Cranberry scones are in the freezer for breakfast."

I would have eaten almost anything at that moment. Even more airplane food. The spread made me forget to roll my eyes at the suggestion the hotel was haunted.

"OMG, cranberries." Tamarind's voice filled the air as she strode into the library. Her short blue hair was wet, and she'd changed her combat boots to bunny slippers. "You're my hero, Rosalyn. Can I come back here each Thanksgiving? Sometimes I feel like nobody besides me fully appreciates the cranberry. It starts out tart on the outside but is sweet once you coax out its flavor. Just like me."

"What's the history of the hotel's name?" I asked Rosalyn.

"My father named this place Tanglewood Inn for the *krummholz* tree you passed coming into the hotel."

"I've never heard of that variety of tree."

"*Krummholz* isn't a type of tree, but a concept. It means 'crooked wood' in German. In cold, windswept places, trees grow like this to shield themselves from the elements and survive."

As Tamarind and I filled our plates, Simon stepped into the room with Dot on his arm, living up to his reputation as a charmer of women of all ages. After his trial, there had been speculation that one or more of the jurors had fallen in love with him, causing the unexpected Not Guilty verdict. I hadn't followed the case closely, but I remembered one part clearly: Simon had an alibi that made it impossible for him to have killed his girlfriend in the park where she was found. Even though forensic evidence suggested he was at the scene, it was his alibi that swayed the jury.

"Rosalyn was going to tell us the story of the hotel," Kenny said. "Nobody is afraid of a ghost story, are they?"

"I'd think your boss would be," Tamarind said. "Especially one told by our host. Isn't that his MO? Afraid of strong women?"

"What's your problem?" Kenny said. "He was found Not Guilty. As in innocent. And it's thanks to his generosity that you're here in this warm hotel for the night instead of stuck at the airport."

Because Tamarind had flattered him before she realized who he was, I thought to myself.

Simon glared at Tamarind, but quickly covered it with a smile. "I'd love to hear the ghost story, Rosalyn," he said.

Dot settled into the sofa close to the fireplace while the rest of us served ourselves plates of food and sat at the round table underneath the candelabra.

"My father bought this hotel years ago," Rosalyn said, pausing to take a bite of sweet potato pie. "I grew up here. It was a wonderful childhood, having this big old house to play in. We'd always been too poor to buy a house, but this place was cheap. Because of the incident."

"The haunting," Simon said calmly, looking at Tamarind.

"Yes," Rosalyn said, picking up a book encased in a glass box. It had been placed apart from the other books on one of the bookshelves. "Our library's avenging ghost."

"The ghost lives in a book?" Tamarind asked.

"Perhaps." Rosalyn shrugged. "As the years go on, the story gets more and more fantastic. I can't complain. It drives up business. What I do know for a fact is that something very strange happened here in the 1930s. The house was already a hotel before we bought it. One of the guests, a Mr. Underhill, died here in this library. This book had something to do with it."

I looked at the glass-encased book in our host's hands. It was difficult to see the title because it was an old hardback book that had lost its dust jacket, and the hinges of the glass container obscured my view further. I stepped closer to see the lettering on the green fabric cover. *Murder on the Orient Express* by Agatha Christie. Four handwritten words had been scrawled on the face of the book in black ink: *You win. I'm guilty.*

"Supposedly," Rosalyn continued, "this book drove him

insane."

"That's what I'm not clear on," Kenny said. "The online descriptions say the police looked into the case as a murder but ultimately ruled it a suicide. Was it a cover-up?"

"Mr. Underhill had ripped books from the shelves here in the library. It wasn't clear if he was doing so in anger or if he was looking for something. The only things we know for sure are one, that it was his handwriting on the Agatha Christie mystery; and two, that he impaled himself on a poker from the fireplace."

"You could add more grisly details for effect," Dot said, not looking up from her knitting.

Kenny laughed.

"What?" Dot said. "'Impaled' is a rather vague word, isn't it? There are much more evocative ways I can think of to describe a—"

"How do you know he stabbed himself?" I asked, not wanting to hear more from Dot's imagination. "It seems like a strange way to commit suicide."

"Because," Rosalyn said, "anything else would have been impossible. Anything, that is, besides a ghost."

"Now this is getting interesting," Simon said. He polished off a bite of pie and leaned back in the upholstered chair. His black hair and light eyes shone under the candelabra.

"While Mr. Underhill was destroying the library, he moved a large table to block the door. This very table, if the stories are to be believed. The table wasn't simply holding the door shut—it was jammed underneath the doorknob. There's no way anyone could have gotten in or out. The authorities had to use a ladder and break the window to get inside."

"Meaning the killer could have gotten out through the windows as well," Kenny said.

Rosalyn shook her head. "Bolted from the inside."

"Locks can be tampered with," I said as I walked to the windows where the heavy curtains were drawn. I pulled back the curtains and was greeted by the twisted tree that gave the hotel its name. "This second floor is pretty high, but the tree is close enough."

"Not quite," Rosalyn said, lifting the sleeve of her sweater to show us a ragged scar on her forearm. "I tried it once when I was a kid. Missed by a mile, but luckily only broke my leg and got this scar. But even if a full-grown adult could reach the tree, it would be much easier to climb down the side of the house. The problem is that the windows were checked by experts after Mr. Underhill's death. Authorities didn't want to believe a supernatural explanation. They wanted to solve it. They focused on the chimney for a while, too, but it's far too small."

"They simply gave up?" Tamarind asked.

She shook her head. "In the investigation, they discovered that Underhill used many names and that he'd been cheating a lot of people out of their life savings. This was right after the Great Depression, so it was even worse. Two of the people he conned killed themselves."

None of us spoke while Rosalyn paused to take a sip of water. She was staring at the glass-encased novel she'd placed on the table. Shadows flickered across her face. That was odd. It was as if the lights were moving. I glanced around. Nobody had entered the room. And we were all sitting still.

"None of the authorities seemed too eager to solve the case after that," she continued. "They ruled it a suicide. Said Mr. Underhill must have snapped from the guilt of leading people to their deaths. But not everyone thought it was his conscience."

"That's when the hotel got its haunted reputation," I said.

Rosalyn nodded. "Because of the supposed connection to a haunting, nobody stayed here for a long time. Not until my dad got the idea to play up the haunting angle. To get people to come here who wanted to see a ghost. It was a 'vigilante ghost,' after all, so nobody else would be in danger. And it's worked for decades. Like the people we had staying here over Thanksgiving weekend. A few families who thought it would be fun to have someone else cook for them while getting the added entertainment of this haunted library, including getting to see the original Agatha Christie book involved in a ghostly murder. I took over as manager after my father died several years ago—and before you ask, he died peacefully of natural causes, not at the hands of the ghost. Nobody else has died in the library." She paused and grinned. "It makes a great story, though, doesn't it? Now, who wants coffee?"

Rosalyn left for the kitchen. I stretched and looked at the books that lined the shelves.

"This place needs a librarian," Tamarind said to me. "Big time. Gothic ghost stories from the nineteenth century are next to natural history books from the twentieth. There's no method here. Damn." She eyed the empty sweet potato pie platter. "Who wants coffee if there's no more pie?" She left in search of the kitchen.

"Can you see if there's nondairy creamer?" Kenny called. When Tamarind didn't answer, he went after her.

"Turmeric is your research assistant?" Simon asked.

"Tamarind," I corrected. "And she is sometimes. But don't let her hear you say that. She's a librarian at the university where I teach."

"She doesn't look like a librarian."

"*Definitely* don't let her hear you say that. You won't survive the night." Self-declared post-punk post-feminist Tamarind Ortega was one of the most brilliant people I'd ever met. She was also big, tall, and tough, an asset at a public university library in the heart of San Francisco.

The electric lights of the candelabra flickered overhead.

"Wouldn't it be something if we were trapped in the dark with the library ghost," Dot said with a laugh. She adjusted the bun on her head, and I noticed it was held in place with knitting needles.

Simon picked up the glass case that held the ghostly copy of *Murder on the Orient Express*. "One of the most ingenious mysteries ever written," he said. "Thrillers are more my forte, but one has to appreciate the genius of Dame Agatha."

"I read mostly nonfiction," I said, "but I remember finding this on my dad's bookshelf when I was a kid." I thought back on my father's own haphazard bookshelves, which he offered up as a neighborhood lending library. My brother Mahilan hated that our Berkeley neighbors would come by at all hours to borrow or drop off a book or snacks, but I loved observing the range of quirky people who'd congregate in our living room. It was a study in human nature. "I remember how well Agatha Christie planted clues about human nature, like being able to tell when people know each other even when they pretend they don't. And her knowledge of poison was impressive."

Rosalyn, Tamarind, and Kenny returned with coffee. The lights overhead flickered again. This time, darkness followed.

Simon swore, but nobody seemed too distressed. We were rational adults, after all. Or perhaps it was the fact that the light from the fireplace was enough to see. Rosalyn walked calmly to a cabinet near the library entryway and removed a box of flashlights. She handed one to each of us. "It happens during storms," she said.

A door slammed in the distance.

This time, we all jumped. A yelp escaped Simon's lips. Even Rosalyn gasped. Dot stopped knitting. The sound of the stairs creaking, step by slow step, filled the silence that followed.

"What the—" Kenny murmured.

"I thought the roads were closed," Tamarind whispered, biting her lip.

The creaking stopped, and a moment later a shadow appeared in the open doorway of the library.

Our taxi driver Ivy stepped inside. Her hair and face were wet with melted snow, making her unruly curls look like strands of wild ivy. "Do you have an extra room? I couldn't make it down the road. We're trapped for the night."

iv.

I awoke with my heart pounding furiously. I shot up in the strange bed. That sound...Where had it come from? My arms prickled with goose bumps. I couldn't tell if it was from the chill in the room or from fright. Had the sound of a muffled scream come from somewhere in the hotel, or from the confines of a dream?

My room was pitch black. Not even numbers on the clock shone through the darkness. The power must have still been out. I felt along the bedside table for my flashlight. Instead I found my phone. Even though I'd plugged it in, the screen was dark. In the darkness, I listened to see if the sound that had woken me would come again. It didn't. All I heard was the sound of the storm walloping the windowpane. That must have been what had startled me awake.

I snuggled back under the lumpy quilt, trying to get comfortable. I wasn't supposed to be here. My brother had scheduled a belated Thanksgiving dinner in San Francisco so I could be there, but with the storm getting worse, as time passed it seemed more and more certain I was going to miss Thanksgiving for a *second* time this week. I was feeling a little sorry for myself— when a man's scream pierced the cool air.

I found the flashlight by accident as I stepped on it jumping out of bed. I pulled a sweater over my camisole and leggings and rushed downstairs in my bare feet. I found Rosalyn and Dot standing outside the closed library door in their pajamas. For Dot that meant silver yoga clothes that matched her hair. Rosalyn looked as if she'd stepped out of another century, with the edges of a lacy white gown poking out beneath a silk robe, and her long black hair wrapped in a braid around her head.

"What was that sound?" I asked.

"That's what we were trying to figure out," Dot said.

"The library door is bolted from the inside," Rosalyn said. "This isn't good."

"I'd say it's very well done," Dot said. "This is a much more dramatic publicity stunt than your telling of the ghost story. Your heart wasn't in it earlier tonight. I didn't *believe* in the ghost. But now—"

"This isn't a stunt," Rosalyn snapped. "But I know how to find out what's going on." She disappeared down the hallway.

"Where's she going?" Kenny asked, appearing on the stairs from the floor above.

"Hopefully to get a key," Dot said, rattling the locked library door.

Ivy and Tamarind were behind Kenny. The three of them had taken time to get dressed, but Kenny was barefoot like me. Rosalyn returned holding both a key and a screwdriver. We were all there except for Simon.

"My father didn't believe in ghosts," Rosalyn said, "in spite of the publicity for our hotel. When he bought this place, he replaced the hinges and locks of this door. That way we could always get inside. Even if something blocked the door again, we could easily remove the hinges and open it in the opposite direction. But I hope it doesn't come to that."

The key unlocked the door. She pushed it open. The library was dark except for the harsh beam of a lone flashlight lying on the floor, casting a narrow swath of light across the room. And across the feet of a fallen man.

Tamarind, Dot, and Kenny rushed forward toward the prone form of Simon Quinn.

I remained in the doorway. Not because I was paralyzed with fear, but because I wanted to take in the room. Something was off about this room. Not only because Simon was lying still on the floor.

Kenny, in the lead, jerked to a stop a few feet from his boss and cried out. Dot and Tamarind crashed into him. Dot's flashlight went flying.

"Oh God," Tamarind said. "What happened? Why did you stop?"

"Glass," Kenny said through gritted teeth, plucking a piece of glass from the ball of his foot. The erratic beam of his flashlight showed fragments of glass strewn across the floor. "Please. Someone who has shoes on and can walk through this mess, please help Simon."

Tamarind reached Simon first. Ivy was close behind. Simon was fully dressed in the clothes he'd worn that evening. Tamarind's flashlight beam illuminated Simon's face, showing his hazel eyes wide open and a twisted expression of horror on his lips. With pale skin and wild eyes caught in a frozen gaze, he looked even more vampiric in death. There was no helping Simon Quinn.

Kenny ran from the room as the two women felt Simon's wrist and neck for a pulse. I looked away as I felt myself shaking but forced myself to look back. Was there a chance I was wrong?

"He's dead," Dot whispered. Her bun came loose and her white hair tumbled over her shoulders. She hadn't secured her bun with knitting needles as she'd done before.

"We need to call an ambulance," I said, and offered to call before remembering my cell phone was dead.

"I'm calling," Rosalyn said. But her hands were shaking so badly she dropped her phone. It landed on a large segment of glass.

"I'll do it," Kenny said, limping back into the room. He was now wearing untied sneakers and stepped through the glass toward Simon. "Is he—?"

"I'm sorry, dear," Dot said, giving his shoulder a squeeze.

As Kenny called 911, Rosalyn placed two battery-operated lamps on the table, illuminating the room and allowing me to see Simon more clearly. The shattered glass wasn't spread across the entire floor, but rather encircled Simon's upper body like a devilish halo. Two of the larger chunks of glass were affixed to hinges, and one to a pewter lock. It was the glass case that had once held the early edition of *Murder on the Orient Express*. The hardback book lay on the floor next to Simon.

"Yes," Kenny said into his phone. "We're certain he's dead." He clutched his flashlight so tightly in his other hand I was afraid it would crack.

I stepped closer, getting a better look but careful to avoid the glass. There was no question Simon was dead. Unlike the first strange death that had taken place in the library, I didn't see any obvious signs of violence—aside from the contorted look of fear on his face. Had the library ghost frightened Simon Quinn to death? It certainly looked like he'd died of fright.

"I understand," Kenny was saying to the 911 operator. He clicked off, tucked the phone into his pocket, and took a deep breath. "It's impossible for anyone to reach us until morning," he said, his gaze falling to Simon.

"That can't be right," Tamarind said. "Isn't that what snow plows are for?"

"They're not going to plow in the middle of the night during a fierce storm," Rosalyn said, "especially since Simon's beyond needing medical help."

"I'll get a sheet to cover him," Ivy said.

"Nobody goes near his body," Kenny said.

Ivy gaped at him. "I don't know where you're from, but it's more respectful to—"

"Not when there's something far more important at stake," Kenny said. "Simon was murdered."

We all stared at him in silence. Even the wind outside calmed for a moment.

"He was in here alone, Kenny," Rosalyn said softly, breaking the silence. "I know it's upsetting, but—"

"Simon was in perfect health," Kenny insisted. "He didn't have a heart condition. He wasn't frightened to death by a ghost. Someone did this to him. I mean, I know we don't know what killed him yet—"

"If you're right," I said, "then that part is easy."

"It is?"

"There are no visible markings on his body," I said. "He was poisoned."

Tamarind gasped.

"But he cried out twice over several minutes," Kenny said, "and he didn't leave the library for help. He kept himself locked inside the library. If nobody was in here with him forcing him to stay in the library, he would have left. How is that possible?"

"I don't know," I said, shivering as I thought of the locked room from the ghost story. "But what I do know is that we're on our own at Tanglewood Inn—and there's a good chance one of us killed Simon Quinn."

v.

"That's ridiculous," Rosalyn said. "This is the twenty-first century. The idea of a murder here at my inn is no more real than the vigilante library ghost. The medical examiner will figure out whatever natural cause killed your friend."

"Simon was murdered," Kenny insisted. "And I know who did it." He pointed the beam of his flashlight at Tamarind. "The librarian."

"That's absurd," I said.

"Your friend hated him."

"So did half of the people who'd heard of him. Probably most of the people in this room."

"Hardly," Kenny said. "Dot, for one, said it must have been an honor for me to work with Simon. She thinks he was a great man."

"It's called sarcasm, dear," Dot said. "Young people are so earnest, aren't they? It was always a challenge to teach students critical thinking. Simon did get away with murder, Kenneth. I thought it would be fascinating to see what he was really like, so I said I was a fan and accepted his offer for a lift to a warm hotel. Rather than waiting on my *gom* son-in-law. But of course I didn't kill Simon."

"He didn't kill his girlfriend," Kenny seethed. "But there's a lot more evidence that points to Tamarind being a killer. She's the one who rushed right to Simon."

"She ran to him at your request," I said, "since you were barefoot and just happened to accidentally contaminate the scene with your blood—"

"Tamarind was the first to reach the body," Kenny said. "I

didn't get near him. But she could have messed with his body. Tampered with evidence—"

"Not that he deserved it, but I was trying to help the jerk," Tamarind said, not helping herself.

"And I saw you messing with his coffee earlier," Kenny said. "I know about poison from my research for Simon. Coffee is a good drink to use since it's bitter. How do I know you didn't slip him a roofie so you could kill him later? Or that you had a time-delay poison—"

"I did no such thing," Tamarind said, crossing her arms. "And you picked the wrong person to mess with. Don't you realize who I'm here with? This is Jaya Jones."

Everyone stared blankly at me.

"Jaya. Jones." Tamarind said again. "*The* Jaya Jones. Seriously, people? Do you all live under rocks?"

Kenny tapped on his phone and looked surprised. "Oh. You're that treasure-hunting historian. You're a lot shorter than I imagined you'd be." He looked me up and down, from my tangled bob of black hair and oversized sweater to my black leggings and bare feet. "But you're good at solving puzzles. Good. Important evidence might be gone by the time the police reach us in the morning."

"You're suggesting I investigate?" I said.

"Don't you want to clear your friend?"

"There's nothing to clear her from," I hissed. This was getting out of hand. And I felt rather ill. Apparently I wasn't the only one.

"You're shivering," Ivy said to Dot. "Rosalyn, could we light the fire?"

"Of course." Snapped out of her daze, Rosalyn went to the hearth.

Tamarind pulled me aside. "You need to investigate," she whispered.

"Why would I—"

"You don't understand, Jaya. I *did* put something in his coffee after dinner."

"*What?*"

"Nothing dangerous," she whispered. "I found a laxative in the kitchen's medicine cabinet when I was looking for honey for my dry throat. He wasn't a good guy, Jaya. I wanted to make his night a miserable one. But I thought better of it as soon as I'd put it in his coffee. That's why I took it away from him and got him a fresh cup. Kenny must have been watching me."

I closed my eyes and rubbed my temples for a few moments.

"I suppose," I said loudly to the group, "it won't hurt to see what I can come up with."

"But you can't touch his body," Ivy said. "Kenny was right. That'll mess with the evidence."

Kenny nodded. "You can put me to work, Jaya. I'll be Watson."

"Hey," Tamarind said. "That's my job. I'm Watsina."

"It shouldn't be *anyone's* job," Rosalyn said. "Nobody should touch anything. Not just the body. It's all evidence."

"We won't touch anything," Kenny said. "We'll just observe."

"Right," I said, wondering where on earth I'd begin. It was true I'd solved several mysteries, but that was because they involved my historical expertise. How was I supposed to solve the impossible murder of infamous author Simon Quinn?

I stepped closer to the newly lit fire. I couldn't stop thinking about the fact that the library door had been bolted from the inside, yet Simon hadn't tried to get out of the room. If he'd been alone, why hadn't he left for help? Even if I was right that he'd been poisoned, he cried out twice over several minutes. That gave him plenty of time to get out.

I knew it wasn't me or Tamarind, which left Simon's assistant Kenny, retired teacher Dot, hotel owner Rosalyn, and driver Ivy. Four suspects. A previous unsolved murder. A ghost story. And a dead man who might have deserved the fate of being killed by the vigilante ghost.

I looked up from the fire and saw everyone looking at me. I realized I should start with what I knew best. *Those who don't know history are doomed to repeat it.*

"We start with history," I said. "Starting with the first death in this room."

"Right," Kenny said. "To find the connection."

"Tell me more about the man who died in this room in the 1930s," I said to Rosalyn.

"I've already told you most of what I know," she said. "What else can help?"

"How about the book. It fits into both murders. Where did the antique Agatha Christie novel come from? Was it Underhill's copy?"

"Remember, the book wasn't antique at the time." Rosalyn walked to the window, opened the curtains, and stood looking out at the flurries of snow falling in the darkness. The sound of the thunderous wind made the room feel physically colder. "That was the 1930s, so *Murder on the Orient Express* had only recently been published. But it was already a bestseller, so it's not surprising it would have been in such a big library."

"So it came from the shelves here?"

"I really don't know." Rosalyn turned from the window. "I'm sorry, but I was only a kid when my father bought this place. I don't know what's fact and what's fiction. Maybe I can see if there's anything in my father's records—"

"None of us goes anywhere on our own," Kenny said.

I gasped as my gaze fell to Simon's body. Where the Agatha Christie book had lain, now only shards of glass remained.

The book was gone.

vi.

"The book was right there." I rushed forward but stopped myself before I got too close. I was still in bare feet. "I'm not imagining it."

"But where could it have—" Kenny began.

"The fire," Tamarind shrieked, lunging toward the hearth.

I grabbed a hefty iron poker and pulled the burning book from the fire. Rosalyn ran for a fire extinguisher, but it was too late. The remains of the book crumbled into ash. The pages were gone. All that remained was the shell of the green spine.

"Looks like the ghost doesn't want its secret to be discovered," Tamarind said.

"You did this," Kenny shouted at her.

"None of us did this," she countered. "None of us had a chance. Only an invisible ghost could have moved it." Tamarind's eyes darted around the room, which looked alive with the flickering light of the fire. "There must really be an avenging library ghost. Because we're all right here. Together."

"Sort of," I said. "We were all in the library, but we were distracted. We were all turned away from Simon and the fire as Rosalyn spoke. Any of us could have picked up the book."

Kenny crossed his arms but spoke without raising his voice. "Seems awfully risky."

"I agree," I said. "There must have been a good reason. We need to find out what that was. I need my shoes. Which means you're all coming with me."

As we crept up the stairs, I considered the faint sound of our footfalls. Could there be someone hiding in this house? I paused and gripped the railing as I thought back to the curtain I'd seen fluttering in my room.

"You're freaking me out, Jaya," Tamarind said softly. "It's like you're in a trance or something."

"Just thinking..."

We reached my room, and I found my heels at the foot of the bed. Instead of leaving, I turned my flashlight toward the window. I saw what I expected I might find. I climbed onto the wide sill and looked up.

"Don't jump!" Tamarind cried. "The ghost has gotten to your head, Jaya. Someone stop her."

Kenny reached me first. He pulled me over his shoulder.

I squirmed, but he was strong. "I'll kick you if you don't put me down."

He set me down harder than was necessary, muttering, "That's what I get for trying to help."

"I wasn't trying to kill myself," I said. I pointed toward the ceiling. "Wires. That's our ghost."

"You think Rosalyn made a manifestation to frighten Simon to death, and then used wires to swing the book into the fire?" Kenny shone his own flashlight over the wires. "It's true Simon wasn't as brave as he looked, but I don't know..."

"Hold on," Rosalyn said. "I admit there are hidden wires. Those wires are how I keep up the act of a haunted hotel. Look at how obvious they are. They're not to kill anyone or elaborate enough to pick up random objects. They're just to make the curtains flutter. That sort of thing. It's fun, like a haunted house. People love being scared. This doesn't have anything to do with what happened to Simon Quinn."

"It's freezing in here," Dot said. "Shall we resume in the library?"

We trekked silently down the stairs. When we reached the library, none of us seemed certain what to do. Dot resumed her knitting by the fire, and Ivy joined her on the couch. Kenny sat at the séance table and lifted his injured foot onto a second chair. Rosalyn checked the light switches again. Tamarind ran her hands over the spines of the hardback books near the door.

"That's it," I said. I knew what had been off about the library. All of the books were treated so haphazardly, even ones that looked expensive. But not *Murder on the Orient Express*. I could understand wanting to protect the famous Agatha Christie novel from theft, but the removable locked glass case didn't achieve that. The book was already damaged, and its value lay in its history rather than condition. What history was the book hiding?

"The poison," I said. "I know how Simon was poisoned."

"Ixnay on the oisonpay," Tamarind whispered.

"He wasn't poisoned in his coffee," I said. "Simon Quinn was poisoned by the Agatha Christie book."

vii.

"A poisoned book?" Dot whispered.

"I think Simon was poisoned by the pages of the book," I said. "Just like Mr. Underhill nearly a hundred years ago."

"No. Way." Tamarind said. "A poisoned book couldn't have stabbed that first guy."

"Of course it could," I said. "Think about the story Rosalyn told us about Underhill. He was going crazy, tossing books off the shelves. Why would he be doing that? If he was alone in the room, he wasn't fighting with anyone. If he was looking for something, why not a more organized search? If he was in a rage and wanted to destroy the room, there were more satisfying objects to break. But if he was poisoned by a drug that caused him to hallucinate—"

"He was fighting an invisible foe," Tamarind said.

"So it was Rosalyn," Kenny said. "She's the one who knew the history of the book. She knew it was poisoned."

Rosalyn's face paled and her eyes looked frantically between us. "I didn't—I didn't poison him."

"I don't think you did," I said. "The ghost killer accidentally struck again."

"Accidentally?" Ivy asked.

"The first killer selected the book for poetic justice," I said. "Think about the solution to *Murder on the Orient Express.* In the book, multiple people were working together to kill a bad man using an assumed name, who many people wished dead. And in real life, our Mr. Underhill conned people during the Great Depression and caused their deaths. A real person or group of people, not a ghost, poisoned the pages of the book. They got away with what many people would consider a justified murder."

"Simon never did respect other people's property," Kenny said softly. "That's one of the reasons his publisher insisted he hire an assistant. I was as much his keeper as his research assistant."

"But why destroy the book in the fire tonight if it was an accident?" Tamarind asked.

"Because Rosalyn *felt* responsible," I said. "I think she knew the truth about how Underhill died, but she kept silent because she wanted to keep the book."

"It was supposed to be safe," Rosalyn whispered into the fire. "That's why it was locked in glass. I wasn't thinking about theft. I was thinking of safety. It was great publicity. Ghost hunters loved to see it. Why did Simon have to break it open?"

viii.

I woke up as the day lingered between night and sunrise. It looked as if the sun was struggling to decide if it should make the effort to push through the haze. Just like I was.

I'd been wrong the night before, I now realized. *Half* wrong.

Rosalyn had told us why it was necessary to burn the book, yet now that I'd gotten some sleep, I realized a fundamental problem with what I'd accepted at the time was a confession. The hotel's owner was the only person who *couldn't* have burned the book. We were all watching her at the window, which was far from the fireplace. Why had she walked to the window as she spoke, when there was nothing to see outside in the darkness?

I found Kenny in the kitchen.

"Kenny, you said you knew about poisons from your research for Simon. What could have still been active after seventy years?"

"It would have to be one of the heavy metals, like arsenic or antimony."

Which didn't cause hallucinations and couldn't have compelled Mr. Underhill to kill himself. And that type of poison wasn't what had killed Simon.

"Coffee or cranberry scones?" Kenny asked. "The storm is over, but I think it'll still be a while before they reach us."

"I'll be back." I left the kitchen and knocked on one of the bedroom doors.

History was repeating itself. As had happened seventy years before, the library ghost was enacting poetic justice again.

Ivy opened the door. Her auburn curls were askew, and dark shadows made her face appear sunken. I doubted she'd slept.

"It wasn't an accident, was it?" I said.

She smiled sadly and shook her head. "No. It wasn't an accident. It was justice. It was the least I could do. You see, it was my fault he went free."

"He lived here in Denver before moving after the trial," I said. "You were here then, too."

She nodded. "I wanted to be a NASCAR driver back then. But I screwed up. I was young. I'd stolen a car to go for a joyride. That night, I saw Simon. He was in the park where he strangled his girlfriend. That park had a great big lot where I thought I could practice my Rockford Spin with the car. I thought it would be empty since the park officially closes at midnight, but when I drove in my headlights shone on the park bench...He never saw my face, only the blinding lights of the stolen car. Simon lied about his alibi. He used his charm to get his friends to back up his story—for all I knew they were probably too drunk to realize they were even lying—and I was too scared to say anything. Confessing to stealing the car would have ruined my life. I didn't get caught that night. But it didn't matter in the end. My nerves were shot after that."

"So when you saw him at the airport today—"

"He's impossible to miss. I turned down other fares so I could 'accidentally' bump into Simon and tell him I had an unoccupied taxi and knew of a hotel."

"But you left after you dropped us off."

Ivy shook her head and laughed ruefully. "I chickened out. But when the storm got so bad I nearly ran off the precarious road, I knew it was fate for me to come back. But you have to understand, I was going to kill *myself*. Not Simon. That's why I had the poison. I've carried it with me for the past year, ever since Simon's last book came out to critical acclaim. And I didn't use it on Simon tonight. Not exactly."

"Then how—?"

"I know Rosalyn," Ivy said. "I've been driving tourists to her inn for years, so we got to know each other well. Nobody else makes the drive to Tanglewood Inn during storms as bad as this one. I

called Rosalyn from the airport to let her know I was bringing some
people to the hotel and it would be better if my passengers didn't
think I'd made the dangerous drive to bring them to a far-away
hotel because I was friends with the owner."

"Which is why we didn't think you two knew each other."

Ivy nodded. "I didn't want her to get in trouble if I was caught.
I knew where she kept her keys, so I knew how to unlock the book. I
didn't tell her what I was going to do, though. I know she tried to
cover for me last night when she realized what I must have done,
since she's always known I believed Simon Quinn was guilty. I
never confided in her what I'd seen a decade ago, but she knew I
felt passionately about his guilt, since it consumed me. But I
wouldn't have let Rosalyn take the fall for me. That was never a
question."

"Even if you originally got the poison for yourself," I said, "you
still killed him."

"I poisoned the edges of the pages of the book," Ivy said, "but I
didn't put the book in Simon's hands. I knocked on the door to his
room after we all went to bed last night. I told him I had evidence of
his guilt, and that it was inside the Agatha Christie book, hidden in
between some of the pages that were stuck together. If he dared
face the library's avenging ghost, he could get the evidence that
proved his guilt and destroy it. If he was innocent, Jaya, why would
he go looking for evidence that didn't exist?"

"He wouldn't," I said.

As I thought of Simon creeping into the library, bolting the
door behind him, and searching for evidence, I knew Ivy was right.
Simon's actions were those of a guilty man. Once he felt the poison
taking hold, he wouldn't have immediately gone for help because he
needed to first find the evidence so people wouldn't learn of his
guilt. That explained why he hadn't left the library for help.

"I'm ready to turn myself in," Ivy said. "My conscience is clear.
I'll accept my fate. It was Simon Quinn's own guilt that killed him."

The Curse of Cloud Castle

This Sanjay Rai short story originally appeared in Asian Pulp, *edited by Tommy Hancock and Morgan McKay and published by Pro Se Productions in 2015.*

Sanjay Rai had escaped from a coffin sinking to the bottom of the Ganges River with a full minute of air left to spare. He had remained calm and composed while appearing on live television wearing nothing but a lungi. He'd even kept a level head to avoid being burned alive when a fellow stage magician had miscalculated an illusion.

Most people would find those situations horrifying. Or, at the very least, stress-inducing. Though Sanjay would never admit it publicly, his heart rate did rise during all of those experiences. However, it was nothing compared to the abject dread he felt as he stood on the dock in front of the small motorboat.

Sanjay didn't hate boats. It was his stomach that did. He felt queasy even contemplating a boat ride.

There was something else making him queasy this morning. Looking across the water, the fog-shrouded island in the distance gave him a sense of foreboding. Sanjay wasn't superstitious. Quite the contrary. As a stage magician, he knew how to see beyond the obvious explanations that most people saw. On more than one occasion, he'd solved crimes that appeared impossible.

But he also knew the power of suggestion. The fact that a curse had been attributed to Cloud Castle played on people's subconscious minds, even when they didn't believe in curses. And

Sanjay Rai did not believe curses.

"It's only a twenty-minute ride," Vik assured him.

"I'm only doing this because it's you." The wind at the edge of the ocean flipped up Sanjay's collar and carried his words out to sea.

"I don't understand," Vikram said with a shake of his head, "how someone who can settle comfortably into a coffin without getting claustrophobic can possibly be so afraid of a little boat ride. We'll be able to see the mainland the whole time."

Vikram, who'd gone by the nickname Vik as soon as he realized he had free will, was one of Sanjay's oldest friends. Vik was two years older, but they'd grown up in the same neighborhood in Palo Alto and bonded as two American born kids of parents from India. ABCD. *American Born Confused Desi.*

Early in life, Sanjay had done what his parents expected. Right up until he dropped out of law school to become a professional stage magician, much to his parents' disappointment. After several years struggling, he'd become a huge success, selling out a long run of shows at a Napa Valley theater and having a short-lived TV show on Indian MTV, which featured the Ganges escape.

After a short phase as a Goth slacker in high school, Vik followed in his computer programmer parents' footsteps, making millions in the latest Silicon Valley dot-com boom. Thanks to his "Om" app, which sent calming and inspiring messages to a cell phone whenever the program detected the user needed to relax, he'd made his first million before he turned twenty-five.

This weekend, Vik was celebrating his thirtieth birthday. With the same gusto that made him successful with his tech start-up, he planned to celebrate his big day by throwing a party on a small island off the coast of Northern California. Nothing too extravagant, by Silicon Valley standards. He was limiting it to forty of his closest friends.

Cloud Castle stood on a private island visible from the mainland only on the clearest of days. Even then, the rocky island was a tiny speck on the horizon, small enough to make one wonder if it was a trick of the light. Aside from a guard outpost next to the dock, the fifty-room mansion was the only building on the island. It was ostensibly the vacation property of a tech billionaire, but the man had lost a fortune in the last stock market crash. To avoid losing his toy castle, he was now forced to rent out the property when he wasn't using it. Luckily for him, the industry was booming again, and there were plenty of young men like Vik who were happy to throw their money around. The castle was rented for getaways ranging from two days to twenty—however long the renter could stand to be away from their cell phone and the Internet. The ethos of the island was to enjoy luxury while taking a break from modern technology.

While Sanjay dragged his feet, a small motorboat waited to shuttle eight guests to the island: Vik, his fiancée Geneva, his little sister Priya, her Welsh husband Broderick, and four friends, including Sanjay. The rest of the guests would be arriving the following day, on Saturday, to stay the night at the castle after the catered party with almost as many hired staff as guests. Sanjay fit into both categories: friend and hired help. He was to be part of the entertainment for the weekend, performing his Hindi Houdini stage show during the party. That's why he'd been invited to come to the island a day early along with Vik's family and closest friends. Sanjay and Vik had once been close, but with the demands of their vastly different careers, they rarely spoke these days.

Vik's fiancée stepped off the boat to join Vik and Sanjay on the dock. Geneva worked long hours as a human rights lawyer, and Sanjay had never seen her without harsh clothes perfectly tailored to her thin six-foot frame, and an even harsher expression. It was partly her name that played into Sanjay's impression. Thirty years before, her mom was presenting a paper at an academic conference in Geneva, Switzerland, while eight months pregnant. She unexpectedly went into labor, and since she and her husband hadn't yet selected a name, Geneva it was. Sanjay knew her name wasn't her fault, but it was telling that the more casual nickname Genny never stuck. As she put her hand on his arm and gave him a warm smile, he wondered if he'd misjudged her. For Vik's sake, Sanjay hoped he'd been wrong about his initial impression of her.

"I don't know how much good it'll do right before you get on the boat," she said, "but I have an extra seasickness patch."

"I'm already wearing two," Sanjay said. "But thanks." With a deep breath big enough to rival that of a Yogi, Sanjay stepped onto the motorboat.

The boat lurched as it pulled away from the dock. Sanjay closed his eyes and focused on breathing.

"Don't you dare throw up so close to us, Sanjay Rai," Priya shouted across the boat from where she stood at the bow, her long black hair swirling around her face. Five years younger than her brother Vik, Priya had tagged along with the two boys when they were kids. She had a crush on Sanjay up until she left for college. She was a sweet kid until then, too, he remembered. Once she got to college, she learned there was a whole world out there beyond the rules imposed by her conservative parents. Unfortunately, one of the first lessons she learned was that her good looks could get her almost anything she wanted.

"If you're going to barf," she continued, "at least lean over the side of the boat."

"Thanks for your concern."

"Haven't you learned to ignore Priya yet?" Vik said, leading Sanjay to the tiny enclosed area of the boat with padded benches. "Engaging only encourages her."

"Why did you invite her, then?"

Vik blinked at him. "She's my sister. How could I not?" He looped his hand into Geneva's and pulled her down to sit on his lap. They were a good-looking couple. Vik was confident enough that he didn't even mind that Geneva was a few inches taller than him.

"It was their parents," Geneva said, lowering her voice and squeezing Vik's hand. "Priya complained to them that she and Broderick were *only* invited to the party on Saturday night, not tonight's pre-party island fun."

"You want to meet the rest of the gang?" Vik asked, nodding

toward the five people at the front of the boat with the hired driver.

"I think he'd rather wait until we're on solid ground," Geneva answered for Sanjay.

For someone so brilliant, Vik could be terribly unobservant. Sanjay smiled weakly, then gripped the edge of his seat. For one startling moment, he could have sworn he was seeing double and feared doubling up on seasickness patches might not have been a good idea. Then he remembered two of Vik's friends were twins.

Emilio and Elena were famous in the tech community for being the brother-sister team who invented a promising social media platform, then sold it for a price that boggled Sanjay's mind. Sanjay hadn't met the twins before, but had heard good things about them through Vik. As he watched them, the wind blew Elena's hat into the ocean. Her long black hair that had been tucked up inside now flowed freely around her. She didn't seem to mind. Her attention was focused on Cloud Castle, slowly coming into view through the fog.

Sanjay hoped the twins would be better company than Priya and her husband Broderick, whom he'd spent more time with than strictly necessary for a well-lived life. For the most part, Sanjay could ignore the vacuous woman Priya had become, but Broderick's gregarious personality ignored all subtle cues that someone didn't wish to speak to him. The tall Welshman was at least ten years Priya's senior. He'd won her over with his suave British accent and his overflowing bank account.

"*Bore da*," Broderick shouted into the wind. "What a beautiful morning for a boat ride."

Priya raised a skeptical eyebrow and stepped across the boat to sit with her brother. "Why is the island covered in fog? There's no fog anywhere else around here."

"Why it's the curse, of course," Vik said with a straight face. But he couldn't hold it. A second later, he burst out laughing. He'd always been a terrible actor.

"Who's that standing with Broderick?" Sanjay asked.

Vik followed Sanjay's gaze. "You don't recognize Kevin?" Kevin was a good friend of Vik's from high school, but Sanjay remembered him as a scrawny kid who didn't remotely resemble the portly man on the boat. On second thought, Sanjay revised his opinion. In baggy jeans, an oversize t-shirt, and floppy brown hair tousled by the wind, Kevin only appeared big and slovenly in such close proximity to Broderick's bespoke suit and close-cropped strawberry blond hair.

"Do you guys know," Sanjay heard Kevin shout over the crashing waves, "what one strand of DNA said to the other? Do these genes make me look fat? Get it? *Genes*, not jeans."

"Why would DNA be talking?" asked Elena.

"It's a joke."

"Oh."

Sanjay closed his eyes and practiced his breathing exercises for the rest of the short boat ride that wasn't nearly short enough. When the sound of the engine changed, he opened his eyes. He was alone on the bench. Everyone else stood at the front of the boat, watching the impressive sight coming into view.

A light fog surrounded them. Cloud Castle dominated the island from its perch on the single hill. Up close, it no longer looked as ominously mysterious as it had from the mainland, yet it was still a strange sight. The secluded Gothic manor that loomed at the top of the hill looked centuries old, though Sanjay was pretty sure the artificial island had been built only ten years before. His best friend Jaya was usually the one who was interested in history, whereas Sanjay preferred to live in the present. But right now, the present was very much caught in the past. The castle and all of its trimmings looked straight out of an Agatha Christie novel.

After the boat dropped them off, Vik punched in a security code at a gate where the dock met land. That broke the spell of Sanjay thinking he'd stepped into a Gothic detective novel—at least for the moment.

With two trunks of magic show equipment, Sanjay was the slowest to make his way to shore. He watched the group walk up the sloping path leading to the castle a few hundred feet beyond.

Now that he stood on the secluded island itself, Sanjay was again struck by an oppressive presence. It filled the path leading from the dock to the mansion. This time, it wasn't his fanciful imagination. The expressions on the faces of the people trekking up to the house told him this was a volatile mix of personalities.

Broderick also lingered behind. "*Uffern dam,*" he mumbled.

Sanjay raised an eyebrow.

The Welshman laughed. "Bloody hell, Sanjay. Bloody hell." He sighed, picked up Priya's bulging suitcase, and followed the others to the castle.

The sound of the boat's motor faded into the distance. They were stranded.

Two watchful gargoyles looked down from their perch atop the stone castle. Sanjay ignored the beasts and followed the others through the twenty-foot-high door that led into the mansion. Stepping into a grand room with Gothic arches above, Sanjay let out a low whistle. He wasn't surprised to see a suit of armor standing next to the door. Two winding staircases led to a mezzanine overlooking the central room.

"All the bedrooms have been made up," Vik said, pointing to the doors on the mezzanine. "Take your pick. The rooms in this main wing are the best."

"Don't we need keys?" Broderick asked.

Vik shook his head. "It's a secure private island. Who's going to steal anything? The rooms lock from the inside for privacy, though. And the bedroom windows don't open. There's central air and heat."

Sanjay selected a bedroom with a king size canopy bed and an antique wooden wardrobe that reminded him of a spirit cabinet he'd used for a spiritualist illusion, then joined the others downstairs for brunch. With the awkward mix of personalities, he was glad it was a champagne brunch.

While the others helped themselves to additional mimosas,

Sanjay slipped away to check out the theater behind the castle where he would be performing the following night. Next to the eighty-seat outdoor theater he found a fire pit, a massive swimming pool, and faux antique wooden tables and benches.

The way the theater was constructed, the audience was given a view of both the Pacific Ocean and the stage. To a magician, this was both good and bad. There were many opportunities for misdirection, but at the same time, fewer places available to hide things from the audience. Planning to begin the show at sunset was the way to go.

He retrieved his wheeled trunks and brought them to the stage. He sought one item in particular. With a smile, he lifted his specially made bowler hat onto his head and got to work. A panel at the side of the stage controlled spotlights. They were more limited than he was used to, but they would do. He decided upon one of his favorite illusions that involved a projector and simple substitution. He practiced a few times until he got it right for this particular stage.

"Bravo!" A deep voice echoed in the distance.

Sanjay squinted past the spotlight. He could have sworn he was alone. During brunch, Vik, Geneva, and Kevin said they wanted to explore the castle, Priya changed into a zebra-print bikini to sunbathe, and Broderick went with her. That left the twins.

"Encore!"

It was a female voice this time. Sanjay stepped forward and jumped down from the stage. Emilio and Elena sat in the last row of seats, their thin shoulders touching.

"You're going to discover my secrets," Sanjay said, but with a smile on his face.

"We'd be happy to sign a non-disclosure agreement," Emilio said.

At first, Sanjay thought he was joking, but Emilio's face was dead serious.

"We like seeing how things work," Elena added.

There was something not quite normal about the twins. At

brunch that morning, they'd sat together at one end of the twenty-seat dining table in the grand room, eating only grapefruit and toast. The kitchen had been fully stocked for the first day of Vik's visit, including prepared meals that only needed to be reheated. An hour after landing, Sanjay was feeling fine, so he'd had plenty of both coffee and champagne in addition to the full English breakfast provided.

Some reporters asserted that the twins were autistic, but Sanjay suspected it was more likely they were geniuses who'd withdrawn from attention after being blindsided by success so early in life. Unlike Sanjay and Vik, they hadn't grown up in privilege. Their parents had been born in a village in Mexico. Emilio and Elena were born in Los Angeles and had grown up with two other siblings in a one-bedroom apartment. Being on the cover of *Wired Magazine* at seventeen must have been overwhelming.

"We could be your assistants tomorrow," Emilio added. "It looks like the box substitution trick could use an—"

"Thanks," Sanjay cut him off. "I think."

"Are you going to use the island's 'curse' reputation in your show?" Emilio asked.

Elena shivered. Her brother drew back and stared at her. "You don't believe in the curse, El."

"Not the curse," Elena said, then hesitated. "Not exactly. But something is going to happen this weekend. Can't you feel it?"

Sanjay practiced for the remaining hours before dinner. Emilio had been right. His substitution was way too obvious in an outdoor theater. He hefted himself onto a boulder overlooking a sheer drop to the ocean and stood facing the mainland, thinking he was most likely on the highest natural spot on the island. Just a few short miles away, the Golden Gate Bridge carried people from Marin to San Francisco where tens of thousands of people were currently wrapping up their work week on a Friday afternoon. Thousands more energetic entrepreneurs would be working all weekend on their start-up ideas, hoping their work would turn them into the next Vik, Broderick, or the team of Emilio and Elena.

As close as that hive of activity was, this island felt like a different world. Sanjay shivered as a gust of sea air surprised him, nearly knocking off his bowler hat. That wouldn't do. He jumped down from the rock and sat next to it, resting his back against the semi-smooth surface.

Like Elena, he couldn't shake the feeling that something was amiss on the island. The whole thing was an artificial construct, both physically and psychologically. A false island with a storybook castle for a man-child with more money than sense. It was flattering that Vik had thought of including him after all these years, but he could no longer claim to understand his friend's motivations.

"What are you doing out here?" Vik loomed above Sanjay, startling the magician out of his fanciful thoughts.

"Waiting until sunset so I can do a run-through."

"I thought you had your act down by now."

"It's different in each setting. Different stages lend themselves to different illusions." Illustrating his point, a gust of wind knocked off his hat. "A secure turban," he added as he ran after his hat, "is the way to go for this show."

Vik grinned. "This is going to be great."

"As long as your guests aren't expecting a concert."

"Everyone gets indie rock bands at their parties," Vik said. "Or sometimes a rapper. Having The Hindi Houdini is much more authentic."

"And memorable."

"All publicity is good publicity. It's a win-win situation. I get to see my old friend, you get to show your stellar show to a new crowd, and on top of all that, my party will stand out. So actually, it's a win-win-win situation."

After doing a satisfactory run-through, Sanjay joined the others at the castle. He found the group inside the conservatory—a glass greenhouse attached to the side of the castle—arguing about a music playlist. It was nearly dark now, and the muted red glow of the sun's fading light shone through the room's glass walls.

Sanjay wondered how often a gardener came to the island to tend to the greenery, an assortment of stunning tropical plants and practical herbs for cooking. Upon closer inspection, he noticed that automatic waterspouts were positioned to tend to each of the plants. Also hidden from view were electric sockets and music player docks. It was over one of these that Vik and Priya were arguing about whose music they should listen to.

"How about heading inside for appetizers," Kevin suggested. The most affable of the group, he'd played peacemaker since they were kids.

The group of eight gathered in the grand room below the mezzanine. A selection of drinks and glassware adorned the top of an antique buffet table. If there had been a butler standing next to it, and there hadn't been bags of potato chips on a nearby tray, Sanjay would have been convinced he'd stepped into the previous century.

"I need to take care of some work," Broderick said. "I'll be back down for dinner."

After Broderick departed, Vik picked up an old-fashioned crystal decanter with a metal nozzle on top. "Is this how you work this thing?" He pointed it at a tumbler and squeezed the trigger. Carbonated water squirted forcefully into the glass.

The sound of muffled barking caused Vik to let go of the seltzer water trigger. "That wasn't this thing," he said. "Was it?"

The barking came again.

"*There are dogs* on the island?" Priya asked. "Vik, you didn't tell me to bring my allergy medication."

"That doesn't sound like a dog," Geneva said.

"A sea lion?" Sanjay suggested. "There could be *sea lions* sunning themselves on the rocks."

"Only one way to find out," Kevin said. He popped a potato

chip into his mouth and led the way outside through the main door.

They followed the sound of the barking, coming from the rocky side of the island past the conservatory. By the time they reached the edge of the rocks, the sound had stopped.

"That was too weird," Kevin said. "They have to be here somewhere. They can't have just disappeared."

Everyone agreed. They split up and circled the small island.

"Looks like we missed them," Geneva said as soon as they regrouped ten minutes later.

"Strange," Vik said. "I read up on this place and nothing mentioned sea lions."

"You rent out this spooky, cursed island," Kevin said, "and you think sea lions are strange?"

"Touché." Vik grinned and led the group back to the house.

Vik and Geneva heated up a dinner that had been delivered the previous day. After Vik declined assistance, Sanjay juggled grapefruits on one side of the kitchen. Emilio and Elena's gaze followed the path of the three pieces of fruit, presumably calculating the angle of the arc to see how it was possible. Priya sat in a window seat with a bored look on her face while Kevin tried to get her to smile by telling her the least funny jokes Sanjay had ever heard. Geneva burned two loaves of bread while Vik looked through the containers of food and complained that the caterers had already taken care of all the fun parts.

"Maybe I should go to cooking school next," Vik said.

"Last year it was magic school," Geneva pointed out.

"Really?" Sanjay's grapefruits dropped to the floor.

A sheepish look crossed Vik's face. "You look like you're having more fun than me. And I've always appreciated the dramatic. That's how Kevin and I became friends in the first place. He was always performing in plays in high school, including that one-man show where he played all the characters. I thought it was much more likely he'd be the one to go on to be a professional stage performer instead of you, Sanjay."

"And that's why my brother chose this dumb island," Priya

said. "*Drama.* Jagged rocks instead of sandy beaches, and because of the stupid curse, Vik thought it was too awesome to pass up."

"Does everyone know the story of the curse?" Vik asked, a mischievous grin spreading across his face. "I should enlighten you." He paused, lit the candles on a candelabra straight out of the sixteenth century, then switched out the overhead light. "It's too bad Broderick will miss the story. You probably all know this is an artificial island created by tech billionaire 'Fearless' Arthur Frank who made his fortune in cloud computing, but that's not entirely accurate. After making his fortune, Fearless Frank retired from life in the Silicon Valley. He'd spent many long nights looking out at the ocean. He wanted his own island. The right island didn't exist, so he created this one himself. There was an existing rocky piece of land here, but it wasn't big enough to be called a proper island. The month after construction of the island castle was completed, he threw a huge house party, much like the one I'm hosting this weekend. On a drunken midnight boat ride, there was an accident. His wife fell overboard. *Her body was never found.*"

"You know I hate this story," Geneva said, rubbing her arms.

"His wife had been a depressed alcoholic for years," Vik continued, "so some people speculated she jumped overboard on purpose. She and Frank had been a happy couple once when they were college sweethearts. Success can bring out the worst in people." Vik paused and looked around the table. Sanjay wondered if he was thinking of anyone in particular.

"Frank," Vik resumed, "didn't seem especially broken up about his wife's death. After all, there were dozens of young women throwing themselves at his money, pretending they were interested in the man himself. I know him. There's no way Frank's admirers were admiring more than his money."

Emilio whispered something to his sister. She nodded, but her eyes remained transfixed on Vik.

"Still," Vik said, "he thought it was best to keep up appearances. He went into mourning and set off for Greece. After six months, he remarried. They returned to California. The wedding was held here on the island. The Monday morning after the weekend wedding, the stock market took a nose dive. Frank was ruined. But he isn't the type of man to give up. He returned to work in the Silicon Valley to remake his fortune. He couldn't bring himself to sell the island castle, so he rents it out for most of the year. Because the two times he'd attempted to live on the island, tragedy had struck, reporters dubbed it a curse. The Curse of Cloud Castle."

A loud beeping noise sounded. Kevin and Emilio jumped.

Geneva laughed. "It's the oven. Dinner's ready. Vik, you'd better grab it yourself. It's likely to explode the moment I touch it."

"I'm glad you know I'm not marrying you for your domestic skills," Vik said.

"I'll go get Broderick," Kevin offered.

In the open floor plan of the main section of the house, they had a view of the first dozen rooms on the mezzanine overlooking the main kitchen and dining area. Kevin climbed the spiral staircase and knocked on Broderick and Priya's bedroom door.

"I'm still working!" Broderick called out.

Priya rolled her eyes and jumped up from the table. She stopped at the foot of the stairs and called up. "You're *always* working."

"You want your bank account to start shrinking?" Broderick asked.

"It's Vik's birthday," Kevin said, jiggling the door handle of the thick door. He turned to face Priya. "He's locked himself in."

"We're not saving you any food!" Priya said before returning to the table. Kevin followed suit.

"Sorry, man," Kevin said to Vik.

"His loss," Vik said. "The part of the curse I'm about to tell you isn't public knowledge." He cleared his throat. "As I was saying, things worked out. For the most part. But about five years ago, a young woman died here at the castle. Alcohol poisoning." Vik paused and made eye contact with each of them, one by one, clearly savoring the moment. "She was said to look eerily similar to Frank's wife."

"You think *I'm* a good actor?" Kevin said. "You're giving me goose bumps, Vik."

"At first," Vik continued quietly, "a few newspapers claimed the curse had struck again, but Frank was able to hush it up. After all, it was most likely the young woman, barely out of her teens, had simply gone too far partying. But that's when he added safety precautions. Even though there's still no cell phone service out here, there's now a satellite phone in the conservatory. Pretty freaky, huh? Two deaths of similar looking women."

"But the deaths were five years apart," Elena interjected, her brow drawn in confusion. "Hundreds, probably thousands, of people have stayed here in the interim."

Sanjay agreed that the human mind likes to draw parallels even when none exist. In the cursed Cloud Castle, with the medieval vaulted arches above them, it was all too easy to succumb to such ideas.

"I didn't come here to be freaked out," Priya said.

Vik laughed. "Don't worry. They were redheads. We don't have any red-headed women here this weekend. You're safe."

Sitting around the long dining table in the grand room, Sanjay helped himself to several platters in the magnificent spread. He avoided the burned loaves of bread but poured a second glass of the free-flowing wine. Vik and Geneva sat at the two ends of the long table, as if they were each holding court. Emilio and Elena sat at the far corner of the long table with Geneva. Sanjay sat next to Vik, directly across from Priya and Kevin.

"I'm cold," Priya said, standing up. "I'm going to get my sweater."

"My jacket is in the entryway," Kevin said. "If you'd like it."

"I think I can handle walking twenty yards to my room," Priya said.

A few moments later, as Sanjay was serving himself a scoop of mashed sweet potatoes, an earsplitting scream rang out through the house.

"She killed him!" It was Priya's voice.

Vik and Sanjay rushed up the broad stairs to the mezzanine. The others stared at each other, stunned. Vik was the first to reach the top of the stairs. Priya ran out of her room and into his arms. She was sobbing so hard she was hiccupping. Vik cradled his little sister in his arms as Sanjay pushed past them into the room.

The scene inside made Sanjay turn away. He wished he hadn't eaten second helpings. Broderick lay sprawled on the hardwood floor. There was no question he was dead. The back of his skull had been bashed in by a bloody hammer that now lay next to the body.

But *how*? The group had been together the whole time. None of them had the opportunity to kill Broderick. Even if it were possible that a deranged murderer was hiding on the island, which Sanjay found extremely unlikely, they would have seen him leave Broderick's room.

Careful to avoid looking at the bloodied dead man, Sanjay turned his attention to the solitary window in the bedroom. Styled with a Gothic arch, the window was easily large enough for a person to climb through. However, there was a glaring problem with that means of escape. None of the windows in the castle opened.

It was impossible for anyone to have killed Broderick.

The only explanation was the curse.

As the others piled into the room, Sanjay forced himself to look back at Broderick. It was hard to believe that the charming entrepreneur, once so full of life, was actually dead. Sanjay felt a pang of guilt for thinking uncharitable thoughts about the man earlier that day.

Broderick's body lay askew with his right arm stretched out in front of him. The tips of his fingers were covered in blood.

Sanjay stared at the message written on the floor with a viscous, dark red substance. Broderick's last act had been to scrawl the name of his killer in blood: ELENA.

Elena gasped when she saw her name. The "A" at the end was only half-formed, trailing off into nothingness, making the message all the more grotesque.

Geneva knelt down at Broderick's side. She took his wrist in her hand. After holding it for a few seconds, she stood up. She shook her head, a grave expression on her face.

"I didn't do this," Elena whispered. "I didn't do this!" She whipped her head around, looking imploringly from Geneva to her brother, and finally settling on Sanjay.

With his arm around his sister's shoulder, Vik stepped into the room. He stopped short when he saw Broderick's body. "Elena?"

"I would never—" Elena stammered. She stepped behind Emilio, becoming the shadow of her twin. The two of them put their heads together, whispering to each other as they often did.

"You little—" Priya's words were cut off by her own sob. Her eyes narrowed as she looked at Elena. Sanjay sensed what was about to happen a moment before she acted. Priya pushed her brother away and flew at Elena. Her hands wrapped around Elena's neck. It took both Vik and Kevin to pull her off Elena.

"I knew she hated me," Priya said, pulling free of the two men as tears streamed down her face. "But I never dreamed she'd take it out on Broderick."

"It's true I had a schoolgirl crush on Broderick a few years ago," Elena said, "after Emilio and I met all of you. But it was nothing beyond that. Nothing! Someone is framing me."

"The police will figure it out," Geneva said, reaching for her phone. Instead of dialing, she swore.

"Why aren't you calling the police so they can lock her up?" Priya wiped her nose on her brother's sleeve and frowned at Geneva.

"Remember there's no phone service here," Vik said, squeezing Priya's shoulder. "We'll have to get the satellite phone."

Sanjay had remained silent during the aftermath of the discovery of the body, taking in the scene, from the room's layout to the group dynamics. Something had changed from a moment ago. What was it? He looked from Broderick's body to the circle of people standing over him. Emilio was missing.

Sanjay bolted from the room.

"Where are you going?" Vik shouted after him.

"We have to stop him!" Sanjay called back, not slowing his pace.

But he wasn't fast enough. When he entered the conservatory, he knew it was too late. The door leading outside stood open. Sanjay reached the doorway just in time to see Emilio throw the satellite phone off the rocky bluff into the ocean. Their only way to communicate with the mainland was destroyed.

Emilio gave a start when he saw Sanjay. "I had to do it," he said. "I had to give her the time she asked for."

"What are you talking about?" Sanjay looked from Emilio to the ocean surrounding them, a mass of black under the night sky.

"I know my sister. She didn't kill anyone. I know people think she's strange—that we both are. Elena is a good person to frame, because she would look guilty to the police and a jury. But she didn't do this. We need this extra time for you to prove she isn't a killer."

"Me?"

"She'll explain why," Emilio said.

Sanjay spun around at the sound of approaching footsteps. The rest of the group caught up with the two men on the windy rocks. Sanjay explained that Emilio had destroyed their only way to communication with civilization.

"They're both insane!" Priya cried. "I always knew there was something wrong with you two."

"Come on, Elena," Vik said. He stood stiffly but spoke with a calming voice. "Why did you ask Emilio to do it? Even without contacting the mainland today, a boat with forty people will arrive tomorrow. You can't get away with this. You're only delaying the inevitable."

"One of you," Elena said, "is framing me." Her large brown eyes locked on Sanjay's. "You're The Hindi Houdini. You've solved things like this before. I've heard how you've used your methods of creating illusions to solve strange crimes. I want you to clear my name."

"I told you she was insane," Priya muttered.

"Think about it," Elena said. "All of you. You saw the way his skull was crushed. There's no way he'd have lived long enough to write my name."

They looked from person to person, none of them able to raise an objection.

"Only a guilty person would be afraid of the truth," Elena continued. "Sanjay, will you help me? You have nothing to lose. Until a boat arrives tomorrow, we're trapped here together."

Ten minutes later, the group of seven gathered around the dining table. Once everyone realized shouting at the twins wouldn't do them any good, they agreed to go inside to figure out next steps. Vik grabbed two bottles of wine before sitting down. They certainly needed it.

"If it wasn't for Elena's name scrawled on the floor," Sanjay said, "I'd swear there was an invisible madman loose on the island."

Priya gasped and gripped her brother's arm. "A madman? Vik, why did you have to plan your birthday on this stupid, cursed island!?"

"It's not a madman," Sanjay said. "Even if he could have secretly escaped from the room somehow, Elena's name spelled out with his dripping blood proves that it was one of us. Only...that's impossible."

"Could you be a little less graphic, Sanj?" Vik said, downing half his glass of wine.

Elena glared at Sanjay. "What do you mean, *it's impossible*?"

"The seven of us," Sanjay said, "were together eating dinner here in the main room while Broderick was killed. He went up to his room to do some work before dinner—a room only accessible by the door since the windows in this castle are sealed—then he told us he was going to keep working. The rest of us were together at the dining table the whole time. Nobody got up until Priya went to get her sweater and found Broderick dead."

Elena looked between Sanjay and her brother. "That can't be right."

"Do any of you remember someone leaving?" Sanjay looked around the table, starting with Vik, Geneva, Priya, Kevin, and finally the twins. Each of them shook their head. Elena's face was deathly pale.

"We were all here," Vik said. "But if that's your line of reasoning, you're not as clever as Elena gave you credit for. It's clear there was a device rigged in the room to kill Broderick."

Sanjay shook his head emphatically. "Before this morning, nobody knew which room Broderick would be in."

"No offense," Kevin said, which undoubtedly meant he was about to be offensive. "I think we'd all better take a look to make sure you're right." He stood up, as did Vik.

"Knock yourselves out," Sanjay said.

Priya's fingers braided and unbraided her long black hair. "I'm not going back into that room."

"You don't have to," Sanjay said. "You can stay down here with me."

Kevin paused at the foot of the stairs. "We can't split up."

"Why not?" Sanjay pointed upstairs. "The room is right there. As long as nobody goes off by themselves, I don't see why you and Vik can't check out the room for hidden murderous devices."

"Um, isn't that dangerous?" Geneva asked.

"Nobody can kill anybody else without us all knowing who did it," Sanjay said. "So nobody is going to try anything."

"That's not what I meant," Geneva said. "I mean if there's a hidden device that killed Broderick, I don't want Vik messing around with it."

"Don't go, Vik," Priya sniffled. "I just lost my husband. I don't want to lose you, too."

"There's no device!" Sanjay shouted. "I'm *not* wrong about this." He hoped he was right.

As Vik and Kevin climbed the stairs, silence descended upon the dining table. Sanjay watched as the two men disappeared into the room with Broderick's dead body.

"Aren't you supposed to be doing something?" Elena inquired, breaking the silence.

"I *am*," Sanjay said. "I'm thinking."

"You're going to go to jail for kidnapping in addition to murder," Priya said to Elena. "It's your fault your stupid brother destroyed our only way to get off of this island."

"If you really believe I'm a killer, why would I care about a kidnapping charge?"

Priya squealed and put her head in her hands. "I can't take this!"

"Let Sanjay think," Geneva said.

After a few minutes, the group began to fidget. They'd already opened the second bottle of wine. Sanjay looked at their frightened faces. They could all hear Vik and Kevin above them, examining the room.

"Let's look at this from a different angle," Sanjay said. "Who would want to harm Broderick?"

"Elena," Priya said. "That's why she—"

"Let's hold off on the accusations," Sanjay cut in. "Elena, you said you once had a crush on him."

Her shoulders slumped. "It was all so overwhelming when Emilio and I moved to Silicon Valley. Everyone wanted something from us. Everyone. We knew their friendship was fake. Until we met Vik. He didn't need us to make money or feel important..."

"But he liked us anyway," Emilio finished for her.

Elena nodded in unison with her brother. "Broderick was like that, too. Vik introduced us at a party, and he was charming with that funny British accent of his."

"It's not funny," Priya mumbled. "It's Welsh."

"Flirting with a man *three years ago*, long before he got together with Priya, doesn't give me a reason to want him dead," Elena said.

"Unless you're a bitter little—"

"Priya," Sanjay snapped.

She rolled her eyes and sat back in her seat. "Vik!" she shouted. "What's taking you guys so long?"

"We'll be back in a minute," he called down. With the door open above them, Sanjay could hear Vik as clearly as he'd heard Broderick the last time he'd spoken.

"I can give you everyone's motives," Emilio said. "If you want to get technical about it, we all had a motive."

"Really?" Sanjay asked. "I thought you all liked him."

"He was a nice guy on the surface," Emilio said, "but he made a lot of money off of other peoples' work. He wasn't a coder and he wasn't an inventor. He was a guy who applied vision to other peoples' ideas. He bought out one of Vik's start-up companies, he took one of Kevin's boring ideas and turned it into something people would actually buy, and he tried to give us a lowball offer for our company. If you're hoping to use motive to solve this, it won't work."

Sanjay groaned. Just then, Vik and Kevin started back down the stairs.

"This isn't right," Kevin mumbled. "Leaving his body there like this."

"You were right, Sanjay," Vik said. "There's nothing rigged in that room. Sorry I doubted you."

"What do we do next?" Kevin asked. All eyes turned to Sanjay.

"I can't think like this," Sanjay said.

"Why don't you go somewhere private like the conservatory?" Vik suggested.

Sanjay swallowed hard. As much as he knew logically that there was no such thing as a curse, and no way a real murderer would strike again now that they were all on high alert, the thought of going off on his own made the hairs on the back of his neck stand up. He realized everyone was staring at him.

"Fine," he said, picking up his glass of wine. "If anyone needs me, I'll be in the conservatory."

Sanjay ambled through the plant menagerie, remembering an illusion he did several years before. A variation on the apocryphal

Indian Rope Trick, in which a rope is thrown into the air and a boy climbs the rope into the sky and disappears. In Sanjay's illusion, his assistant Grace climbed up a strand of winding ivy that grew out of an unassuming basket.

The sprinklers around the plants clicked on, nearly giving Sanjay a heart attack. He was too on edge to think straight. He breathed deeply and paced between the greenery. Back and forth, he walked the distance of the conservatory at least ten times. On his tenth trip to one side, a shiny gleam caught his eye. Someone had left their music player in the dock on this end.

"Sanjay?"

His body tensed at the sight of Elena's silhouette. Like the bedroom doors, the door of the conservatory was so thick he hadn't heard her approaching. As he watched Elena turn sideways to avoid a prickly plant, it dawned on him. *He knew what was going on.*

"You're afraid of me?" she said, visibly hurt.

"No," he said. "I'm not." He walked up to her and stood his ground directly in front of her.

"I saw your face—"

"Yes, but that's not what my expression means."

"Now you look like you're feeling sorry for me! Is that what this is about? You can't solve it?"

"I'm sorry, Elena. But quite the opposite. I'm sorry because I think I've just solved it."

"I don't understand."

He grabbed her hand and ran with her back to the house.

"Emilio and Elena," Sanjay said, standing at the head of the table. "Brother-sister twin wunderkinds. Elena with her long flowing black hair, Emilio with his full shoulder-length hair, very distinctly their own people—except their profiles are the same. How easy would it have been for you all to remember seeing both of them at the dining table, when really it was only Elena who was there!"

Sanjay waited for something—anything—to happen. For Emilio to run, for the crowd to applaud, for Elena to start crying because her brother framed her. Instead, they all stared at him in silence.

"No," Geneva said. "I was there at the far end of the table with both of them. Neither of them got up during dinner."

Sanjay cleared his throat. "You're sure?"

"I'm sure, too," Vik said. "Even though the table is large, I was sitting at the head of the table and could see everyone. You're wrong, Sanj."

"Sanjay Rai," Priya said slowly, walking up to him and putting her hands on his shoulders. Her face was puffy from crying but was now free from tears. "I've known you almost my whole life. I know this is intense, but if you really believe Elena didn't kill Broderick, I know you can prove it." She lowered her voice and spoke so quietly he could barely hear her. "Forget about these guys who think they're smarter than you. They're not. I love my brother, but I know you're the one who can get to the bottom of this. You're the one with the magician's sense of misdirection. What are the rest of us missing?"

Sanjay looked at Priya. She was again the smart, strong girl he remembered from his childhood. And she was right.

"You've just given me the real answer, Priya." Sanjay laughed sadly and looked up at the high stone ceiling. "That was some wonderful misdirection, Kevin."

Kevin froze. "I don't know what you mean."

"Broderick said he had some work to do—odd, given we don't have cell or Internet service. That meant someone here must have given him a reason to think about work. Someone wanted to get him up to his room, so they could get him alone."

"That doesn't work," Vik said. "None of us had a chance to slip away from the dining table while Broderick was upstairs. We already established that."

"Broderick wasn't killed *when* we thought he was," Sanjay said. "He was killed long before we all gathered in the grand room for dinner."

"You're forgetting we talked to him," Priya pointed out.

"Did we?" Sanjay asked. "Or did we hear what a skilled actor wanted us to hear? Kevin was facing the bedroom door with his back to us. He's a performer. I bet he can do a great Welsh accent."

Kevin frowned. "So what if I can? That doesn't prove anything."

"You forgot to factor in how thick these doors in the castle are," Sanjay said. "We heard 'Broderick' loud and clear through the door. But that's not possible. Vik, can you go upstairs?"

Without a word, Vik stood and climbed the stairs. He closed the bedroom door behind him. The muffled sound of "You bastard!" escaped through the door, but just barely.

"Maybe the door was open," Kevin said. His voice was calm, but Sanjay saw beads of sweat forming on his forehead. "I don't remember, but that must have been it."

"No," Priya said. "You shook the door handle and said it was locked."

"Which we only have Kevin's word for," Sanjay added.

Kevin lunged across the table and grabbed the carving knife. Before anyone could react, Kevin landed on his feet next to Priya.

"I don't want to hurt you," he said, grabbing hold of her and holding the knife against her neck. "This was only about Broderick, not you. I hadn't made millions like the rest of you, and he took advantage of that when he bought my idea for hardly any money at all. Don't anyone step closer!" He pushed the knife closer to Priya's neck. Sanjay watched in horror as her eyes narrowed. Not with fear, but with anger. She was going to act.

"If you don't want me to get snot all over you," she sniffled, "at least let me get a tissue from my pocket."

Priya's quivering hand reached into her pocket. Sanjay looked on helplessly as Priya's fingers emerged from her pocket gripping not a tissue, but a small silver canister. After only a moment's hesitation, she raised her arm and sprayed mist into Kevin's eyes. He screamed and let go of his grip, giving Vik and Sanjay the opportunity to tackle him.

"What the hell was that?" Kevin cried.

"This island is shrouded in fog," Priya said, standing over Kevin. "I'm a woman with thick Indian hair. Did anyone think I'd walk around this place without hair defrizzer?"

"It was never supposed to be an impossible crime." Sanjay pressed his knee into Kevin's back. "I bet you didn't think anyone would go up to their rooms until we broke up after dinner when nobody would have an alibi."

Kevin grunted but didn't speak.

"It might have worked," Sanjay said, "if Priya hadn't been cold and left the dinner table to get her sweater."

"When did he do it, then?" Elena asked.

"When the sea lions barked," Sanjay said, struggling to remove a piece of rope from his bowler hat to tie Kevin's wrists. "That was the only time we split up when we all went looking for them. Someone 'accidentally' left a music player behind in the conservatory. I bet when we check it out, we'll find it has the sound of sea lions."

"A distraction," Vik said, holding Kevin as Sanjay secured the rope.

"Thanks, old friend." Sanjay knotted the rope, sat back, and placed his magic bowler hat back on his head.

Tempest in a Teapot

Tempest Raj Mendez, a magician friend of Sanjay's, made her debut appearance in this short story that originally appeared in LAdies Night, A Sisters in Crime Los Angeles Chapter Anthology, edited by Naomi Hirahara, Kate Thornton, and Jeri Westerson, published by Down & Out Books in 2015.

"There's something wrong with this teapot," said the woman dressed in a shiny silver leotard. "The lid doesn't open."

"Don't touch that!" Tempest rushed to Aurora's side and plucked the teapot from the new assistant's clumsy hands.

"Oh my God," Aurora whispered. "Is there poison inside?"

Really, Tempest thought, no good could come of magicians hiring their unskilled girlfriends. Xavier and Zach should both have known better. But she grudgingly admitted that Aurora looked stunning in her sparkly costume, right down to the gold tassels on her four-inch heels. Serving as a distraction was more than half the job of a stage magician's assistant.

"Of course there's no poison inside," Tempest said. "It's a prop for one of my illusions I wanted to show you."

"It doesn't look very exciting."

Tempest scrunched up her nose. "Here, I'll demonstrate. Would you like a drink?"

"You're sure it's not poison?"

Tempest was rethinking her idea of inviting Aurora to join her and some friends for a night out in Burbank later that evening. "Pick a drink. Any drink. I'll make it appear magically from this teapot."

"Seriously? Any drink?"

"Within reason."

Aurora sat down on a wooden trunk at the side of the stage. "What fun is that?"

"I simply meant that it's old magic, so it doesn't know about modern brands. If you were to request a certain distillery's blend of whiskey, for example, the magic teapot would simply give you whiskey."

"I'd love a glass of red wine."

Tempest positioned her hand carefully on the teapot made of dark glass, then picked up a porcelain teacup in her other hand, flipping it to add a little flourish. There was nobody in the audience, but old habits die hard. She poured an ounce of red wine into the teacup and handed it to the bored assistant.

Aurora's eyes widened as she tasted the contents of the teacup. "It's really wine. *Good* wine."

"Of course. What would you like next?"

"How about some tea since it's a teapot." Aurora finished the small amount of wine and handed the cup back to Tempest.

"Black tea or herbal tea?"

"Black."

Out of the spout flowed black tea.

"It's cold," Aurora murmured, a pout forming on her bright red lips.

Tempest shrugged. "Magic is finicky."

"In that case I'd rather have a martini."

Tempest grinned. She loved it when people asked for drinks where a perfect detail could be added. Lifting a tumbler from the side table, she poured a shot of gin from the teapot spout into the glass before handing it to Aurora. While Aurora's attention was still focused on the teapot, Tempest used sleight-of-hand to add two olives to the glass without the other woman noticing.

Aurora was less impressed than Tempest had hoped.

"It's rather an old-fashioned trick, isn't it? Not very flashy."

"I bet you can't guess how it's done."

"Who cares? I'm sure it was a great trick a hundred years ago, but—"

"Those are the best illusions," Tempest said. "They take real ingenuity, not modern technology." She sighed and set the teapot down, making sure it was far from Aurora's reach.

Tempest often felt like she'd been born in the wrong century. Thanks to her mom, she'd always been fascinated by the stage magicians who died long before she was born. Sure, there were skilled magicians today, but it wasn't the same. There was a certain, well, *magic*, missing from modern magic.

Though Tempest was only twenty-six, she had more than a decade of experience as a professional magician. When people saw her, if they didn't remember her embarrassingly public fall from grace, they usually assumed she was a magician's assistant. But she learned that having people underestimate you can be used to your advantage. There were far too few female magicians, not to mention female magicians who looked like her: light brown skin and features that far too many journalists had called "exotic," courtesy of her mixed background with a Scottish mom who was half-white and half-Indian, and a Californian dad with a Mexican mother and black father. So Tempest Raj Mendez pushed all thoughts of critics from her mind and became *The Tempest*.

Aurora hopped down from the oversize trunk of props. "Where are Xavier and Zach? They were supposed to be here ages ago."

"Zach is right here," a deep voice boomed from the back of the theater. Zachary Zookeeper (not his real name) strode down the center aisle toward the stage. The children's performer was dressed in his signature faux-snakeskin suit with a coiled plastic snake as a hat and was carrying a fluffy stuffed elephant in his arms.

Zach and his brother Xavier complemented each other's strengths in their show for kids. Zach was the wacky magician and Xavier the straight-man singer and musician (who refused to let his brother christen him Xavier Xylophone). Sharing the stage with his brother was what Xavier was doing to pay the bills until the masses recognized his brilliance as a solo artist. Xavier had recently fallen for Aurora, an unemployed actress, so he asked his brother to give Aurora a try as their new assistant.

So far, Zach had been far from impressed. But being a good brother, he'd asked Tempest to join them at the small theater, located in a strip mall in Encino, to give Aurora some tips. Tempest was skeptical, but she liked Zach, so she agreed to help.

"Xavier can't make it until later," Zach said, placing the oversized stuffed animal on a seat in the front row. "He's got a meeting with a music producer. And I've got a headache, so I'd rather not do a full run-through today. We can focus on the illusions where you need the most practice. Shall we start with the snake basket illusion?"

Aurora bit her lip. "I'm no good at that one."

"Sure you are." Zach picked up one of the swords from the prop cabinet and pressed it into her hand. "We'll do it just like we practiced it, starting when I say the magic word."

"Isn't that a bit advanced for her?" Tempest asked.

Zach dismissed her concerns with a wave of his hand, his attention focused to the rear of the eight-row theater. "Is someone there?"

"Don't mind me," a husky female voice called from the darkened back row. The ghostly words startled Tempest, who could have sworn they were alone. "I've been in the office doing paperwork, but I'm heading off now."

"Could you lock the door on your way out, Francesca? I'd rather not have any interruptions while we practice."

"Aye aye, cap'n," Francesca said with a faux cockney accent. She'd had a long career as a character actor, and now shared the strip mall theater space with Zach and Xavier to teach method acting to aspiring actors.

"Isn't this illusion too gruesome for kids?" Tempest asked.

"Kids love the macabre," Zack said. "Even though they don't know what macabre means."

Aurora rolled a barrel-size wicker basket into the center of the stage, the harsh stage lights revealing its frayed edges. She showed the elephant audience-member that the basket was empty, then placed it on a stand that raised it a foot off the floor (to illustrate it wasn't sitting on top of a trap door). Skipping his usual banter, Zach tossed his snake hat aside and stepped into the basket. Aurora placed a wicker lid on top, then picked up a sword.

Tempest took a seat in the front row next to the elephant. She'd noticed how much the brothers looked like each other, and now she noticed that Xavier's girlfriend Aurora looked like his older brother Zach's wife. Both women had wavy red hair—a natural auburn red, unlike the flame-red tips of Tempest's hair.

When Zach gave the signal, Tempest counted off the seconds in her mind, hoping Zach knew what he was doing to trust Aurora with this skilled illusion. Tempest saw Aurora's foot tapping and let out a sigh of relief that she was acting with precision.

Aurora thrust the sword downward into the basket.

Tap, tap, tap.

She plunged the sword the opposite side.

Tap, tap.

The sword went into the center.

"Ah!" Zach cried out.

Aurora screamed. The sword clattered to the stage floor.

Tempest jumped onto the stage and rushed to the wicker basket. Flinging the lid aside, she looked inside. Zach was curled up inside the basket, his eyes closed, a pool of blood spreading across his stomach.

"Call for an ambulance," Tempest said. Her voice was calm, though her insides were anything but. Never let the audience see you sweat.

Aurora, however, wasn't a natural performer (which probably explained why she was an out-of-work actress). When Tempest realized Aurora wasn't capable of doing anything besides cry hysterically to the poor 911 operator, Tempest took the phone and explained the situation.

"Take the phone back," Tempest said to Aurora. "I'm supposed to apply pressure to his wound."

"Oh God!"

"Don't worry," Tempest said as she leaned over the basket and pressed a towel to Zach's stomach. "He's unconscious but alive. And it was an accident. He shouldn't have been doing a dangerous illusion when he had a headache. Timing is everything."

"I didn't do this," Aurora said. With shaking hands, she hung up the phone.

"You were supposed to stay on—"

"I didn't do this!"

"Nobody will think it's your fault," Tempest assured her. She looked down at Zach, feeling her heart beating in her throat.

"No, that's not what I mean. Look at the sword." Aurora gestured toward the sword that had fallen to the stage floor. "I couldn't bring myself to use the real sword. I thought it was dumb to use a dangerous sword for a kids' show, so I used a plastic one. There's no way the plastic sword did this to him."

Tempest frowned. Aurora was right. There was no blood on the sword that lay at her feet. Was Aurora a smarter woman than she gave her credit for? Could she have substituted the real sword when Tempest wasn't looking? No, Tempest was sure she would have noticed. She looked to where the real sword lay on top of the trunk. It didn't have blood on it either.

How, then, had Zach been stabbed? One word kept pushing its way to the forefront of Tempest's thoughts: magic.

The paramedics took Zach away in an ambulance, and a police officer questioned Aurora. The police were prepared to dismiss the incident as an unfortunate accident. This was L.A., after all. The police had much more important things to deal with than stage magicians who acted foolishly. It would have been recorded as an accident had it not been for Aurora's insistence that she hadn't stabbed Zach.

She showed the skeptical policeman each of the swords in the theater (there were three, all of which were kept locked up in a prop cabinet) and dared him to find blood on any of them. Daring the police turns out not to be such a good idea. Aurora was taken to the police station for further questioning.

Tempest drove to the hospital to check on Zach. He had regained consciousness and was sitting up in bed. His black hair was disheveled and he looked rather pale.

"Please tell Aurora I'm not upset," he said. "It's my fault, not hers. I should never have made her learn this stupid illusion."

"She swears she didn't stab you," Tempest said. "Not even accidentally."

"I feel awful that she feels so bad she thinks she needs to lie." He ran a hand through his hair and looked down at his hospital gown. "I've just realized something quite disturbing."

Tempest leaned in. "What is it?"

"I think—" He paused and cleared his throat. "I'm pretty sure I feel more naked without my coiled snake hat than I do without my clothes."

Tempest crossed her arms. "Can you focus? I don't think Aurora is lying."

"If she's not lying to protect herself, then she's simply mistaken. I felt a sword hit me."

"There was no blood on the blade, Zach. No blood on any of the swords in the theater."

Zach gave a start, then winced in pain. "It must have gotten wiped off somehow. Maybe on my clothes?"

"There's a problem with that theory. She used the *plastic* sword."

Zach gaped at her. "Then how the hell did I get stabbed?"

Once Xavier and Zach's wife reached the hospital, Tempest departed. She canceled her plans with her friends and instead hurried back to the theater. An idea was forming in her mind that she wanted to explore. If she ever made it back to the theater. Rush hour was beginning and had other ideas. She hoped she'd make it in time.

Her tires screeched as she exited the 101 and peeled into the parking lot. She bounded out of the car and let herself into the theater, relieved it didn't appear to be an evening where Francesca was teaching an acting class. Tempest didn't have her own key, so with Aurora at the police station she'd borrowed Zach's. She tucked the key into the pocket of her jeans and walked straight to center stage.

She knew what she was looking for. Since none of the proper swords had stabbed Zachary, an ingenious device must have been in the basket itself.

A very clever person had meant to kill Zachary Zookeeper.

Twenty minutes later, Tempest lay down next to the man-sized wicker basket in the center of the stage. She stared at the string of lights on the ceiling and ran her fingers over the pewter charm on her necklace, a half-inch bowler hat she'd found in a thrift store that reminded her of her friend Sanjay, a stage magician who lived in San Francisco (not that she'd ever tell him about the charm or wear the necklace in front of him). Holding the necklace didn't give her further insights. Nobody had tampered with the basket. How could she have been so wrong?

She'd briefly considered the possibility that the attempted murderer had come back to the theater to switch baskets before she'd made it back herself, but dismissed the idea as soon as she saw the basket. It had the exact frayed spots she remembered. This was the same wicker basket in which Zach had been stabbed. She kicked the basket in frustration. It toppled, taking its stand with it. Once the basket stopped rolling, all was silent.

Tempest closed her eyes. What was she doing here? She knew the answer, of course. In a world lacking real magic, this situation was magic.

A faint clicking noise sounded. Tempest's eyes popped open.

Click.

"Hello?" She sat up. "Francesca? Xavier?"

Jumping down from the stage, Tempest looked down each row of seats as she walked slowly to the foyer and box office.

"This isn't funny!"

Click.

The noise came from behind her. She whirled around.

Nothing.

Click, click, click.

The sound was coming from the greenroom next to the stage.

Keeping her eyes on the door to the greenroom, Tempest picked up a saw from the shelf of props. It was a rubber saw, but hopefully whoever was inside the greenroom wouldn't know that.

She kicked open the door with her ruby red sneaker. The room was dark. Tempest felt for a light switch and flipped it on.

The room appeared to be empty.

Click, click, click.

A wind-up monkey lay on the floor. One of those annoying creatures that holds cymbals in his tiny plastic monkey hands, banging the instrument together to amuse children and infuriate adults. Only this monkey was missing his left-hand cymbal, causing him to click rather than crash. Tempest shook her head and picked him up. In the dilapidated theater, her kicking the basket must have dislodged the monkey.

Alone in the theater, there was one more thing she could think to do. As a magician, she knew all about secret rooms and hiding places. The sword that stabbed Zach might have been hidden in one such secret spot.

She paused before beginning her search. Even if she found it, what would that tell her? It was still seemingly impossible for the crime to have been committed. Still, the more information she had, the closer she would be to figuring out what was going on.

An hour later, she was regretting that decision. What kind of magician was Zach? There wasn't a single secret room in the whole building. There wasn't even a trap door! She supposed the audiences of a Zachary Zookeeper show had different expectations than her own.

Before leaving the theater, she let herself into Francesca's office, which, she noted, wasn't locked. For a brief moment she thought she might have discovered something important when she found a secret compartment inside the desk. But all it contained was two bottles of vodka.

Tempest turned off the lights and locked up the theater. She stood in the parking lot of the sad strip mall, thinking about her options. Next to the theater was a kid-themed pizza restaurant where many of the children who attended Zach and Xavier's magic show would have a birthday party before or afterward. It was dinnertime, so families drove in and out of the parking lot. There was one empty car in the lot that Tempest knew wasn't going anywhere that night: Zach's beat-up SUV with a cheery advertisement for his magic show painted on the back window.

On the opposite end of the lot was a miniature golf course. From where Tempest stood, she could see one of the holes clearly. Its obstacle was a giant wooden clown head with a mouth that slowly opened and closed, making it necessary to time the swing of your golf club. But in this case, half of the clown's jaw was missing, making him look more like he should be in a horror movie than a kids' attraction.

That's what was wrong with this whole situation, Tempest realized. Zach was a goofy guy who performed magic for kids in a strip mall that had seen better days, not a Las Vegas entertainer making seven figures. Neither money nor jealousy of his life could be a motive. *Who would want to kill Zachary Zookeeper?*

Tempest changed out of her jeans, t-shirt, and sneakers, and donned a little red dress and sparkling red ballet flats. She was no longer Tempest Mendez. Now she was The Tempest. And she knew where to go for inspiration.

The Magic Castle had been L.A.'s clubhouse for professional

magicians since the 1950s. To Tempest, it was the closest thing to the classical era of stage magic that existed long before she was born.

After battling her way through Hollywood traffic to reach the castle, Tempest said the magic words, causing the foyer doors to open for her. She smiled and stepped through the opening in the false wall. She walked through rooms lined with framed photographs and posters as she descended into the magical world.

At the Hat and Hare pub, she ordered The Lovely Assistant, a cocktail that included both vodka and champagne, a combination that was definitely called for that day. A retired magician she knew was having a drink by himself and invited her to join him.

"Tough crowd?" he asked.

"Toughest I've faced to date."

"You know what I do when I've had a day like that?"

"What?"

"I make sure to make a young lady smile." He handed Tempest a necklace with a ring of bright yellow daisies wrapped around it.

"Hey! That's my necklace." She snatched it back, but she was smiling as she smelled the fresh flowers. "I was watching you the whole time. How did you do it?"

"Not the whole time, my dear. I saw your face when you entered the room, when you headed straight for the bar. I knew you needed cheering up. I borrowed your necklace while you were placing your drink order, not here at the table."

"The location," Tempest murmured. "I had the location wrong, didn't I?"

"Don't worry. It happens to the best of us."

At the hospital, Zach was sleeping. But Tempest didn't feel the slightest bit bad when she grabbed his foot to wake him up.

"Hey, I'm an injured man!" he said.

"I know what happened."

"Um, we all do, Tempest. Something went wrong with a prop."

"You're protecting him. Though I suppose it's also protecting yourself. Scandal might be good publicity for musicians, but not so much for a children's entertainer."

"Am I dreaming?" Zach asked. "Because it sounds like you're speaking gibberish."

"Xavier is in love with your wife, isn't he?"

Zach's bloodshot eyes bulged.

"That's what you two were fighting about when he stabbed you," Tempest continued. "Don't bother denying it. I've already told the police my suspicions. They'll find the knife at either your or Xavier's apartment. Now that they know what they're looking for, they'll find the trace evidence."

Zach groaned. It must have been a trick of the severe hospital lights, but his disheveled black hair appeared to have more streaks of gray than it had earlier that day. "It was just an accident. You've got to believe that, Tempest. Things got a little out of hand when Xavier and I were arguing. I didn't want it to come out that my own brother had stabbed me."

"So you came up with a plan to make it look like you'd been accidentally stabbed while on stage practicing your act."

Zach nodded. "It was the perfect plan. I didn't think I'd been hurt too badly, so I drove to the theater and got right to work on the illusion that really could stab me. Xavier had a meeting on the other side of town, so it would look like he had nothing to do with it."

"But you didn't count on Aurora refusing to use a real blade."

"She doesn't have the stomach for stage magic." He shook his head and gave a sad laugh. "And I, apparently, don't have the stomach for being stabbed. It was worse than I thought, so I really did pass out inside the basket."

"Did you always know Xavier was in love with your wife, or only once he started dating her doppelganger?"

"I suspected it, but never knew for sure until I confronted him today. He's my little brother, Tempest. Can't you understand that I'd want to protect him? He didn't know what he was doing when he hurt me. I wish you hadn't sent the police to his apartment."

"I didn't."

"What?"

"This is L.A., Zach. The police have more important things to worry about than two brothers acting stupidly."

"But you said..."

Tempest shrugged. "I needed to know. And if the police don't let Aurora go, you'll need to tell them the truth. Otherwise I won't force you to."

"You're a great magician, Tempest. And an even better person. Thank you."

"I'll leave you to get some rest."

"Now that I'm awake, what do you say about getting us some tea?"

"That," Tempest said, clicking her sparkling red flats together as she turned to leave the room, "is the best idea I've heard all day." She paused in the doorway. "We can figure out how to turn this little mishap into something one of us can use in a show."

A Dark and Stormy Light

This Jaya Jones short story originally appeared in Malice Domestic: Murder Most Conventional, *edited by Verena Rose, Barb Goffman, and Rita Owen, published by Wildside Press in 2016.*

"Why are you looking at that old postcard from India instead of packing for your conference?" My best friend twirled his bowler hat in his hands. A mangled rose petal escaped from the interior of the hat and wafted down to my coffee table. "Damn. I thought I'd solved that problem."

"Did I ever tell you about the second history conference I ever attended?" I asked. "It was back when I was a grad student."

"I don't think so," Sanjay replied, but he was only half paying attention as he fiddled with the secret compartments in his magician's hat. "Boring? We all have to pay our dues, Jaya."

"That wasn't the problem."

"Traumatic?" He tossed the hat onto his head. With his signature hat, perfectly styled thick black hair, and impeccably pressed tuxedo, he looked far more mature than his twenty-eight years. The boyish grin that followed ruined the effect. "I didn't take you for someone who'd get stage fright from public speaking."

"I'm not. It was the most exciting conference imaginable. I'm procrastinating on my packing because I can't imagine any future gathering living up to it. All I have to remember it by is this postcard of Pulicat."

"The conference was in India?"

"No, it was here in the US. And I wish I'd known you then. I could have used your skills of misdirection to figure out what was going on before the situation got out of hand."

"I'm supposed to be the cryptic one, Jaya." Sanjay plucked the postcard deftly from my hand. He's a stage magician, so I couldn't have stopped him if I'd tried. His eyes widened as he looked over the text. "This postcard is signed by Ursula Light. I don't care if I'm late for my dress rehearsal. Now you've got to tell me how you crossed paths with the famous mystery writer. What does she have to do with an academic conference and a postcard from the east coast of India?"

A few years ago, while I was still a graduate student, I began attending Asian History conferences. At the fateful gathering I will always think of as The Conference, we didn't fill up the entire hotel. Instead, we found ourselves sharing the space with a mystery writers' convention.

If I'm being true to the story, I need to say that it began on a dark and stormy night. If it hadn't been for that storm, the whole fiasco would have been avoided.

I was drenched after my brief walk from the metro stop to the hotel. After changing into dry clothes, I was more than ready for a warming drink at the hotel bar. That night I learned that mystery writers are even bigger drinkers than historians. It was barely five o'clock and there wasn't a single free table. Two women invited me to join them. They moved two hulking bags of books to make room for me and my behemoth three-olive martini, even after I confessed I wasn't there for the mystery convention. These mystery folks were a friendly bunch. They introduced themselves as a mystery novelist and a children's librarian.

"What do you think?" The librarian tilted her head toward a gaudily dressed woman standing at the bar. "Is that Ursula Light?"

I'd heard of the famously reclusive mystery novelist, of course. Even though I prefer historical adventure novels, I don't live under a rock. The woman who might have been Ursula Light adjusted an oversized pair of dark sunglasses and the scarf tied around her head.

"Isn't Ursula Light younger?" I asked.

The librarian tried and failed to suppress a smile. "Her book jacket photos are a few years out of date."

"A few decades is more like it," the writer added, raising an eyebrow beyond the confines of her cat-eye glasses.

"Why don't you ask her?" I suggested.

"The convention hasn't officially begun. She's probably trying to get a drink in peace."

"She doesn't look very peaceful." I watched as the woman gripped the stem of a martini glass with a forcefulness usually reserved for killing a mortal enemy. She looked to be in her seventies, but I certainly wouldn't have wanted to tangle with her. She knocked back the drink and scanned the crowd. Was she looking for someone?

"She hates being in public," the librarian said. "She's only here because she's being honored."

"In that case I'm sure she'd be happy to be recognized. She probably feels bad that nobody is talking to her. Why don't we—"

"Jaya!" Stefano Gopal called to me from across the bar and waved for me to join him. He was impossible to miss. He stood over six feet tall, wore the thickest glasses I'd ever seen, and had a full head of white hair that framed his dark brown complexion.

I excused myself from my new friends and joined my professor. As he pulled me farther away from the crowds of the lobby bar, I caught a glimpse of the two women walking up to Ursula Light. A second later, all thoughts of mystery novelists disappeared from my mind.

"Milton York," Stefano said, "is missing."

"What do you mean, *he's missing?*"

"Exactly that. This is a disaster. He's supposed to give the keynote lecture, but he's gone."

"Do you mean he's late arriving? I heard that the storm is

causing flight delays."

"No, it's not that. We had a preconference meeting today. He was there this morning but missed the afternoon half of the meeting."

"He's a grown man. Why are you so worried?"

"He was afraid," Stefano said, his dark eyes filled with intensity, "that something would happen to him."

"Because of that Dutch East India Company discovery he made on his last trip to India?"

"Of course. Milton was paranoid about another historian getting an advance look at his findings. He told me last night that he was certain someone had searched his briefcase. He was quite shaken. And now he's gone."

Milton York was a historian who focused his research on Indian colonialism, the same subject Stefano had spent his long career researching, and the research area I was focusing on at the start of my career. Milton claimed to have discovered a diary that would change some widely held assumptions about why the Dutch lost their stronghold in India. He found the diary in Pulicat, India, amongst the records of a Dutch East India Company cemetery. If his findings were accurate, the life's work of many historians would be called into question. Stefano and I were concerned most specifically with the British Empire's impact on India, so Milton's research didn't affect either of us as directly as it did others, but it was still a big deal.

"So you think someone killed him," I said slowly, "to steal his briefcase?"

"*Ada-kadavulae*, Jaya." Stefano gaped at me.

"What?" I left India at age seven and my Tamil is rusty, but I was fairly confident he hadn't said anything worse than *My God, Jaya*.

"I had no idea you had such a brutal imagination."

"You're the one who said—"

"I'm not afraid he's *dead*," Stefano said. "I'm afraid he got cold feet and left before presenting his controversial findings."

"Oh."

Stefano adjusted his horn-rimmed glasses and appraised me. "It all makes sense now."

"What does?" I looked down at my black slacks, black cashmere sweater, black heels, and pseudo-briefcase. Was I underdressed for a professional conference of historians?

"Your draft dissertation chapters are the least dry chapters I've read in decades. The way you get inside the minds of the figures in the British East India Company you write about, it's like you're writing narrative nonfiction that's being adapted as a screenplay for a big-budget movie."

"Um, is that a compliment?"

"I'm not sure. I—" He broke off and swore creatively in what I'm pretty sure was Italian; Stefano's father was from India, but his mother was Italian. "Reggie, you scared the life out of me. Don't sneak up on an old man like that."

I hadn't seen Reggie Warwick approaching either. Like Stefano, he was a professor of South Asian history, and I don't think he was attempting to be stealthy. He was simply a small man. And I don't say that lightly. He was only a few inches taller than my five feet.

"Sorry, old boy." Reggie slapped Stefano's shoulder, knocking him off balance. What Reggie Warwick lacked in height, he overcompensated for in other areas.

As a grad student, I probably should have thought of Stefano and Reggie as Dr. Stefano Gopal, Professor of Indian History, and Dr. Reginald Forsyth Warwick, Distinguished Herodotus Chair. But Stefano was a casual enough professor that he insisted we all call him by his first name, and Reggie was a snooty enough scholar that he hated it when people, even peers, failed to address him as Dr. Warwick—which, of course, caused everyone to jokingly refer to him not only as Reginald but Reggie.

"Milton still hasn't returned," Reggie said to Stefano. "Quite childish, if you ask me. All so he won't have to give his presentation."

"Reggie, you remember my student, Jaya Jones?" Stefano nodded in my direction.

"A pleasure," Reggie said, barely acknowledging my presence. "He's done a runner, Stefano. Damn shame. I was hoping to give a rebuttal to disprove this nonsense he's claiming. We're going to need a replacement speaker. Even though it's short notice, I might be able to—"

"You're thinking of nominating yourself?" I cut in.

Reggie looked at me directly for the first time. "It would not be the same presentation, of course, since Milton York's was rubbish."

"Nobody even knows the man is gone," I said. "Maybe he got food poisoning and isn't up for answering his phone. Maybe he's simply taking a nap."

"No," Reggie said. "We know. I saw him leave with my own eyes earlier this afternoon. When the rest of us were walking back into the afternoon meeting room, I saw him sneaking out of the lobby with that bedraggled briefcase of his."

"You did?" Stefano frowned. He was nearing retirement, and I knew he worried that he wasn't as sharp as he'd once been.

"Perhaps," a woman's voice said from behind me, "I could be of assistance."

Reggie gawked at the newcomer. It was the flamboyantly dressed woman from the bar.

"I couldn't help overhearing your conversation," she said. "I, Ursula Light, will solve the case!"

"Ursula Light?" Reggie sputtered.

"She's a mystery novelist," I volunteered.

"What business is it of yours?" Reggie asked. "Ursula, was it?" He squared his shoulders. Was he afraid of being upstaged?

Ursula grinned at us. "I've always wanted to solve a real-life mystery."

I was immediately taken with her. In person, she wasn't at all like the press reported. I'd expected her to be socially awkward, but her anxious display at the bar a few minutes before had vanished. A mischievous gleam in her eyes was visible through her sunglasses.

A woman in a purple jumpsuit ran up to our quickly growing circle. "Ms. Light, your assistant said your flight had been delayed and you wouldn't be arriving until tomorrow. I'm so sorry, if only I'd known you were here—"

"Not to worry." Ursula gave the woman a warm smile. "As you can tell, there's something more important than the convention. A man from our neighboring conference is missing."

"Couldn't someone simply see whether or not he's checked out of the hotel?" I suggested.

All eyes turned to me. For a moment, no one spoke. Then everyone began to speak at once. Ursula led the group to the front desk. Stefano and I lingered behind with our drinks—until raised voices carried across the lobby. We rushed over to see what was going on.

"How could his room have been ransacked?" Reggie huffed. "I don't understand how—"

"That's not what I said," the manager insisted. His shiny name tag, matched in brightness by his polished black shoes and glistening helmet of blond hair, identified him as Bertrand Burglund.

Reggie jabbed a thin finger at the bedraggled clerk standing next to the manager. "Your associate says otherwise."

If it had been possible for the manager to supply a more withering look than he was already giving Reggie, I'm sure he would have done so. "That particular maid who reported it has an overly active imagination. The room was *messy*."

The woman in purple from the mystery convention wrung her hands. The two women I'd met earlier tried to calm her. Stefano and Reggie stared at each other.

"There must be some mistake about the room you're looking up," Ursula snapped.

"*Muttal*," Stefano muttered under his breath. I hoped Ursula didn't speak Tamil and wouldn't realize he'd called her an idiot. "You're the one insisting there is something untoward to investigate."

"I simply meant," Ursula said, "that the man that these scholars were speaking of doesn't seem like a messy sort of fellow. I've done extensive research into the criminal mind. If I could gain access to the room and its safe, I could determine—"

"That's entirely impossible," the manager said.

"So he didn't check out," I said, "and his room was potentially ransacked, yet you're not concerned?"

"There was no ransacking!" A lock of the manager's hair escaped and fell onto his forehead.

"Could we talk to the maid?" I asked.

The manager tried to refuse, but between me and Ursula, he was defeated. Ten minutes later, the young maid joined us in a windowless meeting room that smelled of stale coffee. She'd changed into casual street clothes and had a backpack slung over her shoulder.

"No matter what Mr. Burglund says," she told us, "the room was ransacked."

"How could you tell?" Ursula asked. She scrutinized the maid with a troubled frown that caused deep lines across her forehead. Though it seemed like she'd begun this investigation as a game, she was now taking it seriously.

The maid met Ursula's intense gaze with confidence. "I'm working this job to put myself through night school, majoring in criminal justice."

"Why didn't you call the police?" I asked.

She shrugged. "I need this job. I didn't see blood or anything that suggested he was hurt. Just that someone had tossed his room. Instead of cleaning the room, I reported what I found to hotel security. They saw it, too. If we called the police every time I see something weird in a hotel room, they would be here constantly. I'm sorry your friend is missing, but I've gotta get to class. Is there anything else?"

"One last thing," I said. "What time did you go inside the room and see that it had been ransacked?"

"This morning," she said, "shortly before ten o'clock."

Stefano shook his head. "You must be mistaken. A group of us went back to our rooms together during a mid-morning break. One of our colleagues on a delayed flight had contacted us to say she'd arrived at the airport and would be here shortly, and we wanted her to be present for the next item on the agenda. Milton York went into his room at ten thirty, and aside from his minor worries about presenting his findings, he acted perfectly normally when we resumed our meeting at eleven. He didn't disappear until sometime after we broke up for lunch at one and when the two o'clock session began."

"Are you sure?" I asked. "Why wouldn't he say anything about a robbery in his room?"

"It simply means the maid got the time wrong," Reggie said. "I'm sure the tedious days blur together for someone in that line of work."

"I'm right here," the night-school student maid said, crossing her arms. "My name is Martha. And furthermore, *I didn't get the time wrong.*"

"You're sure?" I asked, surprised that Ursula wasn't taking the lead after her earlier declaration.

"I remember," Martha said, "because the guy in the room next to your friend's yelled obscenities at me when I knocked on his door, then gave me a lecture about how he was on vacation and it wasn't even ten o'clock. He swore he'd left the DO NOT DISTURB sign hanging on his doorknob. Those signs are a big headache. They're badly designed and often fall to the floor, so we can't tell if guests are requesting maid service or if they want to be left alone. So yeah, I remember the time. Look, I'm sorry, but I need to go. Best of luck finding your friend." She tightened the straps of her backpack, gave Reggie one last glare, and left.

"Blackmail," Stefano said. Thanks to Ursula's fame, our group had commandeered one of the high tables at the lobby bar. "Maybe the person who searched his room didn't find the Dutch East India

Company diary, so they left him a note telling him not to say anything and to bring the diary to them. They could have threatened him with bodily harm."

I dismissed the idea with a wave of my hand. "Even supposing he's a good enough actor to hide something like that, which I doubt, there's one big hole in that theory: Martha the maid would have seen the note first."

"But that diary *has to be* what the ransacker was after," Stefano said. "Milton was so worried about the repercussions. Do you think he's been kidnapped?"

"Let's not jump to conclusions," Ursula said. "I think we all need a break to think. I'm going to my room." She stood and swooped up an oversized purse.

The tables were packed closely together. A man and a woman at the table closest to me were watching our group with interest. "Aaron," the white-haired woman whispered to her friend, "something isn't right about Ursula." She spoke so quietly that I was surely the only person besides her friend who heard her.

"You've never met the woman, Barbara," her friend replied. "How many G&Ts have you had?"

She barked out a laugh, and they resumed their own conversation.

"Please sit down, Ursula," Reggie said. "I believe I know what happened."

"Do tell," Ursula said dryly. She left her purse on her shoulder but took her seat.

Reggie cleared his throat. "The old boy snapped. Milton realized his findings were bunk, so he ransacked his own room in a fit of insanity, then ran away without checking out. He couldn't face anyone. We should spare him a modicum of dignity and let this go. Thank you for your offer of assistance, Ursula, but there's no mystery to solve."

"Reggie," I said, "that's brilliant."

He beamed at me in spite of the fact that I hadn't called him Dr. Warwick.

"You're completely wrong," I continued, "but you and the woman at the next table have given me the answer."

Reggie frowned. So did Ursula. "I don't know about the rest of you," she said, "but I really do need a break for my mind to function properly. I'm sure better ideas will come to me in the tranquility of my room. Once we have better theories, that imbecile manager will have to let us examine the missing man's room for clues."

"I think you'll find everything you're after right here," I said. "The diary isn't in the safe in his room, Ursula."

Aside from a single flash of surprise that caused her nostrils to flare, Ursula's face retained its mask of mild curiosity. "Why would I care about this historical diary? I'm simply attempting to figure out what happened to your missing friend."

"You're good," I said, "but your motivations aren't exactly what you led us to believe."

Stefano gasped. Reggie choked. Ursula smiled enigmatically.

"The facts, as presented to us, were impossible," I said.

"Indeed?" Ursula said. "I'm intrigued."

"Let's go over what we know," I said. "Milton York discovered a diary on his last research trip to India. He planned on presenting his findings at this conference and told his colleagues that he was worried his findings might meet with a hostile reception. Several people's flights were delayed due to this storm, but not Milton's. He arrived at the hotel last night for a day of preconference meetings today. Milton noticed that his briefcase had been searched that night, but he didn't say the diary had been stolen. This morning, Milton attended the meeting—at what time did it start, Stefano?"

"Nine o'clock on the dot."

"At nine o'clock," I resumed, "Milton York, Reggie Warwick, Stefano Gopal, and several other scholars specializing in South Asian history began their meeting. Sometime before ten o'clock this morning, Milton's room was ransacked—presumably by someone searching for the Dutch East India Company diary. At ten thirty, Stefano, Milton, Reggie, and several others returned to their rooms while waiting for another historian to arrive. Once she did, the group reconvened their meeting at eleven o'clock. And now we come to the key piece of information: Milton acted the same as he had *before* seeing his ransacked room."

"I told you," Reggie said, "that damn maid must have gotten the time wrong."

"She reported it," I said. "I'm sure we can confirm the time. But I don't think that will be necessary. If we only accept the facts that multiple people can confirm and dismiss everything only one person claims to have seen, an answer presents itself."

The din of the bar around us had quieted. All eyes were on me.

"She's an even better storyteller than Ursula," someone at a nearby table whispered. "Who is she?"

"Reggie was right about something important," I said. "Milton ransacked his own room. But not for the reason Reggie asserted. Milton didn't snap. He knew exactly what he was doing."

I paused and looked around at my wide-eyed audience, hoping I was right about what I was about to say. "Everyone thought it was odd that Milton was being secretive about the diary, but it's not unreasonable that he'd want to keep his findings close to his chest. But what if he found out his discovery didn't prove what he thought it did? Or even that it was a fake? Rather than admit his mistake, he would want to save face. What better way to do that than have the diary *disappear* before he could present his findings. Of course, it didn't need to be a real *theft*. All he had to do was leave the diary elsewhere, ransack his own hotel room, then call security and claim to have been robbed."

Stefano exclaimed a mix of Italian and Tamil curses, then shook his head. "But he didn't call security."

"Because," I said, "*he was waiting for the rest of the historians to arrive.* Too many people were delayed by the storm. If he waited, there would be more suspects, and a believable way for the diary to slip through the authorities' fingers and disappear forever."

Reggie groaned and rubbed his eyes.

"What Milton didn't count on," I said, "was that the DO NOT

DISTURB sign on his door would fall to the floor. He didn't plan on the maid entering the room and seeing what he'd done before he was ready for it to be seen."

"Then where is he now?" the librarian asked, gripping her writer friend's arm. "Surely his own disappearance wasn't part of his plan."

"That's where things got muddled," I said. "Milton didn't realize that *someone really was trying to steal the diary*." I turned to face that person. "*Reggie* was the one who had everything to lose if the diary proved to be real. And Reggie was the only person who swore he saw Milton leaving the hotel of his own free will."

"Don't be ridiculous." Reggie glowered at me. "I'm not a common criminal. I'd never break into someone's room or kidnap them."

"I know," I agreed. "But you'd hire someone to act on your behalf. You'd pay someone to steal a document, although from what I've seen of your actions tonight, it looks like kidnapping is a bit much for you. That's why you've been trying so hard to mislead us into thinking Milton left on his own and attempting to convince us we should be done with the matter. You never meant for there to be a kidnapping. You've been trying to let the thief know that you want no part of finding the diary if it includes kidnapping. But it's not working. I'm guessing the thief has a reputation to protect."

Reggie's face went pale.

"You're talking like the thief is here amongst us," Stefano said.

"She is," I said, locking my eyes on the thief's.

The circle of readers, writers, and historians followed my gaze.

"Ursula Light," I said. "Who isn't really Ursula Light. The *real* Ursula Light had her flight delayed due to the storm, as her assistant told the convention organizers, giving our fake Ursula this evening to pretend to be the mystery novelist. Nobody has seen what the reclusive author looks like in many years, so nobody really knows what she looks like up close." I paused as Ursula raised a martini glass and winked at me from across the table.

"When our Ursula was mistaken for the author," I continued,

"she seized the unexpected opportunity. That's why her mood changed for the better so abruptly. A guest of honor at the conference would surely be above suspicion, and as a famous author helping the authorities, she'd be granted greater access to the hotel. Remember, as soon as she began her 'investigation,' she asked the manager if she could see the safe in Milton's room. I suspect that when she searched his briefcase and room last night, she failed to find the diary she was hired to steal—*because the diary was never here at the hotel in the first place.* She confronted Milton when he was alone in between the meeting sessions today, in an attempt to get him to tell her where the diary was. Since he didn't have it, he couldn't give it to her. I'm betting she's got him held captive somewhere nearby, thinking about how she could get him to talk. That's why she looked so tense at the bar, right before she was mistakenly recognized as Ursula Light. She was trying to figure out how to gain access to the safe in his room, which was the only remaining place the diary could be, assuming it was here at the hotel. But..." I trailed off. "Hey, where did she go?"

The woman we knew as Ursula Light, whoever she was, had vanished.

"How does the story end?" Sanjay asked. He'd gotten so wrapped up in my story that he'd been unconsciously picking at his hat. Mangled rose petals surrounded us, filling my apartment with a sweet, calming aroma.

"When hotel security searched the room of the woman who fit the thief's description," I told Sanjay, "they found Milton York bound with comfortable silk ropes. There was no sign of the thief, but faced with evidence of a wire transfer and incriminating e-mails, Reggie Warwick confessed that he'd hired her to steal the diary. He insisted he had nothing to do with the kidnapping and pointed out that he'd tried to get her to stop. He cut a deal to avoid jail time by giving the authorities all the information he had on the fake Ursula Light, but his academic career was over. Milton York, on the other hand, is still teaching. He convinced enough people that my theory about him ransacking his own room wasn't true, and to this day he swears Reggie managed to steal the diary. The real Ursula Light showed up the next day, after the storm ended."

"How long did it take to find fake Ursula?"

I held up the postcard of Pulicat, one of the Dutch East India Company's trading ports in India. "She sent me this postcard a few months after disappearing from the hotel. I have no idea if she's really in India or if she had someone send it for her."

"They never caught her?"

I shook my head. "But I found out some of the information the authorities have collected on her over the years. They're onto her, but she's never been caught. She really is in her seventies. That's her cover that makes her a great thief. Along with her quick thinking. The information they've pieced together on her suggests she only took up a life of crime in her sixties, and she turned out to be quite good. There are several thefts that have been attributed to her."

"I can see why this latest conference you're off to won't live up to that one."

"One never knows. The keynote speaker is Milton York."

The Shadow of the River

This Jaya Jones short story was Gigi's first publication, originally appearing in Fish Tales: The Guppy Anthology, *edited by Ramona DeFelice Long and published by Wildside Press in 2011. It is the only work of fiction featuring Jaya Jones that has a different narrator.*

I arrived ten minutes early outside the office of Dr. Omar Khan, professor of history at the university. That's when everything started to go wrong.

It surprised me when my knock was greeted with silence. In spite of my early arrival, I had been confident Omar would be there.

I knocked again.

"Omar? It's Tarek. I'm here for our appointment."

A faint groan sounded from behind the door.

"Omar?"

I hadn't imagined that sound.

Omar was getting on in years. I knew he took medication for his heart. He'd made a big discovery earlier this week. An ancient map depicting three sacred rivers in India. It was a huge find. Could the excitement have been too much for him?

I tried the door handle. Locked.

I called out again. I pressed my ear to the door. Nothing. But I was sure of what I'd heard.

I ran down the hallway. Skidding to a stop, I pounded on the door of the corner office. This door wasn't locked. It gave way under the force of my fist, swinging open to reveal Dr. Lydia Reynolds,

Chair of the History Department, looking up from her desk at my disheveled self.

"Tarek, what on earth—"

"Do you have keys to the department offices?" I asked. "I think Omar is having a heart attack."

Lydia sprang up from her chair. "No," she said. "With those manuscripts of his, only the campus police have keys."

"But—"

"I know." Lydia rushed past me, moving more quickly than I imagined possible. "There's no time." She disappeared into the office next to hers.

Lydia emerged from the office moments later with a young professor, Bradley Atkins, who was new to the department. Lydia's gray hair bounced against her shoulders as she trotted down the hall with her accomplice jogging after her—all six-and-a-half feet and 250 pounds of him. Watching his sturdy frame, I got an idea of what Lydia had in mind. I sprinted after them.

"You sure?" Bradley said to her, stopping in front of Omar's office.

"You're certain what you heard?" Lydia asked, turning to me.

"Positive." I hoped.

"I take full responsibility," Lydia said.

Bradley gave me a helpless look, which under other circumstances would have been amusing coming from a man who looked like he should have been a linebacker rather than a history professor. He breathed deeply, and then took a few steps back from the door. He ran toward it, lifting his foot just in time to make contact with the edge of the door. A loud thwack echoed down the hallway. The door didn't budge.

At the noise, several heads poked out of doorways down the hallway. One of the visible heads was that of my friend Jaya Jones.

Bradley hurried several paces further back, allowing for a bigger running start. This time the door splintered. He faltered, almost falling onto his hefty back, which would surely have broken several bones of whomever he landed on. Based on my location, they would probably have been mine.

Luckily for me, a stocky man who'd emerged from one of the offices steadied Bradley. With one more heave, the two of them together broke down the door and spilled inside the office. The stocky man— Professor Grant, I believe was his name—landed on the floor at Omar's feet.

Jaya and Lydia stood at my side in the hallway. The three of us followed inside to help Omar. What we saw made us stop just inside the doorway.

Omar was indeed lying helpless on the floor of his office. Only it wasn't his heart. A large patch of blood covered his thinning hair. His large green eyes stared up at the ceiling, unmoving. There was no life left in Omar Khan.

A thick wooden figure lay on the floor next to his body.

It was a statue of a smiling Buddha.

A shrill voice screamed. A deep one did, too. Somebody shouted about calling 911. It might have been me, but I honestly can't quite recall. Those first few moments of seeing the blood on the floor beneath my advisor's head were almost more than I could stand.

Jaya squeezed my hand.

"I thought he'd had a heart attack," I said numbly. "I heard him cry out. That's why we needed to get in."

"Wait," Jaya said. "He doesn't look like he could have—"

"What's all this?"

I nearly jumped out of my skin at the sound of the deep voice next to my ear. Jaya's small body jumped a little as well. She relaxed when she saw the man in the tweed jacket.

"I didn't see you there, Isaac," I said.

"Sorry, didn't mean to scare you," the university's museum director said. "What's happened? Is that Omar who Lydia and Bradley are standing over?"

I nodded but didn't know what to say.

"I wonder..." Jaya murmured. Her hand let go of mine as her voice trailed off. Her lips continued to move almost imperceptibly.

I'd seen her face like that before. It was at the university library, late one night the previous year. I'd walked up to her table and said hello to her, but she hadn't responded. She wasn't being rude; she hadn't heard me. She was so wrapped up in the volume of bound journals in front of her that the rest of the world had been invisible.

"Jaya?" I said. As I expected, she didn't hear me.

Lydia knelt next to Omar's body. She reached out her hand to touch him. Bradley stopped her.

"I'm telling you," Bradley said into his cell phone, "I don't think he needs an ambulance. Just the police."

Jaya wasn't paying attention to any of them. Her olive complexion had paled, but she remained where she was, her eyes scanning the room before stopping on one particular spot. Her focus was directed at the plant on Omar's desk.

I took a look at the plant myself. At first I thought the object next to the plant was only a shadow, but a dried leaf rested on the desk underneath the other leaves of the plant. She took a step toward it, but stopped.

Why was Jaya so interested in a dead leaf?

"I understand," Bradley said, his face grave. He took his phone away from his ear. "There isn't anything we can do for Omar," he said to us. "We need to go wait in the hall. Nobody leave."

That's the moment it truly sank in that Omar wasn't only dead. He had been murdered.

Jaya pulled me into the hallway. She didn't stop there. She's stronger than she looks for her petite five-foot frame. I've seen her flip a six-foot man over her shoulder when he didn't believe she could take care of herself. I nearly tripped as she pulled my elbow until we were around the corner.

"What's going on, Tarek?" she asked.

She poked her head around the wall before I had a chance to answer.

"It's okay," she said. "Nobody followed us. They're all still right outside Omar's office."

"What do you mean what's—?"

"The leaf," Jaya said. "Didn't you see it?"

I had previously thought that Jaya was the smartest graduate student in our history department. Now I wondered if perhaps her genius had crossed over into insanity.

"Didn't you see what was in that room?" Jaya said. "I saw you looking at it, too. We have to tell the police, you know."

I stared blankly at her.

"Next to the plant on his desk," she said.

"A dried leaf?"

"Exactly," Jaya said.

"Why does it matter that Omar forgot to water his plant?"

Jaya threw up her hands. I thought nobody actually did that in exasperation, but Jaya never ceased to amaze me with her varied gestures. She'd been raised in both India and the United States, the respective countries of each of her parents, and had consciously or unconsciously picked up a jumble of body language as well as the spoken languages.

"A scrap of palm leaf was on the edge of his desk," she said. "It looked like a leaf because it *was* a leaf. Just not the kind that came from Omar's plant."

I groaned to myself, finally beginning to understand.

"His great discovery," Jaya said. "It was a torn edge of that map."

"How did you know? I thought he hadn't shown it to anybody yet."

"You've been studying Western history too long, Tarek. You were thinking about Western maps and their inked parchment when Omar told you about the map. But in India, they often used dried palm leaves for paper. We need to find the police and tell them Omar was killed over the map."

Jaya poked her head around the corner of the hall, and then motioned for me to follow her back to the rest of the solemn group of professors and graduate students. She began to pace around, full of nervous energy. Nobody seemed to know what to do. It was a welcome change when the police were ready to talk to us about

Jaya's theory. Two unsmiling detectives led the two of us down the hall and sat us down in Lydia's large corner office. They closed the door behind them.

"There's a fragment of an historic map on his desk," Jaya began. "That's why he was killed. Someone has stolen the rest of that map."

"You saw it happen?" the older of the two detectives asked. He raised a skeptical gray eyebrow.

"No," she admitted, "but when a mild-mannered professor of Middle Eastern and South Asian history discovers a priceless map earlier this week and is bludgeoned to death today—"

"Wait a sec—*priceless* map?"

"Maybe we should start at the beginning," I cut in. "Two days ago, Omar Khan discovered a very valuable map. It was given to us at the last minute to be part of the university museum's collection. It's a map of the Triveni Sangam in India, the meeting point of three sacred rivers: the Ganges, the Yumana, and the 'invisible' Saraswati."

"Why is it so valuable?"

"In this map," I said, "the Saraswati *wasn't* invisible."

"So it was a fake?" The detective rubbed his hand across the deep creases in his forehead. "The forger got it wrong? Then why is it so valu—"

"No, there's a river there. Four thousand years ago, a great earthquake struck India. The river Saraswati was swallowed up by the land, becoming an underground river, said to be bestowed with mystic powers. The site where the two grand rivers converge with this legendary one in Allahabad, northern India, is a sacred place for Hindus. With the sacredness of the site, a map from so long ago that shows a new representation would be worth a lot of money."

"And the ripped edge of the map is on his desk," Jaya said. "Somebody must have torn it from his hands before hitting him with his Buddha statue."

"Know anyone who wanted to hurt the professor?" The detective's face was impassive.

"But I just told you why—" Jaya said.

"If they didn't want to hurt him, they could have stolen this map from his office during the night when he wasn't here," the detective said, cutting her off without raising his voice.

"No way they could have gotten in," I said. "Only Omar and the campus police have keys to his office. He keeps too many valuables to give the key to anyone else."

"Well, somebody else had a key. The dead bolt was locked from the inside. And we're three flights up. No fire escape next to his office."

"Tarek is right," Jaya said. "Nobody else had one."

"His keys were still on him," the younger detective said, speaking for the first time. "We tried them in the lock, and they're the right keys. Someone else must have made a copy. We'll find them."

"Thanks for your help. Here's my card if you think of anything else."

Jaya opened her mouth in protest. It was my turn to pull her away. Her mouth gets her into more trouble than anything else. She let me lead her back to the group in the hallway, a scowl on her face.

Bradley walked over from the opposite direction and stopped next to Isaac and Lydia. He handed Lydia a cup of tepid coffee from the vending machine down the hall. Lydia looked as if she'd aged ten years in the past half hour. Her usually sleek gray hair stood out in all directions, and deep wrinkles bore into her forehead under the expression of horror she wore on her face. She and Omar were two of the old guard in the department, having been at the university for decades together. I had the feeling they had some sort of special bond from their status as a woman and a minority years ago when neither was the norm.

"Do they know anything?" Lydia asked.

I shook my head. "Who would want to hurt Omar?"

"It was clearly an intruder," Isaac said. "Someone not realizing he was here, wanting to steal one of his valuable historical manuscripts—"

"It was that damn map," Jaya said. "That's what they were after."

"You don't know that," Isaac said.

"There was a ripped piece of it on his desk."

Lydia looked on the verge of tears. "Why didn't he just give it to them? It wasn't worth his life."

Isaac gasped. "If you're right, Jaya, I wish I'd never showed him that map."

"There's no need for you to feel guilty, Isaac," I said. "Omar told me he was visiting the storage room of the museum when your latest shipment arrived. He took the initiative himself to look at the latest items. It's not your fault."

A peculiar expression came over Jaya's face.

Isaac was usually so composed that he would never be seen without a pressed handkerchief sticking out of his tweed jacket pocket as he stood confidently with perfect posture. Now, he was slumped against the wall, fidgeting incessantly with his jacket, as if he didn't quite know what to do with his hands. He'd been close to Omar, too, since Omar had been quite involved with the university museum.

Bradley couldn't stand still either. His shoulder and leg were probably sore after his door-breaking adventure. In broad sweeps, he stretched his arms across his chest. After a few swings, he bent his right knee towards his chest in a leg stretch.

"You're making me nervous," Isaac said to Bradley. "What's the matter with you?"

"Sorry." Bradley's face flushed. "I'm not used to breaking down doors. My shoulder is killing me."

"What?" Isaac said. "Oh, yes." But he waited a second too long to say it.

I heard a sharp intake of breath. It was Jaya.

"You weren't there," she said. She was looking at Isaac, her eyes wide. "In the hallway. You weren't there to see Bradley break the door down."

"Oh, of course." Isaac tugged at his jacket. "Yes, you're correct, Jaya. I came upon the scene late. I had to infer who would have—"

"No, you didn't," Jaya said. She spoke calmly, but I could hear a subtle vibration in her voice that wasn't usually there.

"Of course I—"

"You were there as soon as the rest of us got there," Jaya said. "You spoke to Tarek right away. We rushed into the office at the same time, all of us after Professor Grant. He was ahead of Bradley, so that's why you thought Professor Grant was the one who broke the door down. The only way you could have *not* seen that Bradley was one of the men who kicked in the door was if you were inside the room already."

"Jaya," Isaac said, his voice cold. "I know we're all upset—"

"Isaac?" Lydia whispered.

"It explains how someone got out of the room," Jaya said. "You *didn't* get out of the room. Not until we came in. All you had to do was blend in."

"Have you gone mad?" Isaac was no longer so calm. "Why would I want to hurt Omar? You were the one who said a thief wanted the Sangam map. Why would I want to steal my own map, for Christ's sake?"

"Tarek already explained that," Jaya said. "Without knowing he'd done so."

"This is ridiculous," Isaac said and turned away from us.

Bradley put his hand on Isaac's shoulder. "I want to hear what she has to say."

Isaac looked up at Bradley. Or rather, at Bradley's girth.

Jaya's hands were shaking, but she continued in a measured voice. I could imagine the gears turning in her mind, putting the pieces together as she spoke.

"You didn't want to show the map to Omar," Jaya said. "Tarek said Omar happened by when you were unloading a shipment for the museum. He wasn't supposed to be there."

Isaac opened his mouth and drew breath, but didn't speak.

"It's not like our little university museum is the Met," Jaya said. "There's not too much to keep track of. Omar would have known ahead of time if we were receiving something so amazing. Did Omar find it unbelievably strange that this amazing piece was included with no advanced notice? Is that why he took it? To look into it further?"

"Is it true, Isaac?" Lydia asked. She hadn't managed to regain more of her voice than a whisper. "Why were you keeping it a secret? Why would you—" She broke off in a stifled sob.

"You never meant the map to be part of our collection," Jaya said. "A reputable university would serve as a great cover to bring valuable antiquities into the country without strict scrutiny. Only you didn't have time to remove anything from this shipment before Omar saw it."

"What have you got under your jacket?" Bradley asked Isaac, flexing his arm muscle as he did so.

Isaac swallowed hard.

"Oh, lord," he said. He closed his eyes as he pulled out the broken piece of palm leaf from inside his jacket.

The intricate markings of the three rivers seemed to curl around his fingertips. The map was intact except for the missing edge, small enough to be mistaken for a shadow.

Jaya squeezed my shoulder. I gently lifted the palm leaf map into my own hands, wondering if the shadow of this day would one day pass.

Fool's Gold

BONUS NOVELLA

This Jaya Jones and Sanjay Rai novella originally appeared in Other People's Baggage: Three Interconnected Novellas, *along with novellas by Diane Vallere and Kendel Lynn, published by Henery Press in 2012. Each of the novellas stands alone, but if you'd like to learn more about the lost luggage in the story below, and where Jaya's lost luggage ended up, you can seek out "Midnight Ice" by Diane Vallere and "Switch Back" by Kendel Lynn.*

ONE

I stepped onto the stage of the theater. The spotlight blinded me, but after a few seconds my eyes began to adjust. The stage was nearly empty. To my left, a wooden wardrobe cabinet. To my right, a weathered whisky barrel that had seen better days. Rows of plush red seats stretched out in the dark theater, all of them vacant.

"You look awful, Jaya." The voice filled the air, but I remained alone.

I whipped around, looking from the seats to the rafters to the wings, only to be confronted with emptiness. The backstage area had been empty as well, which is why I was now standing here in search of Sanjay.

A moment later, he appeared on the stage a few feet away from me. From where, exactly, I couldn't be sure. Sanjay was a magician. The Hindi Houdini. A bowler hat sat on his head as usual, but today his outfit was a black t-shirt and jeans instead of the tuxedo he usually wore when performing.

"Nice to see you, too," I said.

"I thought you were a good traveler."

"You try being delayed at the Dallas airport for eight hours, then arriving in Edinburgh to find you ended up with someone else's suitcase."

"That explains your ridiculous clothing," Sanjay said. "I thought this magic cabinet had transported me back to 1980."

"Very funny." I smoothed out the florescent pink Edinburgh Fringe Festival t-shirt I was wearing, wondering whether I should have borrowed some of the vintage 1960s clothing I'd found in the suitcase that wasn't mine. It was definitely much more stylish. "At least the night clerk at the hotel was nice enough to open the hotel gift shop at three a.m. so I could grab a t-shirt and leggings. This t-shirt was the only thing that came remotely close to fitting. I left my clothes from the flight with the hotel's laundry service."

"I'm surprised you didn't go shopping this morning."

"I chose sleep." I yawned.

"Now that I'm getting used to it," Sanjay said, looking me up and down, "it's not so bad. I don't think I've ever seen you in pink before. Come to think of it, I don't think I've seen you in anything besides black or gray."

"What about you? No tuxedo? I thought you liked to practice your show in full attire."

"It's not even noon."

"I know," I said. "I should still be sleeping."

Sanjay grinned. "Thanks for coming."

"Sanjay!" A voice with a thick Scottish accent called out from under the stage. "What's the hold up?"

"My friend Jaya's here," Sanjay called back.

A stagehand materialized on the stage next to Sanjay. As had been the case with Sanjay, I wasn't sure exactly how he'd gotten there.

Auburn curls stuck out around the edges of an orange ski cap. "So you're Jaya Jones," the stagehand said. "Sanjay was all broken up that your flight didn't make it in time for you to have dinner with him last night. Can't say I blame him. I'm Ewan."

Sanjay's face flushed as I shook Ewan's hand. I don't know why. Of course it was too bad I couldn't make it on time as planned and was instead relegated to a twenty-four-hour journey from San Francisco to Edinburgh.

I'd only met Sanjay two months before, but he was one of those people who immediately felt like family. He was the best friend I'd made in San Francisco since moving there for my first university teaching job. I finished my PhD in history earlier in the year, after completing the research for my dissertation at the British Library in London.

When Sanjay told me he was performing a magic show at the Edinburgh Fringe Festival, the largest performing arts festival in the world that takes place each August, I knew it was fate—or at least an excellent opportunity. A friend from when I lived in London was also going to be at the festival.

This was going to be a perfect vacation. Flight delays and switched luggage aside, I was ready to enjoy my first real vacation in ages. I'd spent the summer preparing for the four undergraduate history courses I'd be teaching that fall, and I desperately needed a break. I had two weeks before the semester started. I was going to spend this week in Edinburgh relaxing, doing a little sightseeing, and enjoying the festival.

I might have had an ulterior motive as well. I was getting over a breakup. I deserved this treat before diving into real life.

Sanjay narrowed his eyes at the stagehand and cleared his throat. "The show opens tonight," he said, his face slowly returning to normal color. "I'm still working out the kinks of my biggest illusion, so I don't have time to take a break right now. We need to do a full run-through with light and sound as soon as the other member of the crew arrives."

"Do you need any help?" I asked.

"You'd be up for helping?"

"Why not? I've got a little time."

"There's one thing," Sanjay said hesitantly. He pointed to a section of seats close to the stage. "Take a seat in the front on the left, and watch the stage carefully. That's my weak spot. I think I've got it fixed, but I haven't done an audience test yet. Ewan is helping from backstage—"

"Below-stage," Ewan said, "if you want to be accurate." He winked at me.

"The point being that you can't see the illusion from the proper vantage point," Sanjay said.

"Fair enough," Ewan said. "You sure you want her to help?"

"Why wouldn't I help?" I asked.

Ewan shrugged before walking off stage.

"What did he mean by that?" I asked Sanjay.

He gave a non-committal shrug suspiciously similar to Ewan's, and didn't meet my gaze when he spoke. "Who knows?"

"I'm ready whenever you are," Ewan called out, his voice below us.

I jumped down from the stage and sat in the first row.

"Who among our revered audience members," Sanjay began in a booming theatrical voice, "would like to help me ensure the integrity of this illusion? If the lovely lady in the first row with shoulder-length black hair and dangerous heels would assist me?"

I rolled my eyes and hopped back on stage.

"Have we ever met before?" Sanjay asked.

"You can skip the banter," I said. "There's nobody in the audience."

Sanjay sighed. Even the sigh was an overdone theatrical sigh. "Don't you know anything about rehearsing?" he asked.

"Fine." I said. "I don't know you, and am not your confederate."

"Thank you. Now, please select one of the following implements to tie my wrists behind my back."

He lifted a black cloth from the top of the whisky barrel, revealing two types of handcuffs and three kinds of rope. He moved the objects of restraint from the lid, handed them to me, and placed the lid of the barrel on the stage floor. While I inspected the rope and handcuffs, Sanjay took his bowler hat in his hands and rolled his neck back and forth before returning the hat to his head.

"I'll take these two," I said, holding up the more menacing-looking pair of handcuffs and a piece of thick rope.

"Two," Sanjay murmured. "Very nice."

He turned away from me and placed his wrists together behind his back.

"Make them as tight as you'd like," he said.

So I did.

I wouldn't have thought a person could fit into the barrel, especially a man who was five foot ten with his hands tied behind his back, but Sanjay eased inside with little effort.

"If you'll place the lid securely on the barrel before returning to your seat," he said from within his confines.

As I secured the lid, I noticed the barrel rested on a stand that raised it several inches off the floor, so Sanjay wouldn't be able to go through a trap door in the stage.

For a few moments after I returned to my seat, nothing happened. Then the barrel began to rattle. Slowly, at first, for over a minute. As I began to wonder what on earth Sanjay was doing in there, the rattling grew more violent. Just as it was shaking so hard I was sure the lid would burst open, the movement ceased.

The stage was dead silent.

In the silence, a wisp of smoke escaped from the lid of the barrel, followed by a burst of yellow flames through a single hole cut out of the barrel. That couldn't be right.

"Sanjay?"

Silence.

"Sanjay, are you all right?"

More silence.

The flames grew brighter.

"Ewan!" I yelled. "Is this supposed to happen?"

"He's an expert," he called back from below the stage. "I'm sure he'll escape in time." He paused. "Uh...pretty sure."

"You mean he's still in there?"

With my heart thudding in my chest, I jumped onto the stage and ran toward the flaming whisky barrel.

TWO

As I ran toward the flaming barrel, the doors of the cabinet flew open. A hand reached out and grabbed my wrist.

Sanjay whirled me around, stopping me before I reached the fire. We watched from a few yards away as the flames exploded through the top of the whisky barrel. The planks fell flat, revealing only emptiness. The fire was gone too.

"How could you not be inside there?" I asked, shaking free of Sanjay's grip. "I saw the space between the barrel and the stage. There's no way for you to have gotten out."

"A magician never reveals his secrets," Sanjay said. A look of self-satisfaction spread across his face.

"You didn't do that escape in your show at home." I felt my voice shaking as I spoke. I'd been so sure he was burning alive inside that barrel, and he was happy about it. *Men.*

"It's new," Sanjay said. "I thought a whisky barrel would be a good escape for a performance in Scotland. I've performed in England before, but not here."

"That wasn't funny," I grumbled.

"It's Ewan's fault!" Sanjay insisted. "He knew I wasn't still inside. It's supposed to be even more dramatic, with the effect drawn out. Just like Houdini did. But I had to cut it short since you ran onto the stage. What were you planning to do? Throw yourself on the flames?"

I glared at Sanjay. He took a step back.

"You could have told me what you were doing," I said. My voice was close to a growl.

"I had to make sure you wouldn't know what was supposed to

happen," he said, his eyes pleading. "That's the whole point of having you watch, to see if you saw what you weren't supposed to see. I know you like to throw yourself into things, but I didn't think you'd do it so literally here."

"You were right," I said. "I shouldn't have volunteered to help. This is supposed to be a relaxing vacation."

"Why don't you throw yourself into having a relaxing day today. Do some sightseeing and I'll meet up with you later before my show."

"I have other things on my mind."

"Right." Sanjay pursed his lips and a dark expression came over his face. "What with you getting over that breakup and all."

I hadn't actually been thinking about my breakup. *Thanks, Sanjay.* I'd been thinking about whether I had time to buy myself some new clothes before meeting Daniella for the picnic lunch she was having to celebrate the start of her festival show, *Fool's Gold.*

Sanjay shook his head. "Anyway," he said, "the flames in this illusion weren't strong. But it was still very sweet of you to try to save me."

I know I should have left the theater right then, but curiosity about Sanjay's illusion made me decide to watch the trick again. Just one more time.

After I watched Sanjay escape from the empty whisky barrel a fourth time, I still hadn't figured out how it was done.

Each time, Sanjay took the whisky barrel backstage and reconstructed it within minutes, which gave me my first—and only—clue to the illusion. It had been specially constructed to come apart and reassemble easily, and to withstand flames without catching fire. It didn't tell me much. Only that Sanjay was a cruel friend for refusing to tell me how it was done.

The second member of Sanjay's crew arrived as Sanjay stepped out of the cabinet a fourth time and took a bow with his bowler hat in one hand and opened handcuffs and two pieces of rope in his other hand. Though I was tempted to stay even longer, I'd already stuck around longer than I intended. Glancing at the clock on my phone, I knew I was going to be unfashionably late to meet Daniella. I replayed Sanjay's act in my mind as I left the theater. I had yet to figure out a single one of Sanjay's illusions. Even after I knew that Sanjay would materialize in the cabinet on the other side of the stage after squeezing himself into the whisky barrel with his wrists bound, I had no idea how he pulled off the switch.

I paused outside the theater to listen to a new voicemail message and give my eyes a moment to adjust. Dark storm clouds hung low in the distance, but the sun shone brightly above me. It had been darker in the theater than I'd realized. Perhaps that was related to how Sanjay had pulled off his illusion.

My focus shifted when I heard the contents of the voicemail. "I'm so sorry, Jaya." It was Daniella. "Late to my own party...a problem has come up...I'll be there as soon as I—" She broke off and swore before the message cut off abruptly.

I frowned at the phone. It wasn't the words she'd spoken that worried me. If anything, it was a relief to hear I had a little extra time. But I didn't feel relieved. Even before she began swearing, Daniella's voice had been shaking.

This was a woman who regularly performed on stage in front of hundreds, even thousands, of people. I'd never seen her nervous, and never heard her voice tremble like that.

Daniella Stuart had been an actress for years, and this Fringe Festival show was the first play she'd also written. She'd moved from a small Scottish village to London to be an actress when she was a teenager and had become moderately successful on the London stage. But after celebrating her fortieth birthday, Daniella wanted more. I'd met her the previous year at the British Library, where I was doing research on the British East India Company to finish my dissertation, and she was researching historical chess pieces for the two-person play she was writing. Her carefree spirit made her a welcome break from my research in the library's reading rooms.

Whatever was making her that worried, it wasn't good.

THREE

I replayed the voicemail message. The only new thing I noticed was that she gave a slight, nervous laugh after saying she'd be late to her own party. What was going on?

Daniella's play, *Fool's Gold*, was scheduled to begin the following night, so today's picnic was a party her friends were throwing for her. It would have been a dinner except there was a big festival gala happening that evening she planned to attend.

I tried to shake off the bad feeling creeping up the back of my neck. It was probably nothing. I was jetlagged, starving, and dressed like a neon sign. Needless to say, I wasn't at my best. There must have been an innocent explanation. Daniella probably felt bad that I'd flown in from San Francisco and she was running late. Surely that was all there was to it.

I tucked my phone back into my messenger bag and hurried down a street lined with colorful shops at street level and faded stone facades above. The broad sidewalks were full of people watching street performers in town for the festival. I eased my way past a band of fiddlers surrounded by an enthusiastically clapping crowd, and around a teenage comedian who was making small children laugh as he pulled out colorful silk scarves from behind their ears. The energy of the crowd was contagious, and I found myself pushing my worries aside and smiling along with the kids.

The Edinburgh Fringe was an eclectic combination of performances that had begun as side projects to the more formally organized Edinburgh International Festival. It had grown into the largest performing arts festival in the world because they didn't keep anyone out. There were no applications. No juries to approve performances. Actors, comedians, dancers, musical theater troupes, and other performance artists needed to find financing to put on their shows, but there were shoestring budget street performances next to expensive productions. There was room for everyone.

Since Daniella was running late, I had time to stop by my hotel to take a quick shower. I said a silent thanks when I found my laundered clothes waiting for me. I wouldn't have to look like a florescent pink fashion victim when meeting up with Daniella and her friends.

After taking a three-minute shower, I changed clothes and towel-dried my hair while on hold with the airline. A harried employee regretfully informed me they had no idea where my bag was. *Great.* My jeans and sweater would do fine for today—as long as the looming storm held off—but my high heels wouldn't do for the scenic jogging routes or hiking I'd planned. I eyed the stranger's suitcase that looked so much like my own. I never imagined anyone besides me would have a vintage Wedgwood suitcase in blue with white trim. It was one of the things my dad had saved from his childhood in the 1950s, and I'd found it in the back of a closet at his house when I moved out of the house at age sixteen. I made a mental note to never again fail to pack an extra set of clothes in my carry-on bag.

I would also never again pack anything important in a checked bag. Earlier that summer I'd found a faded old letter about a chess game tucked into the pages of a book at a used bookstore in San Francisco, and I packed it to show Daniella, thinking she'd get a kick out of it. Now I wouldn't be arriving at the picnic with a fun conversation piece.

The hotel wasn't far from our designated meeting spot in the Princes Street Gardens. As I entered the gardens, Edinburgh Castle loomed above me, the dark stone enclosure sitting on a mound of volcanic rock high above the center of the city.

The gardens were crowded with people attending the festival, but I was able to find Daniella's group thanks to a bright yellow poster board with hand-drawn black lettering that spelled out

Fool's Gold. Two women sat on a picnic blanket next to the sign. In spite of the crisp wind, they were both dressed as if it was summer in southern California. They were drinking from plastic champagne flutes and speaking animatedly with each other in thick Scottish accents. Though it had taken me almost half an hour to arrive after receiving the voicemail message, there was no sign of Daniella.

As I walked up to the two women, they fell silent. They stared at me, wide-eyed. I was no longer wearing the bright pink gift-shop attire, so I wasn't sure what was so shocking about my appearance. I smoothed my hair, making sure I hadn't accidentally left a comb sticking out of it or some other silly thing I might have done in my sleep-deprived state. When I reached them, I realized it wasn't me they were staring at.

A middle-aged man came up from behind and stopped next to me. Now this was someone with an unforgettable appearance. He was dressed from another era. He wore a perfectly tailored tweed jacket, glasses with thick gold-colored frames, a bright green ascot around his neck, riding boots over jodhpurs, and to top it all off: a deer stalker hat over his salt-and-pepper hair, a la Sherlock Holmes.

"This is Daniella's party?" he said in a posh English accent.

The two women murmured in unison that it was, scrambling to stand up.

"I hope I'm not intruding," he added.

"Not at all," the taller woman said. "It's great to have you. Daniella should be here soon."

"Champagne?" the second woman offered, swinging a bottle in one hand and lifting a platter of cheese and sliced baguette in the other. "Or Brie?" The open bottle swayed in her hand precariously. Clearly she'd had too much champagne and not enough cheese.

"I'd love some cheese," I said. The woman holding the cheese platter looked at me as if seeing me for the first time.

"Sorry!" she said. "You must be Daniella's American friend. She mentioned you were coming."

The women introduced themselves, but I immediately forgot

their names. Between worrying about Daniella and wondering about the man in the outrageous outfit, I was far too distracted for multitasking.

"American, eh?" Sherlock said to me with an overstated wink as he accepted the glass from Daniella's eager friend.

"Guilty," I mumbled through a mouthful of bread and cheese. Travel had left me famished.

"Clayton Barnes," he said, extending his hand.

"Jaya Jones."

Clayton Barnes had one of the most enthusiastic handshakes I'd ever encountered. If his over-the-top attire and handshake were indicators, he was having a lot of fun with life.

The women smiled at him and told him to help himself to anything before giggling and sitting back down on the picnic blanket. They must have been pretty drunk to be giggling so much.

"Here for the festival?" Clayton asked me.

"Daniella and another friend of mine are performing."

"Have you attended before?"

I shook my head as I chewed and wondered if he was consciously trying to look like Sherlock Holmes. *Of course! The festival.* He was in costume.

"You're in for a treat," he said. "I've lived here for over ten years and come to the festival each summer. But this one is special."

"You're in a Sherlock Holmes play?"

He looked at me blankly for a second while I froze, a sinking feeling in my stomach. I might as well have taken off my shoe and stuck my foot in my mouth along with the cheese.

But a moment later he broke into a large grin. "You mean my clothing for a midday picnic," he said with a smile. "I'm a bit old fashioned, I know. It's because of my avocation. You see, I'm an alchemist—"

"An *alchemist*?" I interrupted.

"Yes." Clayton beamed at me, rocking back and forth in his riding boots. "An alchemist."

"You mean you study the history of alchemy?" I asked.

"Oh, no. I'm a practicing alchemist." He took a small sip from his glass, the cheap plastic looking entirely out of place in his hand. "Changing base metals into gold. It's how I made my fortune, you see."

Great. Daniella was late to her own party, possibly because something was horribly wrong, and I was stuck talking to the crazy guy who thought he was in a comic book.

"Uh huh," I said. I glanced over at Daniella's friends, wondering if I could join their conversation on the blanket.

"It's not as glamorous as it sounds," Clayton said. "It took over a decade of rigorous study before I was able to perfect the process. Now I'm connected to the elements to such a degree that I can sense the presence of gold. That's why I was intrigued by Daniella's show and why this year's festival is special. There's a gold and silver chess set—"

"The centerpiece of her show," I said. I'd heard about the idea from Daniella. Antiques dealer Feisal Khattabi was sponsoring Daniella's play at the festival, including the loan of an antique chess set made of gold and silver to be used in the show. It was a replica of the famous Lewis Chessmen. Feisal's gold and silver chess set had been commissioned by an eccentric Scottish laird who'd lost his bid to purchase the original Lewis Chessmen after they were unearthed in a remote region of Scotland in the 1800s.

"It's brilliant," Clayton said.

"I still don't understand the logic of using this chess set to drum up business for an antiques store," I said. "Doesn't the risk outweigh whatever buzz it might create?"

"Hardly," Clayton said. "Feisal has precautions in place. You said you haven't been to the festival before. There are tens of thousands of people here. Performers need to do something to stand out from the crowd. This chess set is great publicity for Feisal's antique business as well as Daniella's play. Here in Scotland, the Lewis Chessmen are a big deal. This gold and silver replica is almost as old—and perhaps even more valuable."

I held my tongue. It still sounded like a terrible idea. Whatever precautions might be in place, flaunting a valuable set in front of thousands of theatergoers wasn't a good idea.

"Do you know the history of the Lewis Chessmen?" he asked, reading my expression.

"I've heard of them," I said, "but don't know much about them. Aren't they in a collection at the British Library in London?"

"Don't remind the Scots," Clayton said with a wink. "Yes, that's them. Some of the pieces are in England, but many of the best pieces from the set are here in Edinburgh, and Scotland wants to get the rest back from England. There's a great deal of national pride wrapped up in those pieces."

"Aren't they supposed to be humorous as well?" I asked.

"You know more than you said." Clayton gave me a mischievous grin.

"It's the curse of a historian," I said. "Whenever I know only a bit of history about something outside of my field, I feel like a fraud to claim to know anything at all."

"That humor you mentioned is one of the reasons the set has fascinated people since their discovery. Aside from the pawns, all the pieces are human figures, and real characters. The artists who carved the pieces created humanity that resonates across time and culture. A scowling king, a shocked queen, a crazed berserker rook. This gold and silver replica doesn't capture the details of the original, but you can see why it's still something that would interest a lot of people."

"All right," I said. "Maybe it doesn't sound like a *terrible* idea. But it's still a stressful idea. I wouldn't want to be the security guard in charge of safekeeping."

Clayton laughed heartily, but I didn't join in. I couldn't shake the memory of the usually confident Daniella's shaking voice on the phone.

"I wonder what's keeping Daniella," I said.

"And Feisal," Clayton said, his smile disappearing. "He wouldn't miss this celebration, either." The worry on his face was obvious, but when he caught me studying his expression he laughed. "Do you know the story of how the chess pieces were discovered? A farmer and his cow discovered the walrus-ivory and whale-tooth carved pieces on his land on the Isle of Lewis in 1831—which is why they're called the Lewis Chessmen. Nobody can agree on where they originally came from, but they are truly works of art."

Past Clayton, I saw Daniella approaching. She was accompanied by a tall, waif-like blonde woman who must have been the other actress in *Fool's Gold*. She gave us all quick hugs and introduced Astrid, all the while with a forced smile. Daniella's short brown hair had always been a bit unruly, but in a stylish punky sort of way. Today it was lifeless and messy, and her face creased with worry.

"Sorry Astrid and I are late," she said. "There was a security problem at the theater."

The sirens of police cars drowned out our voices as they passed us and sped down Princes Street. My eyes followed the cars. They screeched to a halt a block past us.

"What kind of problem were you talking about?" Clayton asked. "Not the chess set, I hope."

"A broken window," Daniella said. "They think it was a drunken prank. The city is crazy right now. But...."

"But what?" Clayton asked, adjusting his Sherlock hat. "As you said, it's festival time."

"It worried Feisal," Daniella said. "And I didn't like the look of it either. He wanted to make sure the theater got it fixed right away."

"Why did Feisal go?" Clayton asked. "That should be security's job."

Astrid gave an unladylike snort, detracting from her stunning appearance. She stood six feet tall in ballet flats, a full foot taller than me, though her bone structure was as small as mine.

Daniella wasn't looking at either Clayton or Astrid. Her gaze was focused past all of us.

"The police cars," she said. "That's our hotel."

She was right. The police cars had stopped directly in front of the Old Town Hotel.

Without giving us a backward glance, Daniella marched away from the picnic, heading straight for the hotel. Clayton squinted at Daniella through his gold-rimmed glasses, his expression unreadable. Astrid's face was set in an angry glare. Nobody made a move to follow Daniella except for me. I hurried to catch up with her.

"What's going on?" I asked when I caught up to her. She had her phone to her ear, but hung up when she saw me.

"I've had a bad feeling ever since this morning," she said, not slowing her pace. "It's always a bad sign for a show when something is sabotaged at the theater."

"What does that have to do with the hotel?" I asked. I was half-jogging to keep up with her. Not an easy feat while walking through a grassy park in heels.

"Maybe nothing," she said. "I hope it's nothing."

Daniella's friends hadn't followed, but Astrid and Clayton caught up with us at the edge of the gardens. The four of us entered the hotel together. We didn't get far. The elevator and stairway off the hotel lobby were being blocked off with police tape, leaving the adjacent bar packed with wall-to-wall people. Families squished themselves into the three tartan-patterned loveseats off to one side, and a lucky few were sitting in the half-a-dozen matching chairs. Everyone else stood wherever there was a free few inches of floor space. The crowd quickly swallowed us up, and I found myself separated from Daniella, Astrid, and Clayton.

I caught a glimpse of Daniella pushing her way through the crowd to the closest police officer. Before reaching him, she paused and changed course. She'd spotted someone.

A tall man with dark, olive-hued skin stepped through the main doors of the hotel lobby. He was easy to spot. The man had presence. This was the type of person you could easily imagine commanding the attention of the room. He wore a dark gray suit that must have cost several thousand dollars. In spite of his businessman's attire, he reminded me of an older version of someone I knew.

Daniella greeted him with a hug. I couldn't hear what they were saying to each other, but their animated body language made it apparent something was wrong. A group of exceptionally tall men with German accents walked past me, and I lost sight of Daniella. This was one of those times when I really hated being short.

Craning my neck, I spotted a deerstalker hat. Clayton Barnes. I made my way in that direction. When I reached him, he was with Astrid and Daniella. The charismatic man wasn't with them.

"It's the chess set," Daniella said, her voice shaking even more than it had on the phone. "A thief used explosives to blow up a safe in the hotel. The chess set has been stolen."

FOUR

"You can't be serious," Clayton said. He shook his head from side to side repeatedly, as if willing his words to be true. His previous calm disposition was nowhere to be seen, replaced by the demeanor of a small child throwing a tantrum. "How could this have happened?

"I don't understand how it happened," Daniella said, looking at the floor as she spoke. "It shouldn't have been possible."

"What do you mean?" I asked.

"We thought we were being so clever," Daniella said, her voice almost a whisper. Her lip quivered and her eyes filled up, but she kept the tears at bay. "We made a show of putting the chess set in the main safe at the hotel desk. But it was a fake set we gave them. Nobody was supposed to know the real chess set was in the safe in our suite."

"How did you learn what happened?" I asked. "Was it from the man I saw you talking with?"

"That was Feisal," Daniella said, nodding and meeting my gaze. "The chess set is his, so the police told him about the theft. He's gone off to the police station with them."

So that was the antiques dealer, Feisal. He reminded me very much of a great uncle of mine I only knew from family photographs. Their faces were superficially similar based on skin color and the shape of their eyes, but my great-great uncle's photographs had captured a bold look in his eyes and in the way he carried himself. I recognized that same adventurous spirit in Feisal.

"I never trusted that security guard of his," Astrid said. Though she didn't seem to speak much, her voice was confident, verging on arrogant. Her accent wasn't Scottish or English, but I couldn't place it.

"You don't mean Izzy," Daniella said.

"Of course I mean Izzy," Astrid said. I placed the accent. Her English accent was tinted with French. "Who else would I mean? You said it yourself—since it was stolen from our suite where the four of us were staying, it had to have been one of us. You, me, Feisal, or Izzy."

Clayton remained silent, looking between Astrid and Daniella with his deerstalker hat pulled low on his brow. He wore an expression that combined anger and confusion.

"He wouldn't—" Daniella began, but stopped short of saying more.

"Well, you and I didn't do it," Astrid said, "and why would Feisal steal his own chess set? I'm telling you, it was Izzy—"

"May I have your attention, everyone!" A fair-haired man in a policeman's uniform stood on a chair near the reception desk to address the crowd with a thick Scottish accent. The din of the crowd lessened slightly, but didn't cease, which was probably because the policeman looked all of twenty years old. As someone who was often mistaken for an undergraduate while I was finishing my PhD, I should have been more forgiving of people who look young but need to exert their authority. In two weeks, I'd be teaching undergraduates as an Assistant Professor of History. I was twenty-nine but had inherited the same small bone structure as my Indian mom. I knew I was a good teacher, so I hoped I'd be perceived by my students as having more authority than this poor policeman.

"The other floors of the hotel will be opened up soon enough," the young officer said, raising his voice to be heard above the chatter. "But not immediately. Please go about your business and you should have access to your rooms again within an hour or two."

The crowd gave a collective groan. The police officer looked in our direction, then jumped down from the chair and walked straight to us. When he reached us, he glanced at the cell phone in his hand. On the screen was an image of the *Fool's Gold* poster with a picture of the two actresses.

"Daniella Stuart and Astrid Moreau?" he asked.

He asked Daniella and Astrid to go to the station for a few questions, since they were staying in the suite with the theft. In spite of the respectful manner in which the request was made, it didn't seem like a voluntary request.

"Of course," Daniella said. "Jaya, I'll meet you back here as soon as we're done."

Instead of finding out why a security guard of questionable character was guarding the chess set, I watched Daniella and Astrid disappear out the door.

Clayton removed his gold glasses and rubbed his eyes. "I hope their input can shed some light on this mess," he said. "God, this is awful. Join me for a pint while we wait?"

I didn't want a beer, but my stomach rumbled loudly. Clayton and I made our way through the lobby toward the hotel's restaurant. At least that's what we tried to do. It was entirely possible I would be crushed to death weaving my way through the crowded lobby. But the policeman's words were beginning to have an effect on the hotel guests. The crowd thinned out and I spotted two seats at the end of the bar.

I passed a woman speaking with her young son, who fell silent and turned to stare open-mouthed at Clayton as we passed. It wasn't just the woman. Several people turned their heads to stare at him as we walked by. Though his outfit was outrageous, the rude behavior surprised me.

I kept on walking until I reached the empty seats. I sat on a high-backed wooden stool and set my messenger bag at my feet. I expected Clayton would remove his Sherlock hat when we sat down, but he left it on.

"I knew Feisal's trusting nature would get him into trouble one of these days," Clayton said. His shoulders slumped as he rested his elbows on the bar.

"You think Feisal's security guard stole the chess set?" I asked.

"I fear so," Clayton said. "I've known Feisal for years. I've bought many antiques from his London shop, and he's become a good friend over the years. He was born in Egypt, educated in London. He fell in love with our great country and has been here ever since. He's a good man, but he lets his emotions get the better of him when it comes to business decisions—such as whom he hires."

We ordered food from the bartender and I asked for a coffee to go with my leg of lamb since it was a bit early in the day for a beer. But as soon as the bartender set down a cup of instant Nescafé front of me, Clayton's dark beer looked much more appealing. I should have known better than to order coffee in a Scottish bar.

"Unless the gold chess pieces are recovered soon," Clayton said as he raised he glass, "I may end up drinking far too many of these."

"The police must know something they aren't sharing," I said. "Otherwise they would have questioned all the guests, not just the four of them staying in the suite."

"I suspect they will be arresting Izzy, if they haven't already."

"Why are you and Astrid so sure he's guilty?" I asked. "Shouldn't a security guard be the least likely person to be suspected?"

"It's his past," Clayton said. I waited for him to go on, but he didn't.

"Which is?" I asked.

"I don't like to gossip about others," Clayton said, drawing his lips together and adjusting his glasses. "It creates a negative energy that isn't good for my alchemical transformations. You needn't concern yourself with our problems. You're here to enjoy the festival. So tell me, what do you do in America?"

I couldn't figure out Clayton Barnes. He seemed sincere in what he was saying and oblivious to the stares brought by his flamboyant Victorian clothing.

He also had a good point. There wasn't anything I could do. I was only being nosy. I would wait for Daniella to return from the police station, since I said I'd wait for her, but then I would go buy myself some clothes and enjoy the city. There was a tour of the castle scheduled in a couple of hours that I had been hoping to attend. I love guided tours because it's interesting to see which parts of history the guides talk about.

"I'm about to begin teaching history at a university in San Francisco," I said.

"Oh, a historian! How lovely. That's why you asked if I studied historic alchemists. You don't study them, do you?"

"I specialize in Indian history," I said. "My research is on the British East India Company."

Clayton squinted at me through his glasses. "You're of Indian descent?"

"My mom was Indian and I was born there. But after she died, my brother and I grew up in California with my dad, who's American with typical mixed European descent."

"There were some extraordinary Indian alchemists," Clayton said. "Arguably the Egyptians did the most to further the study of alchemy, but there's a great tradition of Indian alchemy going back centuries."

"Really?"

"The Bhairavis focus on mercury, not gold, with the goal of prolonging life rather than transforming metals, but the processes are the same."

"Turning lead into gold is the same as the secret to eternal life?"

"They're both about transformation," Clayton said. "There's real science behind these transformations. Modern chemistry is a branch of alchemy. Isaac Newton was an alchemist. He believed his alchemical work to be integral to his scientific studies. Aristotle was an alchemist, as was Socrates."

"You *are* a historian," I said.

"You caught me." He grinned and loosened his ascot. "One needs to study the masters in order to learn their secrets."

"Let me ask you this," I said. "Why doesn't everyone go around turning lead into gold, if it's possible? And why don't we all live forever?"

Clayton frowned. "You're a skeptic. I understand. Most people are. They say I'm eccentric, that I have a screw loose. No, no. It's true. I know what they say. It's only natural. Most people can't achieve the highest forms of alchemy, so it's perfectly reasonable that they doubt what they cannot see for themselves."

"Couldn't you show them?" I asked, thinking about Sanjay's tricks.

"It's not easy to transform metals," Clayton said. "Nor is it easy to transform oneself. And it's not something that can be done in public."

"Since you're one of the few people who have succeeded in this difficult process," I said, "why don't you make enough gold to solve all of the world's problems?"

"As a historian, surely you realize that money alone won't solve the world's problems."

"True enough," I admitted. "But it could help."

"And I do," Clayton said, a huge grin forming on his face. "You're not from here, so you don't know who I am. You see, I'm quite well known. I'm from a prominent old family, and I do a lot with charity causes."

I felt my cheeks flush. That explained why so many people in the crowd had been glancing in our direction. Clayton was famous.

It wasn't the Scottish people who were crazy. It was me who was ignorant. I'd been so caught up in my dissertation the last few years that even when living in London I hadn't heard of him. I hadn't had a television in my flat, and most of my reading was related to my research.

"I'm sorry I didn't realize—"

"Don't be embarrassed," Clayton said. "That's one of the reasons it's been such a pleasure to speak with you. I've spoken more to you about alchemy this afternoon than I've done with anyone in ages, because you haven't treated me condescendingly." He paused and reached into his breast pocket. "I'm hosting a little party for charity at my castle tonight, since so many people are in town for the festival. The process to create gold is draining, so I do what I can, and donate much of it, but I need to convince others to do so as well. I hope you'll attend—no donation expected, of course. You saw how upset Daniella is. You should help her take her mind off of this theft."

The elegant invitation he placed in my hand was printed on thick cream-colored paper with lettering that looked like gold leaf. Behind the letterpress text with information about the event was a light sketch of a stone castle surrounded by a forest.

"I'm supposed to attend the opening night of my friend's magic show tonight," I said, "but if the timing works, I'd love to come. Thank you."

Clayton pursed his lips. I expected he wasn't used to people turning down invitations to his castle.

"I think you would be a big help to Daniella," he said. "You can distract her from this nonsense. The castle is just outside the city, so it takes no time at all to get there."

He tossed off the word "castle" as casually as if he was saying "apartment."

"It's only a small castle," he said, reading my expression. "No real fortifications. It's a glorified manor house with some beautiful gardens. It was owned by a sixteenth century alchemist. That's why I bought it. He's the one who named it Black Dragon Castle."

"Black Dragon?"

"It's an alchemical term," Clayton said. "It symbolizes stages of transformation. The dragon is key to transformations. Integral," he paused, "but dangerous."

FIVE

We'd finished eating and I was halfway through a pint of strong post-lunch beer when a familiar face appeared.

Daniella scanned the bar before spotting us and rushing up to me. She squeezed my hands, looking into my eyes with desperation. Smudges of eyeliner and mascara dotted her cheeks. She looked as if she might burst into a second round of tears any second.

"Is everything all right?" I asked, realizing it was a stupid thing to say as soon as it came out of my mouth.

"Where's Feisal?" Clayton asked. "How did you get here first?"

"Everything is wrong," Daniella said. She wiped an errant tear off her cheek.

"The theft is awful," I said. "But it doesn't sound like anyone got hurt. And surely Feisal has insurance."

"That's the problem," Daniella said. "He does. He spent the last of his reserves insuring this production. He's nearly broke. His business suffered when the economy tanked. This was his last attempt to get the business back on track. The police are still questioning him. They think he stole his own chess set as *insurance fraud*."

"Oh dear," Clayton said. "The police can't really believe Feisal would steal his own chess set, would they?"

"That's what they seem to think," Daniella said.

"Desperate times make people do desperate things," I said.

"I've known him for years," Daniella said. "He's involved in London's theater community. He acquires specialty set pieces for high budget shows."

"I don't believe it either," Clayton said. "Feisal would never do that. I wouldn't say the same of everyone he employs..." He let the unspoken accusation hang in the air.

"Izzy," Daniella said, "would not have done this."

"Well, *somebody* had to have done it," Clayton snapped. "Unless you think it could have vanished into thin air?" His fists were clenched so tightly his knuckles were white. "Sorry," he said a moment later. He looked up at the ceiling as he took two deep breaths. "It's this situation. The gold...I can't believe it's gone."

"This is the worst timing for getting it back," Daniella said. "The police have too much going on with so many people in town for the festival. There's an inexperienced officer assigned to the case. He wants to wrap things up quickly, and the insurance fraud angle is simple."

Clayton groaned.

"Don't police often start with the assumption that it's an inside job?" I said. "That doesn't mean they'll continue to believe it if that's not where the evidence takes them. It doesn't sound so strange that that's where they'd begin."

"That's not the weird part," Daniella said. She turned to Clayton. "You weren't wrong when you said the chess set vanished into thin air."

"What do you mean?" he asked.

"There were a dozen witnesses in the hallway," Daniella said. "A German tour group in town for the festival. After the safe was blown opened, nobody came out of the room through the hotel room door. The police found the door hadn't been forced either. That means it was one of our keys that was used. It's both an inside job and an impossible job. There's no way the thief could have gotten out of that room. The chess set and the thief simply vanished."

SIX

"They can't simply have vanished," I said.

"Obviously," Clayton said with a scoff. "Izzy had to have gotten out somehow."

"Don't," Daniella said. Her voice was soft but firm. "Just because of his past—"

"I warned Feisal not to hire him," Clayton cut in.

"What am I missing?" I asked.

Daniella and Clayton looked sharply at each other, ignoring me. They stared at each other for a few seconds before Daniella looked away. She tucked a lock of her messy hair behind her ear and stared at the floor.

"It doesn't matter what we think," Clayton said. "The police will discover his culpability."

"But he didn't do it!" Daniella cried. "And now they're looking into Feisal. I know he didn't do it either. From what they said to me when they questioned me, I could tell they were just about to arrest him."

"The police aren't going to arrest an innocent man," I said in a voice I hoped sounded much more confident than I felt.

"Feisal!" Clayton called out. "We're over here!"

From a distance, I would have guessed the charismatic Feisal, with his thick black hair and thin build, was a young man. As he joined us I realized he must have been in his fifties. His face was lined with worry, making him appear even older.

"Clayton," Feisal said, shaking his hand heartily as he joined us at the bar. "I'm so sorry I couldn't make it to the picnic."

"What's the matter with you?" Daniella said. "That's the least of your problems."

"Proper respect is of the utmost importance at all times," Feisal said. "That's what will see us through this. I'm Feisal Khattabi," he added, turning to me.

"Jaya Jones."

"Ah, yes, Daniella's American friend," he said, shaking my hand. "You are perhaps part Egyptian? Your beautiful features suggest—"

"I was actually wondering if you were part Indian. You remind me very much of a great uncle of mine—"

"Have you all gone crazy?" Daniella cut in, nearly shouting. "You're exchanging pleasantries and family histories while the chess set is missing, you're possibly going to be thrown in jail, and my play is supposed to open tomorrow!"

"Perhaps we should order Daniella some tea to calm her nerves," Clayton suggested.

"Quite," Feisal agreed.

"I. Don't. Need. Tea!" Daniella cried.

"Yes," Clayton said. "I see your point. This bar is no place for proper tea. Now that you two are here, we can adjourn elsewhere." He raised a finger in an understated motion to catch the attention of the bartender.

I knew about the reserved English, but Daniella had a point. Their forced calm was making my nerves tingle.

"Feisal," I said. "From what Daniella said, I'm surprised to see you here so soon. It sounded like the police were focusing their attention on you."

"They questioned me," Feisal said, "but they had no evidence to hold me. They had a theory about insurance fraud, but they now see that cannot be the case."

"What do you mean?" Daniella asked.

Feisal held his head high and cleared his throat. "After the fees to set up this show and to pay Izzy..." He broke off and looked past us at the row of spirits behind the bar. "I didn't have sufficient assets to adequately insure the set."

"But you told me—" Daniella said.

"I didn't want you to worry, Daniella," Feisal said. "I needed you to feel comfortable acting with the chess set on stage with you. A big part of the publicity needed to be that your play was a marvelous show. I couldn't have you nervous about the chess set."

"Feisal," Clayton said, his voice clipped. "You know better than to go without insurance."

Feisal pulled out a handkerchief from his pocket and wiped his brow. "Quite," he said. "The one time I neglect to get insurance...but never mind." He tucked the handkerchief back into this pocket with a shaky hand. "I'm sure the police will catch the thief and recover the set. Yes, we must have faith in the police. The theft seems impossible...but it can't be, can it?"

"What are the police doing now?" I asked.

"Unfortunately," Feisal said, "I believe they're now focusing their attention on Izzy, because of his background."

"But that's all in the past," Daniella said.

"The police don't see it that way."

"It wasn't his fault," Daniella said. "It was a moment of weakness years ago. Everyone deserves a second chance."

"I don't believe he's guilty either," Feisal said. "I wouldn't have employed him as security if I felt different than you, Daniella."

"I know," Daniella said.

Feisal's eyes were downcast. "I only hope I'll be here to have a job for him once this mess is over. My father never wanted me to stay in this country. He wanted me to learn what I could here, but return home. Home. Such a strange word. Even if I lose my business, Britain is my home. If I lose the money from the chess set, I can rebuild my business. But if I am presumed guilty of this thing I didn't do..."

"You don't mean you could be deported?" I said.

"I'm a permanent resident," Feisal said. "But I don't know what would happen if I were to be found guilty of a crime."

"Don't worry," Clayton said. "We all know you didn't have anything to do with this. The police will see that. Shall we find that tea and leave police matters to the police?"

"I don't want to drink any tea!" Daniella said. Her distressed, bulging eyes reminded me of the rook chess piece who was biting his shield. The bartender gave her a sharp look.

"Feisal," Clayton said. "Even if the ladies don't want tea, how about you and I have a cuppa?"

Daniella and I followed the two men out of the bar. Clayton and Feisal left the hotel, a sea of heads turning in their wake. Daniella wanted to stay at the hotel to wait for Astrid and Izzy, so we found a spot in the corner of the lobby with a good view of the front doors.

"What am I going to do?" Daniella asked.

"Clayton is probably right that the police will get to the bottom of this," I said.

"You don't understand, Jaya. The police will be biased against Izzy."

"With what you told us about the crime," I said, "I might have an idea."

"You do?" She wiped a tear from her cheek.

"I know someone who might be able to help. He thinks...*differently* than the police."

"Differently?"

"He creates seemingly impossible situations for a living."

"Please, Jaya. Anything that could help, please do it."

I pulled my phone from my bag and sent a text message to Sanjay.

Sanjay dissected the seemingly impossible acts of other magicians all the time, and this theft reminded me of such an illusion. If Sanjay could figure out how a thief and chess set vanished, he could help prove it wasn't one of the people involved in the play who'd stolen the set. It looked like Daniella was close to a nervous breakdown about Izzy being persecuted. I couldn't enjoy a relaxing vacation when my friend was convinced an innocent man would go to jail.

Beyond Daniella's worries, an image of Feisal's frightened eyes stuck in my mind. I hated to think about him losing his business and being forced to leave the place he thought of as home.

I'm named Jaya Anand Jones after my great-great uncle Anand, the first of the Indian side of my family to come to the United States in the early 1900s. I'd heard countless heroic stories about him from my mom when I was a kid. Like Anand, Feisal had created a life for himself in a new country, and had been willing to take a chance on someone he believed in.

Daniella bit her lip. "Do you really think your friend will be able to help?" she asked.

"I'm not sure, but it's worth a try." A text message flashed on my screen. "Sanjay texted me back that he'll come over to the hotel as soon as he can."

"Who's Sanjay?" a female voice asked.

"Jaya's friend." Daniella gave Astrid a hug and clung to her for several seconds. "What's going on?"

Astrid gave a graceful shrug. I wouldn't have been surprised if she worked as a model in addition to being an actress.

"Izzy will be along shortly," Astrid said.

"They're not holding him?" Daniella asked.

"He couldn't have done it," Astrid said.

"Thank God the police came to their senses about this being an inside job," Daniella said.

"I didn't say that," Astrid said. "Come, let's go outside. I need a cigarette."

"How can they have cleared the four of us but still say it's an inside job?" Daniella asked as we left the lobby.

The sidewalk outside was even more crowded than the hotel—full of street performers and people in town for the festival—but it felt like a different world outside in the fresh air.

"Who said they cleared us?" Astrid said. "They told you the same thing, that we were to remain available? That means we're all still under suspicion. All of us except for Izzy."

"Can someone please tell me what on earth this Izzy did?" I asked.

Astrid tilted her head back to blow out a puff of smoke. "Of course Daniella wouldn't tell you," she said. "She's sweet on Izzy."

"Just because I think he deserves a second chance," Daniella said, "doesn't mean I have a thing for him." She blushed as she spoke the words.

"He used to be a policeman," Astrid said. "He was caught taking bribes."

"*One* bribe," Daniella snapped. "A weak moment, when his wife was dying of cancer and needed extra care."

Astrid rolled her eyes. "A lot of people agree with her," she said to me. "He hasn't had a problem finding private security gigs. Feisal loves him, and not just because he's such a big guy that he can either scare away or beat up anyone out to steal Feisal's antiques. Oh, and that big size of his?" she turned back to Daniella. "That's why he's off the hook."

"They found how the thief got out?" she asked.

"That's what they implied," Astrid said. "Didn't they ask you about how tall you were, Daniella?"

"They did," Daniella said, "but I didn't think anything of it."

"Well, I asked. They were trying to figure out which of us could have gotten out through the window. Izzy is the only one of us who's obviously too big to have gotten out that way."

"But the suite was five floors up."

Astrid shrugged. "There has to have been some way out. It's not as if it was magic."

SEVEN

In spite of the fact that Sanjay's show premiered that night, he left his theater to meet us outside the hotel.

"A locked room," Sanjay said after he greeted us, already wearing his tuxedo. "How could I resist?"

"That's all you care about?" Daniella said. "The puzzle? This is my life."

Sanjay frowned.

"Finally," Astrid said. "Someone who says what they really mean." She smiled seductively at Sanjay.

"Of course that's not all I care about," Sanjay said.

"Sanjay's magic show opens tonight," I said. "Shall we get down to business?"

"Which is what, exactly?" Daniella asked.

"Let's go over everything you two know," Sanjay said.

"What, you're like one of those fake psychic detectives on television?" Astrid asked. "You can pick out some minuscule detail the police missed?"

Sanjay's shoulders visibly tensed and his eyes narrowed.

"I make my living as a magician and escape artist," he said slowly. "I have never failed in any escape I've attempted, and I have come up with challenges even Houdini never dreamed of. I can free myself from anything anyone can construct. You seem to have an impossible escape. Do you want my help or not?"

Sanjay wasn't known for his modesty.

"We do," Daniella said quickly.

Astrid shrugged.

I went over the basics of who was involved with *Fool's Gold* and the chess set.

"None of us were here at the hotel when the theft took place," Daniella added, "so I'm not sure what more we can tell you."

"Where were you?" Sanjay asked.

"Astrid and I were together," Daniella said. "Jaya was there, too."

"I suppose the police have the hotel room roped off as a crime scene," Sanjay said. "Whose room is it?"

"It's a suite we're sharing," Daniella said. "Feisal and Izzy are sharing one of the bedrooms, and Astrid and I are in the second bedroom of the suite. I suppose we'll all need new rooms tonight." She paused and shook her head. "All these rooms have high-end safes in them, that's why Feisal selected this hotel. It was supposed to be the safest place to keep the chess set when we weren't using it on stage for a performance. We rehearsed with a regular chess set painted gold and silver."

"Who knew the chess set would be in the hotel room safe?" Sanjay asked.

"Only the four of us," Daniella said. "Me, Astrid, Feisal, and Izzy. That must be why the police think it was one of us."

Astrid gave a short laugh. "It wouldn't have been difficult to figure out, would it? Anyone who saw the advertisements about the famous chess set appearing in our show would have known the set had to be locked up somewhere. It's not like we're in disguise when we return to the hotel. We've been here for days. And we used our real names to register."

"That's not true," Daniella said. "I mean, it's true we've been here for days and used our real names, but nobody would have guessed the set was in the hotel room. Feisal made a big deal about pretending to give it to the hotel staff to put it in the hotel's bigger main safe. Anyone paying attention to us would have thought the set was in that safe, not the room safe."

"You mean there's a duplicate fake chess set in the hotel's safe?" Sanjay asked.

"Exactly." Daniella rubbed her eyes, smearing her eye makeup even more. "I'm making this worse, aren't I? Making it seem like it has to be one of us. Feisal gave the front desk a spray-painted fake set, just like the one we're using in our rehearsals. The set's in a box, so unless someone tried to steal it they wouldn't even get a close enough look to know it was fake."

"Interesting," Sanjay said. He placed his fingertips together in an overstated show of thoughtfulness, as if he were performing. "I need to get back to the theater to get ready for my show. Don't you want to walk me out, Jaya?"

"What are you talking about?" I said. "We're already outside."

"Don't be dense," Astrid said. "He wants to talk with you in private. We'll be inside." She stubbed out her cigarette.

"You gotta love the French," Sanjay said after they'd gone inside.

"What couldn't you say in front of them?" I asked. "They didn't steal the set. They have alibis. You heard them. They were together."

"Do you want my cape?" Sanjay asked, pulling a thin red cape from an inner pocket of his tuxedo jacket. "You look like you're freezing to death."

"I wouldn't say no to the jacket."

Sanjay hesitated.

"What?" I said. "You don't trust me with one of your customized magic act jackets?"

"It's not that I don't *trust* you..."

"Never mind," I said, ignoring the goose bumps I felt under my sweater. This was what passed as summertime in Scotland? "I'm fine."

"Anyway," Sanjay said, tucking the thin cape back into his pocket, "all their alibis prove is that they didn't act alone. Any combination of people could be in on it together and even with alibis could have hired someone to steal the set for them."

"Someone who can disappear into thin air," I cut in.

"We'll get to that," Sanjay said. "Daniella seems genuinely

upset. She's a wreck."

"She *is* an actress," I admitted. "But I don't think she's acting. Why would she ask for our help if she's guilty?"

"Agreed," Sanjay said.

"Why didn't you ask more questions?" I said. "I thought you were all about the details?"

"I am," Sanjay said. "But I can't get into that room right now, and I'm not the one who's going to be able to get any useful details from Daniella. You are. She trusts you. You should stay with her."

"She's going to a festival gala tonight."

"Can you go to with her?"

"I have an invitation, but I'm coming to your show tonight."

"I've got nine more performances after tonight," he said. "It's more important that you find out everything you can about what Daniella knows. She'll feel more comfortable with you, especially once she's out drinking."

"You're saying you want me to take my friend out to a gala at a castle and get her drunk."

"You've got a rough life, Jaya, but somebody has to do it."

EIGHT

Sanjay left and I went back inside. I maneuvered through the still-crowded lobby. A man with a shiny bald head was talking with Daniella and Astrid. I guessed this was Izzy. He was large and muscular, and held himself like someone aware of his surroundings.

"I didn't do this," he was saying to Daniella. He put an awkward hand on her shoulder, hesitating for a moment as if unsure if he should follow through and give her a hug. "I swear to you."

"I know," she said.

Izzy squeezed her shoulder, then dropped his arm. Daniella's face fell. She smiled a moment later when she saw me.

"This is Jaya," Daniella said, introducing me to Izzy. "A friend who's in town for my show. She's staying here at the same hotel. Thought we'd have more time to hang out together that way." She gave a bitter laugh. "I suppose that worked out, though not as I imagined."

Izzy gave me a vigorous handshake and looked at me squarely with bright blue eyes. "Good to meet you," he said.

"Why don't you tell her the truth, Izzy?" Astrid said. "That it's *not* nice to meet her, because you'd rather be anywhere but here."

I tried to stop myself from smiling. Astrid was brash, but she was right. All of these English guys were so proper they'd be sure to pop at some point if they didn't let out their frustrations.

"Leave it to you, Astrid," Izzy said, "to make a bad situation even more uncomfortable."

"I'm going back outside to have another cigarette," Astrid said.

"The three of you can stand around exchanging fake pleasantries for the rest of the afternoon. Jaya, it's been real. Really awful."

As Astrid turned and walked out, several male heads turned and watched her.

"She's not normally like that," Daniella said once Astrid was gone. "It's the stress of what's happened."

"Yes, she is," Izzy said. He sighed, his large shoulders swaying close to Daniella. I could have sworn I saw her give him a longing glance, but it only lasted a second.

"Don't worry about me," I said.

I felt like a third wheel, but I knew I couldn't leave. Sanjay was right that I should stay with Daniella if I wanted to help her and Feisal. The two shy lovebirds could figure things out once the theft of the chess set was resolved.

Besides, I wasn't feeling especially generous when it came to other people's romances, since my own recent year-long relationship had ended only a couple months before. I wouldn't exactly say I was bitter. Well...Who was I kidding? I was bitter. This was the start of a new phase of my life. It wasn't being alone that bothered me; I'm used to being on my own. It wasn't even worrying about whether I could pull it off. I was a damn good historian. No, what left me apprehensive was that *everything* in my life was new. A new home, a new career as a professor of history, the start of a new life.

"What did the police tell you, Izzy?" I asked, bringing myself back to the present.

"Not much. They were awfully keen on me at first, but then they found out something else that made them think I didn't do it. There's no way I could fit through the window. They think it's you, Astrid, or Feisal."

"They still think one of us did this?" Daniella asked.

"There was no forced entry into the room," Izzy said.

"Surely that's a mistake." Daniella's voice grew agitated as she spoke.

"What about the window?" I asked. "If someone got out that

way, couldn't they have gotten in that way too?"

"We were the only ones who knew the chess set was there in our suite," Izzy said.

"You remember how tiny those windows were," Daniella said. "Maybe it was one of the acrobats from one of the other performances." Her face lit up at the idea.

Izzy's gaze lingered on Daniella's with fondness. "I wish it was," he said. "But there's no way around it. I agree with them. It has to have been one of us."

NINE

I didn't have time to go shopping for a dress. I didn't think my jeans and black sweater, or my new leggings and florescent pink t-shirt, would be appropriate attire for a fundraising gala for the arts.

It was less than thirty minutes before Daniella said we had to leave. Daniella hadn't been allowed back into her suite, but her luggage was cleared and returned to her, so she had moved into the room of a performer she knew with an extra bed in a different hotel. I hadn't thought about asking her to borrow a dress until she was already gone.

Twenty-five minutes.

I eyed the stranger's suitcase. It couldn't hurt to take a closer look inside. The woman who owned this vintage suitcase had taken good care of it, and she'd taken good care of the contents of the suitcase as well. At least ten carefully folded 1960s-style dresses lay before me. I didn't recognize any of the names on the labels, but these were stylish clothes. A polka-dot polyester dress, a gingham dress suit, a tennis outfit...I could never pull off any of these.

But what about this one? I pulled out a gorgeous black dress with embroidered white details. It was a little big for me, but not too bad. It came with a dainty white belt that cinched the waist. This might just work.

I had black high heels with me. At my height, they were my standard shoes, so I'd worn these stilettos on the flight. I slipped into the dress and stepped into my shoes. I glanced at my scruffy messenger bag lying on the bed. It wouldn't do. The open suitcase lay next to my bag. A shiny white clutch made of vinyl was tucked into the side of the suitcase.

A knock sounded at my door.

"Jaya," Daniella's voice called through the door. "Clayton felt bad for us with the theft, so he's sent a car to take us to the party. It's waiting."

I grabbed the clutch with my wallet and phone, and was out the door.

Downstairs, a gold Bentley waited to escort us to the castle. Astrid was already in the back when Daniella and I climbed inside to the plush seats.

Astrid wore a strapless red dress that went down to her ankles with a slit that went up to her thigh. Her long blonde hair fell over her bare shoulders with a hint of curl. "Your dress is the wrong size," she said to me.

I glared at her. "Long story."

"Astrid is a model," Daniella said. Aside from redness of her eyes giving away she'd been crying, Daniella looked like she could have been a model that night as well. I'd never known her to dress up more formally than jeans and a t-shirt when she wasn't on stage, but tonight she wore a form-fitting silver dress with gold ankle boots. Her short brown hair was spiked stylishly.

"Used to be," Astrid corrected Daniella. "I used to be a model."

"Your outfit," I said to Daniella. "Publicity for your play?"

"Do you like it?" she asked.

Before I could answer, Astrid cut in, "Nobody will notice you're wearing gold and silver because of the play, because nobody cares about the play. There are too many performances at the festival. We should have stayed in London."

With that start to the evening, I was relieved the drive to Clayton's castle took only fifteen minutes. It took longer to drive from my apartment to my university in San Francisco. The castle was in the Edinburgh metro area, right off the A7 freeway.

Edinburgh was a northern enough city that the sun was still high in the sky late into the evening, so for the whole drive I had a perfect view of my surroundings from the window of the luxurious back seat. As soon as the chauffer pulled off the freeway, all evidence of the twenty-first century disappeared. We were swallowed up by a grove of evergreen trees. A bright blue river ran along the side of the winding road. The car slowed as the road and river curved. In a clearing of trees, the turret of a castle overlooked the river.

The Bentley turned off the road and drove up a circular drive; the red stone castle came into full view. I relaxed a little. Though it was a castle, it was mansion-sized rather than football-stadium-sized. I gripped the white clutch in my hand and took a deep breath. I might not be able to handle a gala at a castle, but I could handle a party at a mansion.

I couldn't help shivering while I walked from the car to the castle. It wasn't my nerves. The fickle Scottish weather had turned the crisp breeze from earlier in the day into a full-blown arctic wind.

Champagne flowed freely as guests milled around the grand room of the castle. Tapestries lined two walls. One of the intricately woven pieces of art featured a phoenix rising out of the flames, another a black dragon surrounded by flying pelicans and other winged creatures.

Two winding staircases led from the grand ballroom up to a balcony overlooking the party. On the balcony, a single framed painting stood on an easel. It was this painting that was being used to raise money that evening. A modern painter who critics were praising had painted a scene of Edinburgh Fringe street performers. The painting was being given away as part of a charity raffle that evening. The cost to enter the raffle was £5,000 per ticket.

I spotted Clayton shortly after arriving. He wore a black tuxedo with gold-colored wingtips and a top hat made of gold cloth. When he saw me, he came over and asked if I was doing a good job forgetting about the theft and distracting Daniella from her anxiety about Izzy. I assured him his party was doing a good job helping us both forget our worries.

Astrid had been swept away by a man claiming to be a duke of some sort, and Daniella and I were talking with an elderly couple who'd heard about Daniella's play and were intrigued. Astrid's gloomy prediction hadn't come to pass. They weren't the first people who had come up to Daniella to ask about her show.

"The chess set in *Fool's Gold* is both literal and figurative," Daniella was telling them. "The play is set in the neighborhood I grew up in. The wrong side of the tracks, as my American friend Jaya here would say. The characters Catriona and Alexis were best friends as kids. Catriona's father taught her how to play chess when she was a little girl, before he was killed in an industrial accident. Catriona taught Alexis how to play, and the two of them grew up with chess as their escape. Even though chess meant the most to Catriona, it was Alexis who had the real aptitude for it. She's the one who was able to make it out of there. She got a scholarship to university, leaving Catriona behind. The title *Fool's Gold* is based on the chess term 'fool's mate,' and the gold represents both their friendship and a special chess set they use."

"That's nice, dear," the elderly woman said with a thick brogue. "But what about the *theft*?"

Daniella's face fell. News had leaked that the chess set had been stolen, which was turning out to be even better publicity than showing the gold and silver chess set at the Scottish festival in the first place. She smiled and told them the investigation was ongoing. but she hoped they'd enjoy the show.

"Doesn't anyone care about my play?" she said to me once they'd moved on, downing the last of her third champagne.

"If the news stories get them to come to your play," I said, "then who cares if that's the thing that gets them in the door?"

"Oh God," she said, picking up another champagne from a passing waiter. "What if the police think one of us did this for publicity?"

It wasn't a crazy idea. But I didn't have time to respond before Astrid joined us.

"He wasn't a real duke," Astrid said. "Can you believe it? He's only distantly related to one."

"What about that new guy you said you were seeing?" Daniella asked her.

"What guy?"

"You took a break from rehearsal yesterday morning to call him."

Astrid stared blankly at Daniella. "Oh yes," she said finally. "Him."

But it was a moment too late. She was lying.

TEN

"You forgot you were dating someone?" I asked Astrid.

"You were gushing about him yesterday," Daniella said, followed by a small hiccup.

"Are you two the good-girlfriend police?" Astrid said, her bright red lips set in a pout. "There's got to be some real royalty here somewhere. I'll leave you two prudes to yourselves."

She stormed off, several men turning to watch her as she walked by.

"What's the matter with her?" Daniella asked.

"How well do you know her?" I asked.

"You think Astrid stole the chess set?" She shook her head. "But I was with her."

"She could have hired someone."

"She doesn't have that much imagination," Daniella said. "Oh God! That sounded awful, didn't it? Maybe I've had too many of these." She set her empty champagne class on a nearby side table. "No, I know Astrid can be difficult, but she's not a criminal."

The rest of the party was a bust. Astrid didn't manage to ingratiate herself to royalty. Daniella drank far too much. I felt self-conscious in my ill-fitting dress. Back at the hotel, I had to squeeze out the rest of the contents of the clutch to find the key to my room. How did women use these things? When I pushed open the door, my breath caught in my throat. The light of the room was on. I was certain I'd left it off.

"It's about time," Sanjay said.

"You were about this close to getting my knee in a very uncomfortable place." I flung my key at him. I wasn't surprised that he caught it. It disappeared from sight in the palm of his hand.

"You didn't leave me a choice." Sanjay placed the rematerialized key on the bed stand and sat down in the one chair in the small room. "You weren't answering your cell."

Sanjay was still wearing his tuxedo from his performance. His bow tie hung loose around his neck, and his bowler hat rested on the bed stand.

"My phone barely fit in this little clutch. I thought if I opened it I'd never get it shut again."

"You own a clutch? What happened to the messenger bag that goes everywhere with you?"

"It's not mine. I found it in the suitcase. I didn't think my bag would fit in at the gala."

"You're stealing from this poor woman's suitcase?"

"*Borrowing*," I said. "Where do you think I got this dress? But I bet she's drinking the American whiskey I brought as a gift for Daniella and having the historical letter appraised."

Sanjay leaned back on his elbows and watched me.

"What?" I said, smoothing out the dress. "Do I have a big chunk of lint on me? God, please don't tell me I've got remnants of canapé stuck in my teeth."

"*You* were eating canapé? Where's Jaya and what have you done with her?"

"Very funny."

Sanjay shook his head slowly but didn't say anything. "I was admiring your dress," he said finally. "You look..."

"Silly?" I said, slipping off my heels and flinging them into the corner of the small room. "I know. It's not really my style."

"That's not the word I was thinking of," Sanjay said. "Stunning is more like it. You look absolutely stunning."

"In this?" I looked down at the vintage black and white dress. "It's all wrong for my shape."

"Did anyone ever tell you that you don't know how to take a

compliment?"

"It's hardly a fair assessment coming from a good friend."

Sanjay cleared his throat. "Why don't you dress like that more often?"

"This dress doesn't exactly say 'authority figure.' I start teaching in two weeks. I can't very well go around looking like a nightclub singer."

"I don't know. It has its charm. So who is this woman you stole it from?"

"Borrowed," I corrected him. "I have no idea. She didn't answer the phone number tucked into the suitcase. But she has great taste. The case was full of dresses like this."

I gave a little pirouette. Sanjay laughed.

"Sounds like your show went well," I said.

"Even better than expected. A woman fainted."

"Oh no!"

"That's a good thing," Sanjay said.

"It is?"

"Weren't you paying attention earlier?" he asked.

"Apparently not."

"You were supposed to be scared when the whisky barrel caught fire with me inside it. I cut short the effect when you were there, but with the fully drawn-out presentation, I was brilliant." He grinned as I rolled my eyes.

"What about that poor woman?" I asked.

"She's fine. She came to as soon as Ewan gave her smelling salts. The diversion allowed me to heighten the drama of the illusion."

"I'm sure she's traumatized."

"That's what people pay to see. If people didn't think I was truly putting my life at risk, I wouldn't sell out nearly as many shows as I do. Why do you think Houdini was so famous? He was a mediocre illusionist, but he understood the value of drama. Close-up magic baffled him, but give him the grand venue of an outdoor stage with a challenge to escape from a straitjacket while hanging upside down hundreds of feet above a crowd, and the public ate it up. But enough about my sell-out performance." He paused. "That's not why I'm here. How did the gala go?"

"No fainting was involved," I said, "but Daniella did get fall-down drunk. And even more interesting—Astrid is hiding something."

I sat down on the bed and tucked my legs under me. I went over the little I'd learned about the publicity for both the play and the chess set growing exponentially because of the press surrounding the theft, and I thought about Astrid lying about whatever she had to do away from the group the morning before the theft took place.

"Interesting," Sanjay said.

"That's it? That's all you're going to say? Aren't you going to say something about turning Astrid over to the police for the third degree?"

"That," Sanjay said, "would be jumping the gun." He pulled his cell phone from his pocket. After glancing briefly at the screen, he put it back and looked up at me. "It's late enough," he said.

"Late enough for what? I'm too wound up to sleep. My sneakers are in my missing suitcase so I haven't been able to go running, so I doubt I'll ever sleep again."

"That's not what I'm talking about. Let's go check out the room."

"You're not serious. The scene of the crime? I'm sure it's off limits."

"Of course I'm serious. How else are we going to solve this?"

"I'm sure the police have the room locked up."

Sanjay's forehead crinkled as he raised his eyebrows.

"Right," I said with a sigh. "The lock of that room won't be much different from this one."

"Exactly. You think I let myself into your room for kicks? The hotel is booked, so I needed to practice on a door to a room I knew was empty."

"How long did it take you?"

Sanjay cleared his throat. "Let's not sit around discussing the details of how long it took to open what should have been a straightforward lock."

"Touchy, touchy."

"I've got jet lag." He yawned. "At least this hotel is proud enough of its historic roots that it still uses real old-fashioned keys. Those modern key cards aren't nearly as easy to break into with the set of skills I've got at my disposal."

"I'll remember that the next time I book a hotel room."

"Shall we?" Sanjay said.

I hesitated.

"You can either leave this to the police and see your friends go to jail," Sanjay said, "or we can take a look."

"I'm not going to talk you out of this, am I?"

"If you don't come with me, I'll do it on my own."

"Let me change," I said.

Sanjay's face fell. "Can't you go in that?"

"This is hardly cat burglar attire."

"Exactly. It's the perfect cover. If we're caught, our excuse is that we've just come from one of the festival's parties and we're drunk. That way we'll only get a drunk-and-disorderly warning—or whatever its British equivalent is—rather than being charged with what we're really up to."

I opened my mouth but Sanjay kept speaking.

"But we're not going to get caught," he said. "Especially with you as my lookout. Coming?"

I picked up the white clutch, slipped my heels back on, and followed Sanjay out the door.

"Three minutes, forty-two seconds," Sanjay said.

I turned toward him from where I stood a few paces away in the hallway, holding my heels in my hand and trying to look tipsy to anyone who might see us skulking around the burgled room. Sanjay turned the handle and opened the door.

The room was completely dark. We locked the door behind us and Sanjay turned on the light.

"There's nothing more suspicious than flashlights," Sanjay said.

"You mean if we happened to have flashlights," I pointed out.

"Touché."

The suite wasn't much bigger than a standard hotel room in the US. The door opened into a small hallway. To the right, a bathroom that would have been at home in an airplane. To the left, two bedrooms that looked like they were previously one larger room. Straight ahead, a sitting room barely big enough to fit two chairs, a coffee table, and a loveseat in a tartan print matching the furniture in the lobby. The loveseat faced a television mounted on the wall, and next to the television was a hole where the wall safe had been. The wallpapered wall surrounding the safe was blackened, and the remnants of the safe's metal door hung askew.

In addition to the evidence of the explosion around the safe, the room showed other scars of the theft: the furniture was soaking wet. The sprinkler on the ceiling had done its job.

Neither the sitting room nor the bathroom had a window. That luxury was reserved for the two bedrooms on the opposite side of the hallway, each with one small window. Each bedroom had enough room for two twin-size beds—which looked smaller than standard twin-size to me—about two feet apart. The tall, narrow windows were in the space between the beds. Neither room had built-in closets, but instead had antique wooden wardrobes.

Sanjay ran his fingers along the edging of the floorboards through the whole suite, then did the same thing along the walls. While he made two slow, meticulous circles, I studied the windows. They were small, almost like the openings for archers in a castle. There was no reason to have bigger windows for a view, since the windows faced another old building a few yards away. I looked around the edges of both windows. Typical of hotel windows, these windows didn't open. How had the police thought someone could have gotten out through one of them?

Sanjay came up behind me at the window and rested his chin on my head. I moved out of the way and let him examine the window.

"Nothing out of the ordinary here," he said. "Thick stone walls, solid construction."

"You thought there would be a secret passageway?"

"Not really. But one has to be thorough. Damn. This window doesn't open, either," he said, frowning. He pressed his forehead to the glass and looked down, and then up.

"Fifth floor," he mumbled to himself, staring out the window. "Sprinklers...no fire escape. Even if the thief could have altered one of these windows to open and get out, squeeze through the opening, and slide down a rope—or walk across one to the opposite building, if we want to entertain really outrageous ideas—there wouldn't have been time. They'd need to replace the window to its present state. No, the only way out of this place is that front door."

"Which a whole group of German tourists say didn't happen."

"Something isn't right," Sanjay said. "I don't like this at all, Jaya."

ELEVEN

Sanjay locked the suite behind us. We walked back to my hotel room in silence. I left Sanjay in the room while I used the bathroom to change.

"I've been thinking about the witnesses," Sanjay said when I emerged in my bright pink t-shirt and leggings.

"Unless this is an amazingly huge conspiracy we're stuck in the middle of, the tour group of Germans isn't lying."

"But what if they weren't lying," Sanjay said. "What if there was a way for the thief to get out of that suite through the door and have the witnesses think they never saw anyone come through the door?"

I eyed Sanjay skeptically. He was again seated in the desk chair, his elbows resting on his knees as he leaned forward and spoke earnestly.

"Don't you see?" he said. "A *diversion*."

"You mean like one of your stage tricks with smoke and mirrors."

"Something like that," he said. "Not smoke and mirrors literally, but an illusion of the same kind."

"You think they all looked away at a cute puppy at the same exact moment, right after an explosion sounded?"

"What if—" he leaned forward even closer and spoke in a reverent whisper. "What if the thief changed the room numbers on the outside of the doors?" He sat back and clasped his hands behind his head. "It's a magician's trick. Making you think you're looking at one door, but then changing the decoration—in this case the room numbers—so you don't realize it's a different door."

I thought about it for a minute. Could the thief have made a simple switch that made him invisible without being invisible?

"Brilliant, isn't it?" Sanjay said.

"You're forgetting something," I said. "The Germans didn't care about the room number—they heard the room the explosion came from and saw the smoke. So unless this thief is a mastermind genius who has figured out how to move the sound of an explosion and the accompanying smoke from one floor to another, that explanation doesn't work."

Sanjay dropped his hands and grabbed his bowler hat. He ran his fingers along the rim like he always did when he was thinking.

"I don't like this," he said again.

"I don't either. This whole thing is a big mess for Daniella's play and Feisal's business."

"Not just that," Sanjay said. He stopped tracing the hat with his fingers. "This isn't a normal crime. I don't like that we don't know what we're dealing with—and that you're wrapped up in it."

"What do you mean? You think I'm in danger?" I hadn't stopped to consider the possibility. I don't think of myself as easily frightened, but a wave of mild panic came over me as Sanjay spoke in a more serious tone than I'd ever heard him use before.

"I shouldn't have asked you to investigate with Daniella and Astrid tonight," Sanjay said. "Since it seems like Astrid is somehow involved—"

"Weren't you listening?" I said, trying to convince myself as much as Sanjay. "Astrid was with Daniella during the theft."

"Your point being?"

"You know what my point is," I snapped. "That would mean Daniella is lying, too, and that she's involved. Then why would she ask for our help? We already went through this."

"I know," Sanjay said. "But we're missing something important. Maybe she wanted to throw suspicion off of herself."

"She already has an alibi of Astrid," I said. "Why would she risk us figuring out she was involved if she was already in the clear?"

"She could be a dupe," Sanjay said.

"Of Astrid, you mean? So what do you want to do?"

Sanjay and I stared dumbly at each other for a full minute, neither of us attempting to speak.

"Police?" I said.

"Police," Sanjay agreed.

"Now?"

"It's almost three o'clock in the morning."

"Good point." I yawned. "We can go in the morning. Meet me back here an hour before your show."

"Not enough time. But that doesn't matter. I'm sleeping here—on the sofa. Until we know what's going on, I'd feel a lot better keeping you in my sight."

"*Excuse me?*"

"I said that badly. But you know what I mean."

"Do I? Why don't you enlighten me?"

Since I only reached five feet tall in thick socks, when I was a teenager my dad made sure I could take care of myself. He drove me in his VW van all around the greater Berkeley area to every kind of martial arts class that existed. I stuck with jiu jitsu the longest, and I was fairly certain I could overpower Sanjay. I hated it when people underestimated me.

Sanjay swallowed hard. "I mean...you're handy to have around. If we get cornered, I can make myself disappear and you can arm wrestle the bad guy." He looked at me expectantly.

I smiled and gave him a kiss on the cheek. "I know that's not what you were going to say," I said, "but thank you. Together, I think we'll be fine. And sure, to save time, that makes the most sense for you to stay here. That's stupid for you to sleep on the tiny sofa, though. The bed is big enough for both of us."

"Uh..."

"What? You're like my brother, Sanjay. Why does it matter?"

"I'll be fine on the sofa," he snapped. He stepped into the bathroom and shut the door harder than was necessary.

What was the matter with him?

THE CAMBODIAN CURSE & OTHER STORIES

*   *   *

The next thing I remembered, something was tugging on my foot. I opened my eyes. It was Sanjay. He stood at the foot of the bed in his tuxedo trousers and a fitted white undershirt, his normally perfect thick black hair standing at all angles like he'd been struck by a bolt of lightning. I had assumed Sanjay's hair—which his fans swooned over—was effortlessly perfect, but clearly that wasn't the case.

"We overslept," he said. "I only have half an hour before I'm supposed to be at the theater for the matinee. We're going to have to go to the police after the show."

"Damn."

"Look, I'm going to catch a cab back to my hotel to take a quick shower and grab a new tux—"

"You travel with multiple tuxedos?"

"Of course. At least six. Magic is dangerous business." He winked at me, then turned serious again as he glanced at the time on his phone. "Catch a cab to my show, okay?"

"But it's only a few blocks from here."

"Humor me," he said.

"Fine," I said. I had no intention of taking a cab for what would be a five-minute walk, but Sanjay didn't need to know that and worry for no reason.

Sanjay sighed. "All right. Don't take a cab. But be careful, okay?"

With that mind reading, he was out the door. Maybe there really was some magic in the air. If there was, I definitely needed it. I didn't know what I was doing. This wasn't the relaxing vacation I'd imagined.

On my walk to the theater I stopped at a take-out fish and chips shop to grab some fried food to placate my growling stomach. The cashier's accent was so thick that I'm not sure what it was that I ordered, but the fried breading made up the largest percentage of the meal wrapped in newspaper, and it was delicious. The magic show was sold out by the time I got there, but the ticket taker had been left with a note from Sanjay to allow me backstage.

The lights flickered as I entered the theater, the sign that the show would begin shortly and everyone should take their seats. I didn't walk through the seats to get to backstage, so I couldn't see the crowd, but I could hear the overlapping excited voices with accents from across the world. I reached the dark backstage area near the stage as the curtain went up.

A solitary stage light illuminated the stage. Or rather, it illuminated a small part of the stage. Sanjay stood at the back of the stage in the shadows, his bowler hat resting on his head. He began to chant in a slow, rhythmic voice. He spoke in Punjabi, so I didn't understand what he was saying. But one didn't need to understand the words to feel what he was saying. As he spoke, one more light turned on, and a series of shadows flashed across the back of the stage. He was telling a story with simple cut-out figures that danced along the wall.

"Do you like it?" a soft voice asked in my ear.

Sanjay's voice. I think I jumped about a foot into the air.

"Jesus, Sanjay," I whispered back. "I thought you were on stage."

"What, that voice over? Do you like it? It's new." He straightened his bow tie. "That's just a shadow of me. A little more detailed than the projection of the stick figures, but pretty simple."

"That's not even another person up there?" My heart rate slowed closer to normal as I looked between the real Sanjay and the shadow on stage that I could have sworn was him.

"Nope. Just a projection. People see what they want to see. In this context, people assume it's me. The key to shows at the Fringe is to keep things simple. Things are crazy enough putting on a complex show with bare bones staff. That's how I came up with this idea. The whisky barrel escape is the most complex of the illusions I'm doing here, but even that one is pretty simple—if you know the trick."

I gasped. It must have been a bit loud. Sanjay put his finger to his lips.

"Sanjay," I said. "I know how the thief did it."

"You do?"

"Sanjay," another voice whispered. I jumped again. I really hated how dark it was backstage. Ewan, the red-headed stagehand, came up beside us. "Cutting it close, aren't you?"

Sanjay swore. "Don't go anywhere," he said to me.

He turned and took the few steps to the edge of the stage. The stage lights shifted and the shadow I had assumed was Sanjay disappeared a fraction of a second before the real man stepped onto the stage. Applause sounded as I ran further backstage to think.

Just as Sanjay had led the audience to believe he was on that stage, the thief had done the same thing in that hotel room. Sanjay had been on the right track when he suggested a diversion that was an illusion.

The safe exploding was the illusion. By the time the explosion blew open the door of the safe, *the chess set was already gone.*

That meant the theft was no longer tied to an exact time we knew of. It could have been Astrid. But it could have been any of them. Our list of suspects with alibis was wrong. All wrong.

TWELVE

By the time Sanjay found me backstage in the green room after the show, I'd filled several pages of notepaper with thoughts about what was going on. Most of it was scratched out. My revelation meant we knew less than before.

"Not cool," Sanjay said, closing the door behind us and tossing his bowler hat onto the hook behind the door. "I need full concentration for my performance. Which I didn't have today."

Sanjay's tuxedo did look more wrinkled than usual. A couple beads of sweat ran down the side of his face. Come to think of it, I don't think I'd ever seen Sanjay look that disheveled.

"Did anything go wrong?" I asked.

"Not exactly."

"Then what—"

"Never mind. The audience may not have been as wowed by the flaming whisky barrel as they should have been, but I know what my illusions made you realize: the timing of the theft was wrong. When the explosion occurred, the chess set was already gone."

I nodded. "That's what I realized too. The explosion was a clever way to create the impression that that's when the chess set had been stolen. Just like you were never the shadow on that stage, and you were already gone from the whisky barrel by the time it caught fire. I bet you were gone just as soon as I closed the lid of the barrel."

"I admit nothing," Sanjay said. "But I should have thought of it before this." He shook his head. "It must be the jet lag."

I rolled my eyes as Sanjay picked me up by the elbow.

"Where are we going?"

"You'll see."

Sanjay led me through the maze of the backstage area and out a back door leading to an alley. My eyes had grown accustomed to the backstage light, and I'd forgotten it was only early afternoon. I shielded my eyes from the sun on this cloudless summer day. We cut through the alley to the front of the theater. Theatergoers streamed out of the main doors, and we cut through them, heading to the box office. But instead of a ticket taker, someone else was waiting for us.

"Astrid," Sanjay said. "I'm glad you could use the complementary ticket I left for you."

"How could I resist your message?" she said.

I glared at Sanjay.

"I didn't have time to tell you," he said to me before turning back to Astrid. "I thought the three of us could take a trip to the police station together."

Astrid's eyes darted angrily between us. Beyond the anger, there was fear. She wasn't her normally composed self.

"You conveniently forgot your boyfriend last night," I began. "The one you went to call the morning of the theft."

"Yes, so what?" Astrid said. "Men. They aren't worth remembering." She sneered at Sanjay.

"Some of them are," Sanjay said. "Like the police officers who are going to check your phone records."

Astrid's thin body began to tremble. She looked between us like a cornered animal.

"We know you stole the chess set before the explosion," I said. "When you weren't with Daniella."

"How do you—" Astrid stopped herself.

"As soon as the police learn they have the timing of the theft wrong," I said, "they'll know your alibi doesn't hold up."

"I didn't do it!" Astrid cried. "I only helped."

Sanjay and I glanced at each other. Sanjay's face mirrored the surprise I felt.

"I'm sure the police will be lenient if you tell them who stole the chess set," Sanjay said.

"Don't you see?" Astrid said. "I don't know where the chess set is. I don't even know who I'm working for!"

"But you—"

"I was supposed to leave the key," Astrid said, "and to create a small security problem at the theater, something that Izzy would have to fix—to set him up. Simple! It was supposed to be so simple. Those two little tasks...I'm turning forty this year, you know. Who wants to hire a forty-year-old model?"

"Come on," Sanjay said, trying to grab Astrid's elbow.

She pulled her arm away. "I won't tell them anything," she said, spitting out the words. "You have no proof, do you? Even though I don't have an alibi, it's not a crime to lie about who I called on the phone."

"Maybe not," I said. "But I wonder if the police would be interested in hearing this?" I pulled my phone out. The "record" button was on.

Astrid's eyes grew wide. She lurched for the phone. Sanjay stepped to my side as I leaped backward away from Astrid's reach. Astrid tripped and fell forward, landing hard on the box office floor. Sanjay took the phone from my hand and slipped it into a hidden pocket of his tuxedo.

At the police station, Astrid was led away for questioning, and I had to leave my phone with the police as evidence. I filled out some paperwork to get it back later. While I was filling out a form, a uniformed constable came up to us.

"Funny case," he said.

"What do you mean?" I asked

"Why would the thief return *half* of the chess men?"

"What?"

"You didn't hear?" he said.

"No," I said, shaking my head and forgetting all about the form in front of me.

"The silver half of the chess set was dropped off by courier earlier this morning."

THIRTEEN

I stretched my legs over the back of a theater seat, a borrowed laptop from Daniella in my hands. I was hooked up to the Wi-Fi from the Pizza Hut next door to the theater, where I'd eaten several pieces of pizza.

Daniella was rehearsing Izzy, who had told her he'd watched her show enough times that he knew Astrid's part by heart and could play the part of Alexis as Alex. But even with Izzy filling in, they still didn't have the chess set.

"I can't concentrate with you back there!" Sanjay called out from the stage.

"I thought you wanted me to stay," I called back.

Sanjay hopped down from the stage, walked up the aisle, and sat down next to me. "I can't win," he said. "I can't concentrate either way. You have this mysterious theory that you came up with after the silver half of the chess set was returned. Are you ready to tell me what you've got?"

"Clayton Barnes isn't crazy."

"The philanthropist alchemist guy?" Sanjay said. "Why does his sanity matter? I thought you were going to figure out what happened to the chess set for Daniella's show?"

"That's exactly what I'm doing," I said. "Check it out. Clayton Barnes, the descendant of an old inbred English family who've been wealthy for centuries. A family of selfish jerks who blew all their money gambling and spending lavishly—until Clayton came along. The black sheep of the family with a few screws loose. But he turned their fortune around. He's been forgiven by British society and the public because he's from this prominent family and because he's seen as a nice guy in spite of his eccentricities. He's donated millions to various charities, and loaned out many of his gold acquisitions to charities to put on display to raise money from other wealthy donors. In other words, he's done a lot of good."

"That's great history, Jaya. I get it that you're a historian so you like researching this stuff. But what does this have to do with the theft of the chess set?"

"His charities of choice," I said. "They're all arts organizations. They give him memberships and also special invitations to private showings—all related to his interest in alchemy."

"Gold," Sanjay said.

"Exactly. And for every few special gold exhibits he's attended, there's been a theft within the following year."

Sanjay perked up.

"And that's just the exhibits where he's been listed by the press."

"He was casing the places," Sanjay said.

I nodded. "Clayton acted upset about the theft of the gold chess set, but he wasn't nearly as upset until he found out Feisal didn't have insurance. I don't think he meant to hurt his friend. He never wanted Feisal to be implicated. That's why he set things up to make Izzy look guilty, and why he returned the silver half of the chess set after he learned Feisal hadn't insured it. He wanted Feisal to at least be able to recoup some of his losses. But he kept the gold."

"Sounds like he's even crazier than people think," Sanjay said. "Hoarding all that gold."

"He's not crazy," I said. "He let his guard down with me, since I didn't have any preconceived notions about him. He didn't think I'd look into the theft—in fact, he's been trying awfully hard to convince me to forget about it, and to make Daniella forget about it, too. I don't think he realized how much people cared about Izzy. Izzy isn't turning out to be the simple fall guy he and Astrid thought he would be."

"Hang on," Sanjay said. "How could someone so recognizable

pull off all these thefts?"

"Can you tell me what he looks like?" I asked.

"Seriously? He's got to be one of the most recognizable—"

"His clothes are recognizable," I said. "And his gold glasses and Sherlock Holmes hat. But what about *him*? Do you know what color eyes he has? Or even what color hair?"

"Do you?" Sanjay said.

"No," I said. "I don't. That's the point. If he takes off those silly 'eccentric' clothes of his, puts on jeans and a dress shirt, and leaves the hat and glasses at home, would anybody recognize him? I doubt it."

"I should have thought of it," Sanjay grumbled.

"This is a calculated plan," I said. "Clayton Barnes is a thief and con artist who's been selling gold treasures to finance his family's crumbling fortune."

FOURTEEN

I shut the computer and looked for my phone to call the police with what I'd found out. After a few seconds of searching through my messenger bag, I remembered the police had my phone.

"Let me use your phone," I said to Sanjay.

"Why?"

"I'm calling the police."

"With your theory that Clayton isn't crazy and is a criminal mastermind?"

"Yes," I said. "But with less dramatic language. Now let me use your phone."

Sanjay punched in some numbers on his phone. I held out my hand, but he refused to hand it to me. A few moments later, he was put through to the detective in charge. I listened as he gave a brief summary of my research—with the key difference being that he said eccentric Clayton Barnes was hoarding gold. When he was done speaking, he listened in silence for almost a minute.

"Oh," he said, frowning. "Yes. Mmm hmm. Yes, of course."

He hung up.

"What is it?"

"It seems," Sanjay said, "that the police have suspected Clayton for quite some time. They put two and two together, just like you did. But they've never been able to prove it. Apparently they're out at his castle right now with a search warrant. Clayton is at the police station and said they were welcome to search his home. That doesn't sound like the reaction of someone who's guilty."

I swore. Why had I thought I could figure out something like this that the police couldn't solve?

"Don't beat yourself up," Sanjay said, putting his hand on my shoulder. "It was a good idea. Too bad both you and the police were wrong."

"I don't think so," I said.

"But didn't you just hear? He's given them permission to search—"

"He's guilty, all right," I said. "But the gold isn't hidden at his mansion where the police can find it."

I stood up.

"Where are you going?" Sanjay asked.

"I'm going to do what I do best. Historical research. I was stupid and arrogant to think I could identify a suspect, when that's what the police do best. But history is what I do best. I know how to find the set and save Daniella's show, clear Izzy from suspicion, and save Feisal's business and his home."

"How?"

"Clayton said he bought his castle because it was once owned by an alchemist. What do you want to bet there are hidden areas of that house the police will never be able to find, even with their thorough search?"

"You've just discovered the police aren't stupid, Jaya. I'm sure they have the blueprints to the house."

"That's where I know more than the police. Historical buildings built by people with something to hide—like persecuted alchemists—often made fake blueprints. I'm looking for local history books about alchemy that mention this historic castle."

Sanjay glanced at his phone. "Five hours until Daniella's show," he said.

"Then we'd better get going."

I knew what I was after, so I was able to find it within two hours. The cab we caught at the Edinburgh University library dropped us off around the bend from the castle. We went on foot from there.

Three hours until show time.

The fountain stood where the historical description said it would. Water cascaded down the worn stone, pouring through the waterspout mouths of four gargoyles that faced outward around the circle.

"It's a working fountain," Sanjay said, circling the structure. "I wasn't expecting that. How is that a good entrance to a secret lair?"

"It wouldn't be a very good hiding place if it wasn't working."

"If you tell me I have to swim to the bottom of that algae-filled fountain to reach this alchemy lab, I'm going to go get the police. I know that means they'll hang onto the chess pieces as evidence for too long for Daniella and Feisal to use in the show as the draw. But I draw the line somewhere. And that line is slimy algae."

"I'm sure there's a way in that wouldn't leave the alchemists sopping wet when they reach their lab."

"Those historical documents you found didn't say?"

"It wasn't a how-to guide."

Without stepping inside, Sanjay leaned over the edge of the fountain and pressed the nose of the gargoyle in front of him. He leaned back and waited a moment. When nothing happened, he walked around the fountain to the second of two gargoyles and did the same.

If I'd been an alchemist—a real believer—during a time of persecution, I'd have wanted the safest hiding place I could think of for my alchemical lab. Putting it outside the main house, and under a fountain, was a great idea.

I sat down on the stone bench a few feet from the fountain. The bench faced both the fountain and the rose garden that lay beyond it on the way to the mansion. Beauty filled the grounds. Compared to the rest of the ornamentation, the stone bench was rather plain. A stone slab without any flourishes, but it looked like the same centuries-old stone. The flat slab itself was solid, but one of the cobblestones in front of it was loose. I stepped on it and it shifted a little. I knelt down and pressed on it. It moved a little but didn't give.

"Sanjay," I said. He stood at the last of the gargoyles, scowling at the little monster. "Come over here and put your trapdoor skills to use."

"It wouldn't be on the ground," he said. "Too easy for a gardener to accidentally step on. But here..."

He reached his hand under the bench. He ran his fingers along the base for a few moments. When his hand emerged, a faint sound of scraping stone echoed underground. But we didn't see anything.

"Oh, that's ingenious," he said.

"I don't see it."

"It's a two-part mechanism," Sanjay said. "Clayton Barnes hasn't kept up greasing his door very well. We shouldn't have heard that sound. We're supposed to think pushing the button didn't do anything."

"It didn't."

"Oh yes it did," Sanjay said. "It unlocked the secret passageway."

I stepped aside as Sanjay pushed at the slab of the stone bench. The first side he tried didn't budge. He moved to the other side. The stone swung wide, revealing a narrow set of stone stairs leading down.

FIFTEEN

Sanjay and I looked at each other for a moment before following the steps.

As we descended, it was clear the surrounding shrubbery had been strategically placed around the fountain and bench so that nobody outside of the immediate vicinity would see whoever was taking the hidden staircase.

I was so in awe of the historical room we'd discovered that I wasn't paying enough attention. When my foot hit the bottom step, the stone moved.

Unlike the loose stone above ground, this stone wasn't nearly tilting from age—it was sinking. I gasped and instinctively backed up, bumping into Sanjay. He swore in Punjabi at the same time another noise sounded. The stone bench was closing above us.

Sanjay realized what the sinking stone had done, too. He turned on his heel and ran up the steps. It was too late. The thick stones came together, closing us off from the world.

I didn't think of myself as being afraid of the dark, but fear gripped me as pitch black enveloped us. This was definitely not the relaxing vacation I'd signed up for.

The darkness lasted only a few moments. As soon as the stones clicked firmly into place, lights came on. The scene before us was amazing enough that I forgot my fear. A series of gas lamps hung along the stone walls, but that wasn't what lit the room. A set of modern bulbs had been strung along the walls, leading to a room roughly the size of my San Francisco studio apartment.

The room was a combination of old and modern. It hadn't been professionally upgraded. A man of Clayton's wealth could have afforded to do so, but he must have wanted to keep his secret from everyone.

The high-ceilinged room was stocked like an old-fashioned chemistry lab. In the back of the cave-like room was a large clay oven. Two stone dragons stood taller than me on either side of the oven. A small trickle of water dripped down one side of the open mouth of the oven. The ceiling in that section of the room was lower than the rest of the room. That wall must have been directly under the fountain. Wooden tables lined the two walls flanking the oven, with crowded shelves above. Glass jars filled with powders of metallic colors, beakers of liquid, metal tongs for lifting hot vessels. In a corner near the oven, a primitive faucet hung over a copper bowl.

"The alchemist's lab," I said. "The fountain even gives it running water."

"It looks like a chemistry lab from Houdini's time," Sanjay said. "He's preserved it perfectly. It's not even dusty."

An acidic smell filled the air. Fresh, not musty. That was curious. Even more curious: a small glass bowl of gold flakes lay on the table closest to us.

One look at Sanjay and I knew he was as confused as me.

"You don't think he actually...?" Sanjay's voice trailed off.

"No," I said, more confidently than I felt. "Definitely not. This isn't real. There has to be a logical explanation."

Sanjay picked up the bowl of gold, raising it to eye level.

"It looks real," he said.

"What do you know about gold?"

"I'm just saying."

"I'm waiting for a host from a reality TV show to jump out from behind the clay oven," I said.

Sanjay walked over to the oven.

"I didn't really mean—" I began.

"I know," he said. "Can I see that magnifying glass you always carry around?"

"You could if it hadn't disappeared with the rest of my

luggage." I mentally kicked myself again for putting so many things I didn't want to lose into that checked bag.

"Look at these ashes," Sanjay said, kneeling down. He picked up a handful of blackened ashes and watched them flutter through the air as they slipped through his fingers. "This oven is in use. Why would it be in use if he wasn't practicing alchemy?"

"Burning evidence?" I suggested.

Brushing off his hands, Sanjay considered the idea with a thoughtful expression. "Speaking of which," he said, "I don't see the gold half of a chess set anywhere. You don't think you were wrong about him, do you?"

"No," I said. "My theory makes sense. It's a con. He's hiding something. You saw how well hidden this lab is."

As I spoke the words, I was reminded we were trapped in a room nobody besides Clayton Barnes knew existed. I shivered, and I wasn't sure if it was from the damp chill.

"If he believes he's an alchemist," Sanjay said, "then he believes he needs to hide this lab so he won't be persecuted. I mean really, look at this place—"

"Sanjay," I interrupted. "There's got to be a way out of here, right?"

"Yeah," he said quietly, looking away. "The problem is we need to find it."

"You're good at this stuff," I said. "You found the way in here."

"That was one clever entry system," Sanjay said. "This lab is hidden away below several feet of stone. We need to find the way out ourselves. Nobody is going to find us here."

SIXTEEN

Sanjay's cell phone didn't get any reception, even from the highest step we could climb. For the next thirty minutes, he meticulously tapped every few inches of the walls, floor, and stairway, looking for our way out. I picked up the containers on the tables and went over the table tops and legs. None of it revealed the opening of a secret door. When we regrouped in front of the fireplace, Sanjay's knuckles were raw.

"The stone door we came through is the only way out," he said. "There has to be a trigger, but I'll be damned if I know what it is."

I had been so confident Sanjay would figure it out. I trusted him completely. Just like I knew my own strengths that led us to this alchemy lab, I knew Sanjay's. I hadn't been as frightened as I knew I should have been because I knew he would be able to escape from this room. But what if I was wrong?

Sanjay sighed and sat down on the well-swept floor. He leaned his back against one of the dragons. Watching him, an idea clicked into place in my mind.

"The dragon," I said.

"I already tried it," Sanjay snapped. "I tried everything."

"The black dragon," I said.

"There's no black dragon. They're both gray stone."

"But the scales carved into the stone," I said. "Look at this. There's a black one."

"That's natural discoloration," Sanjay said. "It's been worn..."

His voice trailed off as I pushed on the black scale on the chest of the dragon. It didn't move.

"The black dragon is a meaningful term to alchemists," I said.

"Clayton mentioned it, and there was also a tapestry of a black dragon in his castle."

I pushed harder on the black stone. It shifted. The carved stone scale was a lever. The movement dislodged something I hadn't planned on. A large stone fell forward.

I jumped back, but I wasn't fast enough.

The rock smashed into my left arm, a jagged edge tearing through my sweater. I horrid crack sounded. I screamed as pain enveloped me.

As searing pain shot through my arm, I realized the bone was most likely broken. Not only did I have a broken bone that needed medical attention, but I was trapped in an underground cave with no cell phone reception, and nobody knew where I was.

"Jaya!" Sanjay cried, pulling me further back from the avalanche. But it was only the one stone that fell.

Pain made its way from my forearm up to my neck. I hadn't broken a bone since I was a kid, but the memories flooded back. I was five years old when I fell out of a tree along the water near our house in Goa. More than the pain, the thing that stuck out in my mind was the difference in what I smelled—I associated a broken arm with fresh air and the scent of bananas, but now the air was stifling and musty. I felt as if I might choke.

"You're bleeding," Sanjay said, kneeling to examine my arm. He pulled a handkerchief out of his pocket. Then another. I must have been seeing double. No, that wasn't it. It was a set of five white handkerchiefs tied together. They must have been for one of his tricks.

"I think it's broken," I said, my head spinning. I closed my eyes and the sound of scraping stone filled my ears. Was I hallucinating?

"Stay there," he said, as if I was going to go anywhere.

I opened my eyes as a new shot of pain surged through my arm.

Sanjay used the handkerchiefs to tie a wooden spoon from the lab to my arm as a makeshift splint.

"We have to get you out of here," he said. "I'll go over every inch of the room again."

"You don't need to," I said, pointing to the stone stairs with my good arm.

Natural light cascaded over the steps. I hadn't imagined the sound of scraping stone. The doorway down to the lab had opened back up. I'd never been so happy to see the light of day.

"The dragon opened up the door," Sanjay said, following my gaze.

"We didn't hear it because of the falling rock."

"Come on," he said. "I can carry you up the stairs."

"I can walk," I said.

My voice was shaky and I wasn't sure I believed my own words. But the thought of being carried to my rescue like a damsel in distress wasn't much more appealing than being stuck down in that alchemist lab. "I just need a second."

Sanjay held my good arm to help me across the room. Hot pain throbbed each time I took a step. Drops of blood followed in my wake.

"Wait!" I said.

"Do you need me to carry you after all?"

"No," I said, holding my arm in my other hand. I winced in pain. "This is another diversion."

"That's great, Jaya. We can talk about diversions later. Now come on."

"Stop," I said. "I need to think."

"No, you don't," Sanjay said. "You need to get to a hospital."

"Clayton is smart," I said. "Really smart. Just like how he dresses so outrageously so he can hide in plain sight when he wears more normal clothing, this lab is the same false front." I paused and steadied myself on the edge of a table. "If someone happened to find their way into this lab, all it would do is tell them that he takes his alchemy seriously. Those gold flakes are a prop. This place has another hiding place—the real one."

"That's great, Jaya, but this accident—"

"Don't you get it? That wasn't an accident. It wasn't that a rock was so unstable that it fell when the doorway opened back up. That rock fell because we were too close to his hiding place. It's a booby trap. A booby trap that opens the door back up, for the person who got caught in the trap to be relieved to have a way out—instead of searching for the real hiding place. We were looking for a way out, so we weren't looking for a hiding place. Those dragons are the perfect hiding place."

"You're not going to let this go," Sanjay said.

"No," I said, ignoring the growing bloodstain on the splint wrapped tightly around my arm.

Sanjay's shoulders sagged and he closed his eyes. "All right," he said. "Two minutes. Then we get you out of here."

"The dragon's mouth," I said as I reached the dragon. "The stone tongue is a different piece of stone, not a continuous carving."

Sanjay inspected the mouth of the dragon, grumbling about how I didn't have the magnifying glass I use for historical documents. His grumbling cut off abruptly.

"What is it?" I asked.

"A key hole in the back of the dragon's mouth," he said.

"We don't have the key," I said.

"Who do you think you're talking to?" Sanjay pulled one of the tools from his escape acts and poked it into the dragon's mouth.

A few moments later, a sharp click sounded. Sanjay lifted out the tongue of the dragon. Beyond it were three black velvet bags.

Opening the first drawstring bag, a smile spread across Sanjay's face. He pulled out the gold chess figure of a crazed rook biting his shield.

SEVENTEEN

Two hours later I sat in a reserved box watching *Fool's Gold*. My arm rested on a pillow in its new cast.

The house was packed. The media was having a field day with the fact that Clayton Barnes had been arrested for stealing the gold and silver Lewis Chessmen and was suspected of countless other thefts of gold treasures.

The media attention was great for business. Not only had Daniella's show sold out all its scheduled performances, but Feisal had a bidding war for the chess set.

Sanjay had insisted we go straight to the hospital, rather than stopping at the theater to hand over the gold chess pieces to Feisal. But while I was getting my cast, Sanjay had called Feisal who came by to pick up the pieces that Sanjay and I happened to have "forgotten" were in my bag when we handed over the other evidence to the police.

"I don't know how to thank you," Feisal had said, bowing and kissing my fingers that poked out from the cast.

Clayton made a full confession after being assured he would get a deal for returning several missing treasures. He couldn't return all of the treasures he'd stolen, though. He hadn't been selling the pieces intact. He's been melting down treasures in his alchemy lab. It was easier—and safer—to sell gold once it had been disguised.

Clayton's theft of the chess set was never meant to be an impossible crime. His plan had been to have an alibi for the time when the theft was supposed to have taken place, and for Izzy to be the one person without an alibi. With Izzy's past, he was sure the police would have things wrapped up quickly. The German tour group in the hallway ruined the simple plan.

Clayton had used the key, which Astrid left at an appointed spot, to get into the suite and break into the safe early that morning. He'd set an explosion on a timer to go off during the picnic. He was a good thief, and part of his MO was that he was exceedingly careful, taking steps such as never having an accomplice know his identity. That's why even though the police had long suspected him, they had never been able to prove anything.

Clayton needed Astrid's key because he hadn't wanted to be seen picking a lock in a crowded hallway. He could open the safe himself when he had more time and knew Astrid would be making sure the suite's occupants were otherwise occupied. Astrid's other role was to make sure Izzy would be fixing a security problem at the theater while everyone else had the alibi of the picnic. Clayton hadn't counted on Daniella being suspicious of the theater's security breach or of the depth of her feeling for Izzy. That's why he tried to get me to distract Daniella, so we wouldn't look carefully into what had happened.

In retrospect, Clayton should have anticipated human emotions to get in the way, since it was precisely his own feelings that had tripped him up. He knew he would be inconveniencing Feisal by stealing the chess set, but he never imagined Feisal wouldn't have insurance. When he learned Feisal had cut corners and didn't have insurance, he decided to anonymously return the silver half of the chess set, so Feisal could recoup some of his losses. The only reason Clayton had decided on this theft in the first place was because he was desperate. He was running low on funds and didn't see an alternative. He got sloppy.

I heard about Clayton's confession from Feisal when I arrived at the theater from the hospital. Being the good man that he was, Feisal was already talking about forgiving Clayton.

"Is your cast dry yet?" Sanjay asked as the stage lights flickered and signaled that Fool's Gold would begin soon.

"I think so," I said. "Why?"

As the lights when down, Sanjay whipped out a black marker from a hidden pocket and signed his name across the cast with a flourish.

Izzy wasn't the greatest actor, but it didn't matter. He wasn't lying when he said he knew the part of Alex, and now that Daniella's usual confidence was back, she had enough talent to carry the show. Besides, half the audience only cared about the sensationalist chess set mystery they were able to be a part of. From the way Daniella and Izzy were looking at each other, Daniella didn't seem to care.

I hadn't ever thought that Sanjay's illusions as The Hindi Houdini could help solve crimes, but it was those clever deceptions of his that had been the key to piecing together how the theft was done. I also hadn't previously thought my research skills as a historian could help catch a criminal, but maybe there was something to it.

I never did get that relaxing vacation I was after. But sitting in the theater box with Sanjay after we'd caught a clever thief, seeing Daniella and Izzy find happiness, and knowing I'd helped save Feisal's antiques business and ensure he'd get to stay in the country that has become home, I wouldn't have had it any other way.

Author's Note

I've always loved the Golden Age of detective fiction, when puzzle plot mysteries and short stories were popular. Authors like John Dickson Carr, Clayton Rawson, and Ellery Queen (the pseudonym for Frederic Dannay and Manfred Lee) took the challenge to readers even further, often writing locked room or otherwise impossible crime stories (the definition of which is explained by Doug Greene in the Foreword).

From the time I sat down to write my first short story, I knew it would be this type of "fair play" puzzle plot, where the writer plays fair with the reader by planting all the clues in plain sight. I wasn't sure if I was a skilled enough writer yet to successfully write an impossible crime story, but I knew I wanted to try. I wrote "The Shadow of the River" in longhand one afternoon at the San Francisco Public Library. It was a simple twist, but I was so proud of finishing that story that I submitted it to an anthology competition of blind submissions—where it was accepted. My subsequent stories became more complex as I became a better storyteller, and I always challenged myself to come up with an impossible crime twist that would baffle readers as they had fun trying to figure it out.

While Doug Greene and I were chatting at Malice Domestic last year, he asked me about the locked room methods I used in my stories. I hadn't realized until that moment that each of my stories used a different method, each of them one of the methods laid out by John Dickson Carr in his famous Locked Room Lecture. I had pushed myself to make each story surprising and different, but I hadn't realized just how much I was following in the tradition of the authors who'd inspired me.

So now I will issue my own challenge to you, the reader: Did you spot the different methods used in each story as they followed the categories of the famous Locked Room Lecture? Hint: There's at least one story that features more than one method.

And one more challenge: There are several "Easter eggs" hidden in these stories—fun hidden references to literary characters and authors I love. Fans of Elizabeth Peters, Aaron Elkins, and Juliet Blackwell, I hope you caught the nods to these fabulous authors.

Thanks for reading! To stay up to date with my latest publications, you can sign up for my email newsletter at www.gigipandian.com/newsletter/

GIGI PANDIAN

USA Today bestselling author Gigi Pandian is the child of cultural anthropologists from New Mexico and the southern tip of India. She spent her childhood being dragged around the world, and now lives in the San Francisco Bay Area. Gigi writes the Jaya Jones Treasure Hunt mysteries, the Accidental Alchemist mysteries, and locked-room mystery short stories. Gigi's fiction has been awarded the Malice Domestic Grant and Lefty Awards, and been nominated for Macavity and Agatha Awards. Find her online at www.gigipandian.com.

The Jaya Jones Treasure Hunt Mystery Series
by Gigi Pandian

<u>Novels</u>

ARTIFACT (#1)
PIRATE VISHNU (#2)
QUICKSAND (#3)
MICHELANGELO'S GHOST (#4)
THE NINJA'S ILLUSION (#5)

<u>Short Stories</u>

THE LIBRARY GHOST OF TANGLEWOOD INN
THE CAMBODIAN CURSE & OTHER STORIES

Henery Press Mystery Books

And finally, before you go...
Here are a few other mysteries
you might enjoy:

COUNTERFEIT CONSPIRACIES
Ritter Ames

A Bodies of Art Mystery (#1)

Laurel Beacham may have been born with a silver spoon in her mouth, but she has long since lost it digging herself out of trouble. Her father gambled and womanized his way through the family fortune before skiing off an Alp, leaving her with more tarnish than trust fund. Quick wits and connections have gained her a reputation as one of the world's premier art recovery experts. The police may catch the thief, but she reclaims the missing masterpieces.

The latest assignment, however, may be her undoing. Using every ounce of luck and larceny she possesses, Laurel must locate a priceless art icon and rescue a co-worker (and ex-lover) from a master criminal, all the while matching wits with a charming new nemesis. Unfortunately, he seems to know where the bodies are buried—and she prefers hers isn't next.

Available at booksellers nationwide and online

Visit www.henerypress.com for details

MURDER IN G MAJOR

Alexia Gordon

A Gethsemane Brown Mystery (#1)

With few other options, African-American classical musician Gethsemane Brown accepts a less-than-ideal position turning a group of rowdy schoolboys into an award-winning orchestra. Stranded without luggage or money in the Irish countryside, she figures any job is better than none. The perk? Housesitting a lovely cliffside cottage. The catch? The ghost of the cottage's murdered owner haunts the place. Falsely accused of killing his wife (and himself), he begs Gethsemane to clear his name so he can rest in peace.

Gethsemane's reluctant investigation provokes a dormant killer and she soon finds herself in grave danger. As Gethsemane races to prevent a deadly encore, will she uncover the truth or star in her own farewell performance?

Available at booksellers nationwide and online

Visit www.henerypress.com for details

THE SEMESTER OF OUR DISCONTENT

Cynthia Kuhn

A Lila Maclean Academic Mystery (#1)

English professor Lila Maclean is thrilled about her new job at prestigious Stonedale University, until she finds one of her colleagues dead. She soon learns that everyone, from the chancellor to the detective working the case, believes Lila—or someone she is protecting—may be responsible for the horrific event, so she assigns herself the task of identifying the killer.

Putting her scholarly skills to the test, Lila gathers evidence, but her search is complicated by an unexpected nemesis, a suspicious investigator, and an ominous secret society. Rather than earning an "A" for effort, she receives a threat featuring the mysterious emblem and must act quickly to avoid failing her assignment...and becoming the next victim.

Available at booksellers nationwide and online

Visit www.henerypress.com for details

PUMPKINS IN PARADISE

Kathi Daley

A Tj Jensen Mystery (#1)

Between volunteering for the annual pumpkin festival and coaching her girls to the state soccer finals, high school teacher Tj Jensen finds her good friend Zachary Collins dead in his favorite chair.

When the handsome new deputy closes the case without so much as a "why" or "how," Tj turns her attention from chili cook-offs and pumpkin carving to complex puzzles, prophetic riddles, and a decades-old secret she seems destined to unravel.

Available at booksellers nationwide and online

Visit www.henerypress.com for details

CPSIA information can be obtained
at www.ICGtesting.com
Printed in the USA
LVHW04s0926091018
592787LV00025BA/1430/P

9 781635 114188